Tempting Taste

A HOT OPPOSITES-ATTRACT ROMANCE

SARA WHITNEY

THE CINNAMON ROLL ALPHAS SERIES

Tempting Taste
Cinnamon Roll Alphas

Copyright © 2020 Sara Whitney
Published by LoveSpark Press, Peoria, IL

This book is a work of fiction. Names, characters, places, and incidents are either products of the author's imagination or used fictitiously. Any resemblance to actual events, locales, or persons, living or dead, is entirely coincidental.

All rights reserved. No part of this publication can be reproduced or transmitted in any form or by any means, electronic or mechanical, without permission in writing from the author or publisher.

Developmental Editor: Sue Brown-Moore
Editor: Victory Editing
Sensitivity Reader: Tessera Editorial

Ebook ISBN: 978-1-953565-05-1
Print ISBN: 978-1-953565-01-3

First Edition: February 2020
v. 2.3

To Kate the Great,
a real-life defender of women on public transportation.

And to Tara, who said,
"Hey, you should write something about Josie."
Thanks for believing in her, and in me.

The grumpier the guy, the harder they fall.

All Josie Ryan wanted was some cake. She didn't mean to flambé a man's life. But since her teeny little fight with a cake shop owner cost the head baker his job, she'll just have to help the charming grump open his own bakery.

Erik Andersson craves stability, but the gorgeous PR whiz who's promising to turn his talent into a wedding cake empire is nothing but chaos. Too bad he needs her business savvy almost as much as he needs to bury his hands in her fiery red hair.

Soon enough Josie and Erik are exploring their sweet-and-salty dynamic in the kitchen and out. But when their definitions of success collide, can they find the perfect fusion, or will they always be a recipe for disaster?

Keep in touch!

Subscribe to Sara's newsletter to stay up on
new releases, sales, and giveaways!
sarawhitney.com/newsletter

CONTENTS

Chapter 1	1
Chapter 2	9
Chapter 3	17
Chapter 4	25
Chapter 5	35
Chapter 6	45
Chapter 7	53
Chapter 8	63
Chapter 9	73
Chapter 10	85
Chapter 11	91
Chapter 12	99
Chapter 13	109
Chapter 14	119
Chapter 15	129
Chapter 16	139
Chapter 17	147
Chapter 18	157
Chapter 19	169
Chapter 20	179
Chapter 21	187
Chapter 22	193
Chapter 23	203
Chapter 24	211
Chapter 25	221
Chapter 26	229
Chapter 27	237
Chapter 28	245
Chapter 29	255
Chapter 30	261
Chapter 31	269

Chapter 32	277
Chapter 33	285
Chapter 34	295
Epilogue	303
Author's Note	309
Also by Sara Whitney	311
About the Author	315

ONE

Josie Ryan jerked awake. Yellow lights swam in her vision, and her hands slid across clammy vinyl as she groped for her phone.

Almost 2:00 a.m. No wonder she'd nodded off on the train carrying her home. Every business in the Chicago area wanted to launch new products and host grand openings as soon as April ushered in slightly warmer temperatures, and Josie had been sprinting from event to event for her marketing firm all month long, including this Friday-night bash to celebrate a downtown club opening. Good thing she'd woken up before she missed her River North stop. But what had pulled her out of sleep?

She checked her phone again as the L creaked around a curve, confirming what she already suspected: she hadn't been woken up by a return text from her mother. Apparently praise from one of Chicago's top lifestyle blogs for tonight's event wasn't enough to spur Pamela Ryan's elegant fingers into motion, despite Josie's cheerful "So excited by this write-up!" opening salvo.

She jammed her phone back into her purse, frustrated

that she'd expected anything different. That's when she heard the noise.

"Come on, baby. I'm just being friendly."

She shifted in her seat to look for the source. Her mother's lack of reply might have left her restless, but the man's whiny tone was pushing her right toward the edge of twitchy. Then another voice reached her ears.

"I *said* I'm not interested."

The quaver in the woman's words prickled the skin on the back of Josie's neck and spiked her adrenaline.

"You should be grateful." Belligerent anger colored the man's voice now. "Somebody like me thinks you're worth talking to? You should be fuckin' grateful."

Josie was on her feet and in the aisle before she could think twice. A woman cowered against the window two rows back while a thin, hardmouthed man pressed against her with his arm across the back of the seat.

"Excuse me." Josie adopted her bossiest tone. "Is he bothering you?"

The woman's terrified eyes met Josie's, and she nodded vigorously. The man didn't drop his arm, but he did crane his neck to growl, "Fuck off."

Josie flicked her gaze left, then right, confirming that she was alone on the train with the creep and his target. A mix of unease and outrage thrummed under her breastbone. The smart move here would be to mind her own business. Then again, she wasn't known for choosing the smart move, especially when it came to bullies; too many people had minded their own business back when she'd been the target.

Time to do something stupid.

"Actually, I don't think I can fuck off, as tempting as that offer is. See, that's my friend. We went to school together." Josie bent her lips into a ferocious smile and addressed the trembling woman. "I haven't seen you in ages! Not since graduation, right?"

The woman was obviously half a decade younger than Josie's twenty-six, but she nodded anyway. "R-right. Not since g-graduation." Her wide eyes never left Josie's face.

"That's way too long." Josie advanced a step with a ramrod spine but wobbly knees. "I'd love to catch up with you right now. How about you ditch that asshole and come sit next to me?"

"Who you calling an asshole?" The man exploded from his seat just as the train's brakes started to screech. Josie hid her flinch and held her ground, knowing from experience that people like this guy fed on weakness. As the train lurched to a stop, the doors at the front and the back of the car hissed open. In a flash, the other woman slid across the bench and darted out the closest exit, a mouse escaping the cobra's jaws.

The guy didn't turn to watch her go; he had new prey now. "Somebody needs to teach your fancy ass some manners, you know that?" He eyed Josie with distaste, his hands curling into fists, and a whisper of panic slithered through her veins. He was wiry and not much taller than her own five foot four, but he looked *pissed*.

Then she lifted her chin. Her redhead had been activated, so he ought to look scared. *Poor motherfucker.*

"My manners are fine, thanks." She rocked back on her heels, looking him up and down with a sneer. "*I'm* not the one pawing a woman on the train like some kind of escaped zoo animal. Couldn't find any of your own species to mate with, huh?"

The guy surged forward until his putrid breath

burned all the way to Josie's sinuses. "What the fuck is your problem?"

"What the fuck is *yours*?" she shouted back. "How do you not understand that no means no, asshole?"

Her heartbeat throbbed in her ears. Next time she'd be smarter about how she let her temper out. Next time she'd try harder to de-escalate instead of rushing straight to *fuck you, buddy, let's go* mode. But that was next time. She was here now, and she'd just have to take care of herself like she always did.

The man growled, and she loosened her stance so she was prepared to dodge if he grabbed for her, frantically trying to recall where they'd told her to gouge during that self-defense class she'd taken at the Y last year. Eyes, right? And groin?

Suddenly the man's face paled, and he took three big steps back. "Look, I'm sorry, okay?" All his bravado drained away, and the whine returned to his voice. "Jesus, I was just chatting up a cute girl. No harm intended."

He lifted his hands in surrender and backed toward the same exit Josie's "friend" had taken at the earlier stop, and oh, watching a humiliated harasser scramble down the steps and jog away as soon as the car slowed felt *great*.

"Yeah, that's right! You step right off and keep stepping!" she yelled at his retreating form through the closed train doors. "And *mind your fucking manners* next time!"

She jabbed a finger in his direction with each word, smugly satisfied with her ability to handle herself and defend a victim of bullying no matter the personal risk. He'd recognized her inner predator, and he'd bowed before it. She was the biggest, baddest badass on this now-empty train. With a toss of her hair, she spun on her heel to return to her seat... and slammed into a solid wall of man.

She sprang backward with a strangled cry, arms windmilling as she tried to catch her balance. The *true* biggest badass on the train clasped her upper arm with one massive hand, and she suddenly realized what had sent her harasser running. The man steadying her might just be the biggest human she'd ever seen up close, all muscled and scowly and towering over her by at least a foot. Her pulse fluttered like a hummingbird at the base of her throat as she considered all the ways his strength and size were superior to hers— nothing at all like the diminutive man who'd just bolted. And this time she truly *was* on her own. Her earlier alarm came roaring back even more acutely than before, and just as she was about to catapult into panic mode, the big stranger released her and backed away, raising his hands in the universal gesture of "no harm intended."

She grabbed the back of the closest seat as the train jolted back into motion, relieved to be able to breathe again now that he'd put a few feet between them. "W-where the hell did you come from?" Her voice held none of its earlier fire, and the brute took another step in the opposite direction, his broad shoulders shifting as he jerked a thumb toward the door she'd had her back to.

"Since when does this train make a stop in Asgard?" Now that she didn't seem to be in imminent danger, her smartass streak was reasserting itself. But he merely looked back at her blankly, so she tried again. "Asgard? Where Thor lives? Just saying, what with you all..."

"With me all...?"

Her cheeks burned at the amused rumble of his voice, but it didn't stop her from waving a hand down the length of his six-foot-plus frame, all buff and Hemsworth-y. "Just... you know." He even had his dark blond hair pulled back into a bun, for God's sake. But instead of nodding or smiling or playing along in any way, his gaze remained flat and steady.

"Gah, never mind." She whirled away with a huff and reclaimed her seat, her heart thrumming for an entirely different reason now, while her unwanted rescuer dropped onto the bench running lengthwise down the train. Without a second glance her way, he plugged in a set of earbuds, leaned against the window, and closed his eyes, apparently done with the conversation.

She wasn't though. Her pleasure at helping the frightened woman had curdled, and it was this guy's fault. This guy and Harasser McGee and, what the hell, her mother too, while she was assigning blame. If Pamela had just sent a reply text, Josie might not have gone looking for a fight.

Who was she kidding? She was *still* looking for a fight.

"I was fine, by the way," she called to the god of thunder. "I was *handling it.*"

His only response was to crack open one eye, shrug, and link his fingers over his battered moto jacket.

"Well?" she demanded. De-escalation was apparently not an option for her tonight, even with a man as big as he was.

The guy pulled one of the earbuds from his ear with a sharp tug and looked at her with a raised eyebrow, clearly indicating *Well, what?* When she continued to glower, he heaved a sigh. "Sorry."

"For?"

He gave her an opaque look. "For whatever's got you so angry."

She shut her mouth so hard her teeth clicked together. "Well, that's a terrible apology. You're just putting the burden on the injured party. Care to try again?" She crossed her arms over her chest, but he merely blinked and returned to his precious earbuds, leaving her to fume unnoticed.

Before long though, the aloof chill he radiated from six feet away wrapped its tendrils around her and poked a hole in her fight! instinct. As the buzzing in her head quieted, regret trickled in, like usual. Had she been too harsh with the huge, hot guy? He'd presumably thought she was in trouble and stepped in to help, and she'd yelled at him for it. It wasn't his fault that she'd been startled by his size and angry that she'd needed rescuing.

Dammit. *She* was the one who needed to apologize.

She peeked at him under the pretense of checking her phone. His eyes were peacefully closed, as if their interaction never happened. Still, guilt swelled in her chest until she called, "I'm sorry" over the seat in front of her.

His lips quirked even though his eyes stayed shut and his earbuds remained in place. "Why? Aren't you the injured party?"

Yeah, she deserved that. She stood and trudged toward him, her pinched toes crying for mercy after a long day in her tallest heels. "Okay, so I'm not *injured*, per se. But I—"

"—could've handled it. I heard." His eyes snapped open. "I believe you."

He tugged his earbuds out again as his bright blue gaze traveled from the top of her head down to her shoes.

She puffed out her chest, conveying as much toughness as possible in her Brooks Brothers business suit.

"You're goddamn right," she insisted. "I have *skills*. I know self-defense."

He twitched those full lips again. "Sure. You could probably teach Lady Sif a thing or two."

His reference to the Asgardian warrior pulled a surprised laugh from her. "You *did* get the reference."

That earned her another nonverbal response along the lines of *Well, obviously*. She shook her head and had started to pivot away when the rough velvet of his voice stopped her.

"I'm curious."

She turned back to find his head cocked in her direction.

"Your self-defense style. Is it mostly shin-kicking and yelling 'fuck you' from a distance?"

Heat coursed through her as his gaze moved across her face, both from her anger at his suggestion and her awareness of how well he wore that smirk on his lips. She was so caught off guard by her reaction that for once she couldn't find the words for a comeback.

He shrugged and crammed those damn earbuds back into his ears. "It'd scare me off anyway." Then he closed his eyes and had the audacity to ignore her for the rest of the trip.

TWO

A persistent ring pulled Josie from sleep.

"No. Go away," she groaned as she reached for her phone.

It was way too early on a Saturday morning, particularly after sleep had eluded her following the previous night's train encounter.

Both of the train encounters.

She slid her finger to accept the call but could only muster a moan into the speaker.

"Where is my ring bearer?"

The unusual note of strain in Richard's voice sent her scrambling to untangle herself from the sheets. "No! Oh my God, I completely forgot!"

He clucked his tongue. "You'd think this wasn't your wedding too."

"Ha."

Her best friend Richard was getting married in two months, and she'd volunteered to help with a few final details while his fiancé was out of town. This wasn't a great start.

"What time was I supposed to be there?" She staggered to the bathroom, fatigue pulling at her like molasses. The reflection in the mirror startled the last of the sleep from her brain, and she poked at the straggly mess of curls.

"Five minutes ago, so leave right now."

Again with the sharp tone. Something was stressing him out, which was unusual enough to make her skip her usual normal beauty routine.

"I'll be there, but I might not be too cute," she warned after another glance at the mirror revealed that her pale cheeks were now accessorized with under-eye rings. Sexy.

"Sweet potato pie, you're always cute," he said. "Just hurry."

She smacked a kiss into the phone and hung up, then raced through washing her face and brushing her teeth. She threw on the first semiclean clothes she could find and tiptoed past her roommate Finn's shut bedroom door, behind which she was presumably sound asleep with her boyfriend.

Once Josie was clear of the apartment, she sprinted down the stairs and burst out of the building. Thankfully, the little bakery that had been generating buzz on the Chicago wedding scene was only a few blocks from her place, so she could hoof it in her flats without any trouble.

By the time she arrived at the Cake Shoppe, her fingers were tingling from the brisk morning air, and she was grateful she'd layered a fleece over her long-sleeved T-shirt. A bell jingled when she pushed open the door to the little shop, but the scene she encountered was anything but cheerful.

Richard was seated at a round café table next to a grim-faced sixtysomething woman, who said peevishly,

"Is this her? Finally?" The woman's mouth tightened so much her lips disappeared in a mass of wrinkles.

Josie's friend stood smoothly and wrapped her into a hug, whispering, "Thank God" as he kissed her cheek. Then he guided her to the open seat in front of an array of cake slices.

Josie flashed the woman an apologetic smile. "I'm so sorry. Late night last night."

The woman just scowled and adjusted the headband holding her cottony white hair off her forehead. "Well, now that everyone's finally here, we can start. I'm Dora, the owner."

She didn't extend her hand for Josie to shake, but Josie hadn't worked in marketing for five years for nothing. "Hi, Dora! I'm so thrilled to finally check out your bakery," she enthused. "I've heard so much about your gorgeous cakes over the past few months!"

Dora's watery blue eyes flicked over Josie's North Face fleece jacket and leggings. Damn, she'd grabbed the pair with a hole over the knee. Why hadn't she tossed them out last week when she'd noticed the snag? Her hand fidgeted to cover the exposed patch of skin, but she forced herself to stay still and act like she'd intentionally chosen distressed athleisure wear.

Dora sniffed. "Yes, I'm delighted that the good word is starting to get out. It's thrilling to have the... best parts of Chicago society take notice."

Shit. She should've taken more care with her appearance before she left the apartment. In her haste to get out the door, she'd ignored the first lesson her mother had taught her as a child: dress the way you want people to treat you. But over her Spandex-clad dead body would she let Richard and Byron get anything less than stellar service because of her.

"The best part of Chicago's sitting right here," she said, squeezing Richard's elbow in its impeccably fitted suit. Thank God he was classy enough for both of them. "What flavor shall we start with?"

Richard pointed at the cake nearest him. "With chocolate, of course."

"Of course." She grinned at him and grabbed a fork.

Some people might have trouble gorging on cake before nine in the morning, but Josie wasn't among them. She and Richard moaned their way through the chocolate fudge ganache with a hazelnut filling, the vanilla-raspberry, and the pistachio crunch, all under Dora's disapproving gaze.

"Did I read that you've been in business for close to three decades?" Josie asked around a mouthful of Boston cream.

Any hopes she had that talking about herself might soften Dora up were dashed when the woman simply nodded as she watched Richard lifting his next bite to his lips. Josie forked up another mouthful and tried again. "So what made you explode on the wedding scene so recently, do you think?"

Dora sniffed and straightened the cuff of her floral-patterned sweater. "Payoff from years of hard work." Then she lapsed back into silence, which was broken only by the scrape of Richard's fork tines against the plain white china.

What appalling customer-service skills. The only other human being Josie had this much trouble conversing with was her own mother—and come to think of it, the two women did seem to share a certain disdain for people in general and Josie in particular. But unlike Josie's mother, Dora at least brought some genuinely delicious cake with her.

"So what do you think?" Josie abandoned her attempt at conversation with Dour Dora and turned to Richard. "Byron's going to flip for the hazelnut, no?"

Dora looked up from the pad where she was jotting notes, a thin smile on her face. "And who's Byron?"

Richard's whole body melted into besotted joy. "My fiancé. He's out of town for the next few weeks, but we knew we needed to…"

He trailed off when Dora stood sharply, the chair scraping against the floor.

"Byron? *He?*"

"Yes. He." Richard's voice was calm, but Josie felt his leg tense where it brushed against hers under the table. Her heart sank. *Please don't go where I think this is going to go.*

Dora's eyes darted between Richard and Josie as she connected the dots. "Well. Well, that just…" Her accusing gaze landed on Josie. "You didn't specify the couple's names when you called to make the reservation."

"You didn't ask," she said slowly. "You just took my name and made some assumptions." She pressed her shoulder against Richard's in a show of solidarity. "I'm his maid of honor. Or best woman. Did we ever decide?"

"It's your call," Richard said in a deceptively light tone, his deep brown eyes never wavering from Dora's face. "Are we going to have a problem here, ma'am?"

Dora began jerkily whisking the cake plates off the table, dumping them into the nearby bin reserved for dirty dishes.

"Well," she huffed. "It was bad enough when I thought..."

Her voice trailed off as her eyes darted between Richard and Josie again, and Josie's temper spiked for the second time in less than twelve hours. "It was bad enough when *what?*"

Dora had no answer, but Josie could make an educated guess. She sucked in a deep breath. *Keep it together. Don't escalate, remember?*

Richard was doing a better job of maintaining his calm. He casually leaned his elbows on the table, pointing first to himself and then to Josie. "It was bad enough when you thought I was marrying this pretty white girl, right?"

Dora pinched her mouth shut, but her narrowed eyes answered for her. "I think you should leave," she blurted, circles of red burning in her powder-caked cheeks. "We won't be able to accommodate your wedding."

Richard flowed to his feet and spoke in a lethally polite voice. "This is a shortsighted way for you to run a business. I'd urge you to reconsider."

Dora sneered. "I don't need money from *you.*"

The disdain in the woman's voice held such a strong echo from Josie's own childhood that her fragile grip on her temper snapped. She'd *had it* with bigots and bullies today, and it wasn't even noon yet. "Do you know what year it is, lady?" She surged to her feet, almost knocking her chair to the tile floor.

"Trouble, Dora?"

At the sound of the deep voice, all three heads whipped to the bakery counter where a man had stepped from the back room.

A mountain of a man. A *familiar* mountain of a man.

"You!" Josie gasped, not caring that she sounded like a character in a melodrama.

The big brute who'd rescued her on the L last night stood behind the counter, swathed in an apron, dusted with flour, and wearing those damn earbuds again. Not even a flicker of recognition registered on his face, and for a split second, Josie was crushed that she was so forgettable. But this particular moment wasn't about her.

"Talk some sense into your boss please," she snapped. "Refusing to bake cakes for two men in love is vile."

Train guy's stony expression didn't budge as Richard rose and tugged his suit coat into place. "Don't bother," Richard said with a sniff. "I'll serve our guests stale bread before I'll serve them anything from here." He linked his arm with hers and addressed Dora coldly. "You're a dinosaur, and sooner or later a meteor's headed your way. Enjoy extinction."

He steered Josie toward the exit, but before they sailed through the door, she glared over her shoulder at the man behind the counter. "Thanks a lot. Guess we had to handle this one on our own."

The tinkling of the bell over the door punctuated her words, and then she and Richard were on the street and hustling down the sidewalk. Once they'd turned the corner, Richard jerked to a halt, his body trembling.

"The whole time we've been planning our wedding, I've been braced for something like that. Was expecting it even. But when it actually happens..."

She pulled him into a hug. "Let's go back and tear that place to the fucking ground."

He gave a small sob and wrapped his arms around her to squeeze back. "I wish. I wish we could."

He sounded so resigned that Josie's heart ached. As

awful as that scene had been for her, she couldn't even begin to understand the pain it had caused her friend. So she kept her arms around him as his tears fell.

Once his breathing had returned to normal, she asked, "What do you want to do now?"

Richard exhaled hard. "Do you have time to get coffee and start researching other bakeries?"

"Absolutely. There's a coffee place a few blocks over."

They'd walked several steps before Richard sighed. "What a damn shame. That hazelnut filling was to die for."

THREE

The slamming of the door echoed through the bakery as Erik Andersson pieced together the influx of information he'd absorbed in the past two minutes.

First he'd received the shock of his life when he'd recognized the funny, smart-mouthed redhead from the L at the tasting table. Then his oh-so-helpful brain had pointed out that she looked just as good in stretchy black pants and a fleece as she did in her tight suit the night before. Then there'd been the brief, unexpected pang when he thought she was there to pick out a wedding cake with her suit-wearing fiancé. And finally, she'd started shouting, which reminded him that as hot as she was, she was exactly the kind of woman he'd tried to avoid his whole life.

It was enough to make him long for the safety of his kitchen. But this time he couldn't walk away. He'd avoided this discussion for too long.

"What just happened?"

Dora's color was high on her round cheeks as she collected the tub of dishes and marched behind the counter. "Nothing. Nothing at all. Just a pair of look-but-don't-buy types. I asked them to leave."

She brushed past him and moved to the back where she scraped the cake remains into the trash with angry motions while Erik turned over what he'd heard.

"Dora," he said slowly, "how often do you turn people away?"

She didn't meet his eyes. "Not often. Just couples who aren't..."

His stomach roiled as he waited for her answer.

Finally Dora lifted her nose and announced, "If I don't approve of someone, I don't have to take their money. It's my right."

Goddammit. This was worse than he'd thought.

Dora had hired him as her head baker five months ago, and within a few weeks, his discomfort with her constant negativity had bloomed into full-blown loathing of her closed-mindedness about certain "people and lifestyles" as she put it. But he'd finally landed his ideal job after half a year of grunt work in some of the worst kitchens of Chicago, so he'd kept his head down and his earbuds in and did his best to ignore his boss unless she spoke directly to him. He'd told himself he could endure just about anything if she truly was as close to retirement as she swore she was when she'd hired him.

This though? This was too fucking far. How many people had she turned away since he'd started working for her? Muttered comments were one thing, but to actually refuse to bake for someone? Dammit, he shouldn't have spent so much time drowning her out with music. He should've paid better attention. Bile burned the back of his throat.

"My business, my decisions." She interrupted his

thoughts, and when he didn't respond, her voice sharpened. "Are we going to have a problem, Erik?"

He lowered his brows and shook his head. Nope. No problem he couldn't solve.

"Good." She pulled her ever-present notebook out of her pocket and flipped to the newest page, muttering the whole time. "My baker doesn't say more than twenty words a day, and this morning he decides to use them all to question my business judgment."

Her eye roll made it clear what she thought of his opinions, and he clenched his jaw. She really didn't know the first thing about him.

Dora plucked a printed sheet from the counter. "Here's today's schedule. How are you coming with the Parker-Wilson cake? Get me a sketch for the design they requested by noon."

Without a smile or a thank-you, she turned and swished out of the kitchen, leaving Erik alone in the kitchen that he'd made his own. He might actively dislike his boss, but he loved this place: the spotless ovens, the industrial fridge full of creative possibilities, the shelves lined with baking staples and rarities.

An odd, energizing melancholy swept through him. He knew what he had to do. It'd be hard as fuck, but it was the right thing. He'd been ignoring his conscience for too long, and it was finally time.

A glance at today's task sheet confirmed that one thing at least was going his way. He crammed the paper into the back pocket of his jeans, then slipped his apron over his head and hung it on the hook on the wall for the last time. Shoving the few personal items scattered throughout the kitchen into his backpack, he took one more look around the place that had given him his break in the big city. Then with a long sigh, he slung the bag over his shoulder and pushed through the door.

Dora was shifting tables to prep for the next batch of tasters due in later that morning. Good luck to her with that. "Are the rest of today's samples ready?" she asked.

He gestured behind him to the kitchen, where he'd left a neat row of glossily iced cakes. "Done. Along with this weekend's orders."

She nodded absently, not glancing up from the chairs she was nudging into precise right angles. "Good. Carla and Chuck will handle the setup."

He walked to the exit, more certain about his decision with each step. The dread was still there of course, but he needed to do his part to *handle it,* as the shouty redhead might say. "Cakes for the next two weeks are in the freezer for you to decorate."

That got her attention. Her head snapped up, and her mean little eyes zeroed in on his face. "What do you mean? Where are you going? I didn't authorize vacation."

"I quit." No take backs now. Those two little words were both horrifying and freeing, like that moment of suspended euphoria when you jump off a cliff but before gravity grabs your ankle and drags you to your doom.

"What?" Dora screeched. "Not funny, Erik. Get back to the kitchen. We have people due in thirty minutes."

If he wasn't all twisted into anxious knots, he might have enjoyed the utter confusion on her face when he didn't leap to obey. Too bad for her if she was only now noticing that her baker had a mind of his own.

"You can't just quit like this." She started sputtering. "It's... it's irresponsible. It's unprofessional!"

He paused with his hand on the doorknob and studied her with all the compassion she'd shown anyone different from her—which was to say none. "I'm ashamed that I stayed as long as I did." Then he voiced a suspicion that had occurred to him more than once since he'd started working at the Cake Shoppe. "Were you ever really planning to retire and let me take over?"

Her eyes narrowed, confirming his darkest thoughts. She'd been stringing him along, and he'd been so hungry for the promise of a safe future that he'd let it happen.

"Doesn't matter," he said. "I'm leaving before that meteor hits."

Dora's face registered a moment of blank shock before twisting in anger. "Don't be ridiculous. You're quitting the best job you'll ever have over... *those people?*"

His jaw worked silently as he gathered the control he'd need to speak civilly. "People like my best friend, you mean? And the pastry chef who trained me?" Her face hardened with each word, but he pushed past his disgust to continue. "Or how about my favorite high school teacher? Our city's mayor? The guy who just left here? And what about every single couple you've turned away that I don't even know about? Hell *yes,* I'm quitting."

The guilt and discomfort he'd been shoving down for months came boiling out, and his rush of words still hung in the air as he pushed open the door and walked out, the tinkle of the bell clashing with the painful throb of his heart as he took his first steps into an unknown future.

He'd made it close to three blocks before his pulse slowed and his legs stopped devouring the pavement. He'd paused in front of an empty CTA bus bench, so he sat down. Well, collapsed, more accurately. Now that he was clear of Dora, every cell in his risk-averse body was screaming in disbelief. He was alone in Chicago with no job and no prospects on the horizon.

What the fuck had he just done?

He slumped forward to rest his head in his hands, and for a moment he was ten years old again and being tossed around during a rootless, chaotic childhood. The acid churning in his stomach reminded him of the promise he'd made to himself all those years ago: he would never again be unsure of where he'd be sleeping that night and what he'd be doing the following day. For all her vast flaws, Dora had always provided him with that.

He pinched the bridge of his nose and exhaled slowly. Okay, it wasn't as bad as it could be. When he'd first come to this unfamiliar city, he'd dragged himself to every restaurant and bakery in the area, forcing himself to make small talk with strangers until he'd landed the job with Dora. Finding work hadn't killed him then, and it wouldn't kill him now. Probably. At least he knew a few more people in the industry this time, and he had the Cake Shoppe's recent track record to point to, assuming Dora didn't poison his reputation all over town.

"Fuck," he said softly. The Cake Shoppe's success had been the result of his unique flavors and decorative flourishes, and he was well aware of the value he brought to the kitchen. But even the thought of having to prove all that to a new boss settled heavy on his bones. He leaned back against the bench, closed his eyes, and tilted his face toward the morning sun.

Two paths branched in front of him. One was slow and steady and safe. The other required risk and uncertainty. And he had to choose.

If only it were a few years from now and he was in a better position to open his own shop. If he'd spent more time researching possible locations. If he were an entirely different person who had any kind of handle on marketing and publicity and all the nonbaking things it took to get a new business off the ground.

Pointless fantasies, boy. His grandfather's warning rang in his head so clearly the scowling man might as well be sitting on the bench next to him. And in the end, it wasn't a choice; he'd been opting for safe ever since his mother had dropped him at Pops's door, a scrawny kid with a dirty face and an empty belly, desperate for discipline and boundaries.

Time to push aside his dream and make the rounds of the area bakeries again. The faster he locked down his next job, the better he'd sleep at night and the sooner he'd know what he'd be doing the next day. At least he had one lead.

He reached into his back pocket to retrieve the crumpled paper with one crucial notation on it: SATURDAY, 8 A.M., followed by a phone number but no name. Shit.

He heaved a breath, dialed, and braced himself. He hated phone calls in general, but this one was infinitely worse because the train redhead was the kind of confident, fashionable woman who left him even more tongue-tied than usual. He listened to the phone ring and willed himself not to think about the light, citrusy smell of her hair, which had lingered like a phantom the whole train ride home last night.

"This is Josie." The voice on the other end of the phone was crisp and professional and nothing like the confrontational tone he was expecting.

"Is, uh, is this the redhead?" His mouth suddenly felt too full of saliva, and oh, he hated this. Talking on the phone amplified every bit of awkwardness he brought with him in all his interactions with strangers.

At first he only heard background clatter, and then a

hiss came over the line. "Listen, asshole, I don't know who you are or how you got this number, but I'm not—"

An unexpected laugh rolled through him, taking him by surprise and loosening the tightness in his chest. He'd boarded the train last night to find a fierce little tyrant staring down a harasser with violence shining in his eyes. Of course the same woman who didn't back down in the face of obvious danger and then yelled at her rescuer would try to start shit over the phone.

"My God, is your default setting Fight?" With effort, he wrestled his amused surprise into submission and flattened his voice. "This is Erik Andersson from the bakery. And the L."

That shut her up.

"I... okay. What do you want? And how'd you get my number?"

He blew out a breath. "Bakery paperwork. Are you still with your friend?"

"Yes," she said cautiously.

"Can we talk? I have a proposition."

Now *she* was the one huffing a short laugh. "Wow. Sure. Um, we're at Blake's Coffee, a few blocks away. You know it?"

"Yeah."

"Want to join us there?"

No. But he needed to make this work. "See you soon."

FOUR

"Well. You'll never guess who that was." Josie raised her mug to her lips and studied Richard over the rim. The grim brackets around his mouth showed that he was still shaken by their experience with Dora the Destroyer, but he forced a smile.

"Hot cross bun from the bakery. He wants to fall at our feet and apologize."

She set the mug down in astonishment. "How do you always know?"

He grinned and slicked a hand over his tight black curls. "Context clues and a top-notch brain."

Josie scraped her chair closer to the table to let a man squeeze past in the cramped seating area. "I don't actually know that he's coming to apologize," she warned as the guy's overcoat sleeve dipped perilously close to her coffee. "Maybe he's going to demand payment for the free cake we scammed. Byron better earn a bonus this month to cover our dessert bills."

Richard's mouth tugged down, and Josie nudged his ankle with her Tieks-clad toe.

"Missing him?"

He nodded. "Wishing he could be more involved. I know he doesn't control his travel schedule, but..."

"Yeah."

Richard, Byron, Josie, and Josie's roommate, Finn, were all in the PR/marketing biz in various capacities, but Byron was the only one whose work regularly took him out of town to meet the vendors whose accounts he managed.

"Where is it this week?" she asked.

"La Crosse." Richard's voice was so gloomy Wisconsin might as well be Siberia, so she returned to the subject that had pulled a reluctant smile from him earlier.

"About Mr. Man Bun. Did you see those arms? I bet he could bench-press me. Maybe you and me at the same time even." She fanned herself with a lazy hand.

Richard's teeth flashed, then vanished just as quickly. "Girl, he could hang one of us from each bicep and do curls. If that guy doesn't have a thirst-trap Insta account with a billion workout ab shots, then I quit life."

Her fingers involuntarily twitched toward her phone to search "hot Chicago baker," but she forced them to behave. "Too bad he's not my type."

He paused with his coffee cup halfway to his lips. "Excuse me? I thought Nordic god-men were everyone's type."

She reached for another sugar packet. "Big and brooding's nice to look at, but I'm more into confidence and a three-piece suit." She dumped the crystals into her already-sweet coffee and stirred, looking up when Richard snorted.

"Oh yeah? And how did your last five dates with the suit-wearing 'so-confident-it-borders-on-narcissism' guys go?" Richard just laughed when she stirred her coffee harder. "I'm not saying date the hot baker, and anyway, you probably already scared him off. But I am saying maybe what you think is your type is really more your mom's type, and you're only dating them to win her approval."

"Hey!" Her mug hit the table with a thunk, and Richard raised his hands in surrender.

"Ooooh, sorry. I retract. It's your fault and your fault alone that you're the most single girl in Chicago."

"Damn righ— Hey!" she said again, but he just laughed evilly and went to fetch another refill for himself.

She twisted in her chair to call after him, "Everybody loves a man in a suit!" but her words were lost in the scream of the cappuccino machine. She exhaled a similar gust of hot, agitated air and turned back around in time to see the door swing open to admit the big blond baker. Erik, he'd said. And her eyes hadn't deceived her during their previous two meetings. He was, to dust off a word she hadn't had much use for previously, positively strapping. All he needed was an ax and a blue ox.

Nope. Definitely not her type.

Bright blue eyes swept the crowded shop and landed on her. As before, not even the tiniest flicker in his somber expression showed that he recognized her as he weaved through the packed tables with surprising grace for such a big man. When he reached the table, he stood close enough that the scent of vanilla on his skin edged out the acrid burn of coffee beans.

"Hi." She tipped her head up, up, up. "Do me a solid and sit down before I permanently damage my neck."

He complied and laced his fingers together on the table in front of him. "Hello," he said, studying her with a frown hovering at the edge of those unreadable blue eyes. Yet again, she was reminded of her uncharacteristically frazzled appearance. She couldn't have paused to apply a little lip gloss at some point?

She was about to fall into a vanity-induced downward spiral when Richard returned to take control of the situation.

"If you're not here to apologize, don't bother getting comfortable." Her friend took his seat like royalty reclaiming the throne, and the big man across from him grimaced.

"I *am* here to apologize. And to make you an offer."

Richard sipped his coffee and said nothing. Mr. Strong but Silent cast her a glance she couldn't interpret before turning back to Richard, his massive shoulders heaving upward before slumping back down. "I let myself spend too much time in the back. I had no idea she was..." The muscles in his jaw bunched and released. "I'm sorry."

Richard's mouth hardened. "That's great, but I'm sorry doesn't cut it when—"

"And I quit."

His words stopped Richard short.

"I should've quit a long time ago." Erik unlocked his fingers and flattened them on the table. "And if you're still looking for a baker, I could use the work. I'm..." Pink invaded the blades of his cheeks above his golden scruff. "I made and decorated the cakes at the Cake Shoppe. I'm the reason it's been successful."

"How long did you work there?" Josie asked.

"Close to half a year."

Richard glanced at her. "Right around the time the bakery started getting buzz for those gorgeous designs."

"And the flavors," Erik added, ducking his head.

He ducked his head. Josie blinked. Had she just witnessed a genuine apology followed by genuine bashful modesty? She clearly spent too much time with marketing bros who never apologized and never missed the chance to brag. This denim-clad creature in front of her was some entirely new style of masculinity.

"We weren't properly introduced before." Richard set his drink on the table. "I'm Richard Washington. This is Josie Ryan. And you are?"

"Erik Andersson."

Richard leaned forward with a hard gleam in his eye. "Was she pissed when you left?"

Erik's lips twitched. "Not as pissed as she'll be when she realizes I didn't leave any of my recipes behind."

"Hey! Good for you!" Josie held her hand up for a high five, and after a moment's hesitation, he delivered the world's most gentle smack to her palm. His dinner-plate hand dwarfed hers. *Mmmm. Big hands, big—*

"So the hazelnut," Richard said. Damn his timing. "That was you? And the pistachio?"

Erik nodded.

"Hired. You're hired." Just then, Richard's phone buzzed. He glanced at the screen. "It's Byron. You two keep chatting. This Georgia boy needs to talk to his peach." He shot Josie a quick wink as he pushed away from the table, weaving through the maze of coffee drinkers and leaving her alone with a big, broody, not-at-all-her-type man who had a distinctly pained look on his face.

Well, damn. Maybe she wasn't *his* type either, and didn't that thought chafe a bit?

"So what do you plan to do n—" she started to ask, but Richard's return interrupted her.

His whole body was rigid, and he held the phone tight to his ear. "What? When?" He listened to a staccato voice on the other end. "Okay. Okay, thank you. I'll be there as soon as I can." When he ended the call, the phone slipped from his fingers to clatter on the table. "Byron was in a car accident in La Crosse."

Josie gasped. "Oh no. Is he...?"

"He's in surgery. They took him to the Mayo Clinic by helicopter. I guess it's the closest level-one trauma center." Richard's voice wavered, and he swallowed a few times before continuing. "They're worried about a head injury, and he's also got broken ribs and God knows what else."

Josie placed her hand over his and squeezed. "What do you need?"

His eyes snapped to hers, suddenly focused. "I have to go. I have to get there. I have to be there when he wakes up."

Her planning brain spun into gear. "Of course you do. Okay, you leave right now and go home to pack. Take enough for a long stay just in case. Do you want me to rent you a car?"

"It's a six-hour drive. Might be faster for him to fly."

Erik's voice startled her; she'd actually forgotten he was still at the table with them.

Richard shook his head helplessly. "I can't. I-I need to—"

"Just go," Josie ordered. "I'll do the research and book you whatever's the quickest. I'll send you details."

Richard stood, and she stood too to pull him into a quick, hard hug.

"He'll be okay," she whispered.

"He'd better be." He pulled away, wiped his eyes, and jogged from the coffee shop.

Okay. Time to figure out the best way to get Richard out of town. She woke up her phone and started pecking at the screen.

"What city's the Mayo Clinic even in?" she muttered.

"Rochester, Minnesota." Erik's answer was immediate even though she hadn't really been asking him.

"Thanks, human Google," she said distractedly as she waited for the results to load. Too slow. Was it worth dashing back to her apartment to do this on an actual computer?

"Here." Erik reached into his bag and produced something wonderful: a MacBook.

"Oh, bless you," she breathed. She opened a flight search in one tab, pulled up information on the nearest car rental place in another, and zoomed in on a map showing hotels in Rochester in a third.

"Got it. Good. This can work." Once she'd decided on the best plan, she fished her credit card out of her wallet and started entering information into the required fields.

On public Wi-Fi. On a stranger's computer. Her fingers hesitated over the keys.

She shook her head and kept typing. Take care of Richard first, deal with any identity fraud fallout later. A few keystrokes and it was done. She switched to her phone and, in a flurry of swipes, forwarded the confirmation emails to Richard, then dialed his number.

Voicemail picked up as Erik said, "Tell him to pack layers. The rooms in Mayo can be cold."

She nodded, then spoke into the phone. "Nonstop to Rochester leaves from O'Hare in two hours. The flight's an hour and ten minutes. I'll text you the info. I also emailed you information for the three hotels closest to the Mayo Clinic, but maybe you'll want to stay with Byron tonight if they'll let you. Let me know. Oh, and your new baker says to pack layers for the hospital. I love you."

She hung up the phone and slowly became aware of a warmth between her shoulder blades where Erik's massive hand rested with the lightest possible pressure. As soon as she noticed, he pulled it away.

"Mayo also has twenty-four-hour family waiting rooms."

The gentleness of his tone surprised her, and that's when she realized her cheeks were wet with tears. "Oh wow," she said shakily, dabbing at her eyes with the cuff of her fleece, the coffeehouse chatter rushing back to flood her senses now that she was out of hyperfocus mode. "I didn't mean to..." She blew out a breath and met his bright blue gaze. "Thanks for staying."

"Where else do I have to be?" For the first time in their strange acquaintance, he smiled at her for real, with teeth and everything. Despite her concern for Byron, she almost fell out of her chair at how damn attractive he looked when he wasn't frowning at her.

"You know a lot about the Mayo Clinic. Did you—"

The buzzing of her phone cut her off, and she scooped it up. A fraction of the tension drained from her neck and shoulders as she read the text.

"Richard's in an Uber on the way to the airport. He'll send an update once he's there." When she took a final swig of now-cold coffee and stood, Erik stood too.

"Thanks again for..." Blood rushed to her cheeks at the memory of this quiet stranger's hand warming her with his simple, calming touch. Her flustered reaction made no sense whatsoever, so she rushed to finish her sentence in the most neutral way she could think of. "Thanks for the laptop. I'll give Richard your number so he can call to talk cake when he's ready."

"Sounds good."

"Okay then. See you maybe." She got three steps from the table when something occurred to her and she whipped around. Even seated, he was a head taller than anyone else in this crowded coffee shop. "Thanks for quitting today."

That earned her another smile, smaller than before, although it still crinkled the corners of his eyes. "I handled it."

"That you did." She smiled back, then left to continue worrying in the privacy of her apartment.

FIVE

This was dumb.

This was dumb, and he shouldn't do it.

Yet there went his thumbs, acting independently of his brain, tapping out the text message he'd been mulling over sending for days, mostly because he was a decent human being, partly because he needed the business, and a tiny sliver because he had a perverse need to see what Josie Redhead would be like over text.

How's your friend's fiancé?

The deed done, he dropped his phone like it was as hot as that red hair of hers had looked under the sun streaming through the coffeehouse windows on Saturday. Would she somehow try to pick a fight with him via emoji? The thought made him chuckle quietly even as the rational part of his brain reminded him that no good had ever come from him interacting with a woman like her in anything other than a professional capacity.

Yeah, he shouldn't have sent that fucking text.

The thought had him pacing the length of his apartment, which took him all of five steps. "Paltry" overstated the percent of his financial resources he'd been willing to allocate for housing in Chicago, and the coffin-sized living space reflected that. Still, it meant when his phone rang from across the room, he was able to reach it in two seconds.

"You answer texts with a call?" he grumbled.

Josie's laughter tickled his ear. "And you answer the phone without saying hello."

He grunted, and after a beat she got the hint and picked up the conversational ball.

"Thank you for asking. Byron's going to be okay."

"Good." And he meant it, even though he didn't know Richard or his fiancé at all. Just seeing the man's distress on Saturday morning had been enough to keep them on his mind.

Josie wasn't done with her report. "He's got a concussion, broken ribs, a broken pelvis. Richard's going to telecommute from Rochester for at least a few weeks while Byron's recuperating at Mayo. And do you know what's wild?"

Wild was Erik having a conversation with Josie Redhead on the phone. Everything about her, from her fashionable clothes to her friendly chatter to her fight-me attitude, should've made him run in the opposite direction. But instead of ending the call, he waited for her to tell him.

After a long couple of seconds, she sighed. "C'mon, Man Bun. You're supposed to answer with a 'What?' or an 'I don't know.'"

He wasn't a nickname guy. "I don't know. What?" He flopped on his couch in irritation, and it creaked as he searched for a comfortable spot.

"Why, thank you for asking." She laughed. "What's

wild is that I volunteered to take care of the last of their wedding details while they're both out of town."

She paused, and Erik forced himself to make the effort. "Why's that wild?" Look at him, chatting on the phone with a girl. If only Pops could see him now, he might've worried about his solitary, long-haired grandson a little less.

"It's wild because I'm the perpetually single lady in our group," she said matter-of-factly. "I've never even come close to getting engaged, let alone married, and they're leaving *me* in charge of all the details until they're back? Madness!"

From the little he'd seen, she was an emotionally expressive woman with fancy shoes and lots of hair. That basically described every bride he'd ever worked with. She might not appreciate that comparison though, so he packed away the comment.

"Anyway," she said, "it's good that you called me because—"

"I didn't. You did."

She gave an exasperated sigh. "Pedantic. Okay, so it's good that *I* called. You were on my list. Did you mean it about making the cake for the wedding?"

"Of course." Had she forgotten he was out of a job? He'd bake them a cake every week if it would cover his living expenses while he searched for permanent work.

"Oh yay!" she squealed. She actually squealed. He should hate that overly loud enthusiasm, but for some reason it made him smile, maybe because he'd seen her interact with Richard and believed she was actually that excited to be helping her friend. "When can we meet to hash out the details?"

"You're the client. Your call." His own days were terrifyingly empty.

She hummed in thought. "Let's see, tomorrow's Thursday, and I've got a late-afternoon meeting in Schaumburg. Could we do evening? Like eight? We could meet at Blake's again since we both know where it is."

"Sure." So that conversation was done. Was it time to hang up yet?

"So how's the job search coming?"

Apparently not. He shifted on the couch, and it creaked again. With his luck, it'd finally splinter into wood shards just when he *really* shouldn't spend money on a replacement. "It's coming."

While he choked back the panic that came from hearing nonstop "sorry, but no" for days, she said brightly, "Well, if all else fails, you could always open your own shop, right?"

She tossed the suggestion off lightly, and he almost dropped the phone at hearing her voice the dream he was afraid to let himself want. Before he could muster a response, she wrapped up the call with a chirpy, "Okay then, see you tomorrow!"

He sank farther into his couch, allowing himself five minutes of blissful blankness before he hauled himself to his feet. Time to bake.

ERIK'S FINGERS drummed out a rhythm on the table as he waited for Josie to arrive on Thursday night. Unlike Saturday morning, Blake's was almost deserted, so his heavy *tap tap tapping* was audible in the small shop. When he noticed the reedy barista glancing his way, he forced himself to stop the fidgety action. He wasn't nervous; it's just that his life was in a state of anxiety, and waiting for the inevitable chaos of the manic-pixie wedding planner wasn't helping things.

His phone buzzed to life on the table next to him, and he flipped it over to find a message from Gina on the screen, probably wanting to talk about her upcoming move to Chicago. He picked up the phone to let her know he'd call her later, but Josie chose that moment to burst through the door, all wild hair and pink cheeks.

"Hi! Sorry I'm late!" She dropped her bag and shrugged out of her tan coat. "I'm desperate for a chai tea. Give me a sec?"

He forgot all about the text to Gina as he watched the Technicolor tornado of perfume and pointy shoes spin to the counter, direct far more words than the situation warranted at the barista, and return to claim a seat.

"Thanks for coming." She beamed. "I talked to Richard this morning, and when he heard we were meeting, the first thing he asked about was your chocolate hazelnut cake."

"Good choice." He didn't hold back his smile. He'd never get tired of hearing praise for his creations. "First some paperwork." He tapped his thumb on the notebook in front of him. "Groom names?"

"Richard Washington and Byron Cutter."

"Guest count?"

She pulled out her phone and consulted a screen of notes. "About eighty. How big a cake is that?" She grinned as she peered at him over the top of her phone. "And by that I mean, how many of your amazing flavors can we have?"

You can have as many of my flavors as you want. He

frowned as the come-on floated through his mind. He wasn't a pickup-line guy, and even if he was, he'd like to think he'd never use one that cheesy on any woman, let alone someone as sophisticated as Josie in her tight dress and frighteningly tall high heels.

He cleared his throat. "We could do three layers. Four if the guys are okay with leftovers."

"Cool." She typed away on her phone, oblivious to his wandering thoughts. "I'm sure they'll want leftovers." When the barista appeared at their table with her drink order, she looked up with such a dazzling smile that the kid almost upended her tea. "My hero! You're a beverage artist. Thank you."

The barista smoothed a hand over one of his exuberant sideburns and stammered out a dazed combination of "thank you" and "you're welcome" and "refills on the house" before escaping behind the counter, looking as if he'd just stared into the face of the sun. Erik sympathized. The woman across from him, sipping her tea with a euphoric look on her face, was... a lot.

"Mmm. *So* good," she said. "Anyway, they'll want one chocolate hazelnut, for sure. What else do you suggest?"

Yes. Back to cakes. Here went nothing. He reached into his backpack and pulled out two plastic containers. "Richard said he's from Georgia?"

Josie nodded.

"Thought so. Here." He nudged the first container over to her, along with a plastic fork he'd scrounged from the coffee station. It was a far cry from Dora's guest china at the Cake Shoppe, but the result should speak for itself.

Josie wasted no time trying a sample, moaning as the first bite hit her tongue. "Oh my God. Heaven. What is this?"

Pointedly *not* thinking about how good her moans of pleasure sounded, he said, "Peach cake with a pecan filling."

"For Georgia!" she exclaimed around her mouthful. "He'll love that."

Pride swelled in his chest; he'd come up with the recipe on the fly, hoping it would mean something to Richard. Beyond the good word of mouth, it sounded like the guy could use a little happiness right now.

He slid the other container toward her. "I also have a cardamom cake that you didn't try on Saturday. I think it's a strong counterpoint to the sweeter flavors, but Dora always said it was 'too ethnic.'"

Josie rolled her eyes. "Of course she did." Her expression turned rapturous as she sampled the new selection, and Erik congratulated himself on correctly estimating the range of her palate.

"Amazing!" She was typing again. "Options for layers: chocolate hazelnut, Georgia peach, and bigots-be-gone cardamom. Oh, and Richard loved the pistachio too."

She grabbed a second mouthful of cardamom cake. Another moan. Another sound for him to ignore as it crossed those velvety lips.

"I prefer buttercream icing if they're okay with that." Abrupt, but it kept the meeting on track.

"Oh sure," she said. "Fondant's gross."

"Exactly. I want my cakes as delicious on the outside as they are on the inside."

She set her fork down with a gasp. "That's great! That's your tagline."

"My what?"

"For your new bakery!" She sketched a rainbow arc

through the air with her hands. "Hot Buns: Delicious outside, delicious inside."

"I'm not calling my shop Hot Buns," he muttered, feeling ridiculous even joking about it with someone else.

She slapped a hand against the table with a hoot, causing the barista to peer around the cappuccino machine to make sure his new customer-girlfriend was safe.

"Aha! You *are* considering opening your own bakery." She shot him a smug grin, and he gave her his most forbidding look in return to get her to drop it.

It worked too well. The teasing light vanished from her face, and she frowned down at the notes on her phone while he battled back the urge to apologize for frightening the joy out of her. But wanting to coax that smile back to her face wasn't the smartest impulse in the long run; she was only here to help pick out a wedding cake, and he wouldn't see her again until the wedding itself, if even then. No need to confide in her like she was his friend.

Smarter to stick to the facts. "When's their wedding date?" Not that it mattered since he had no other work on the horizon at this point, but it got them back on track. Of course, it also reminded him that *he had no other work on the horizon at this point*. Panic roiled in his belly again.

"June twenty-eighth. Fast, right?" She was smiling again, but it was a little less bright this time. "They only got engaged in February, and they still have tons of decisions to make."

She swapped containers and took a big bite of the peach cake, rolling her eyes heavenward as the fork hit her tongue. She might be far too vivid for his everyday life, but her over-the-top expressions made her his ideal cake-tasting client.

"So that's why I'm freaking out," she said around another mouthful. "I offered to take care of some of the details while they're both in Rochester since I'm the best maid and the only semilocal family is Byron's brother, who's way too bro-ish to bother with 'girly wedding shit.'"

So many words to convey such simple ideas. Yet even though their business was mostly concluded, he wasn't ready to go back to his empty apartment. So he did the unthinkable and kept the conversation going. "Nothing girly about wedding prep. What's already done?"

She twirled her fork in the air as she thought it through. "Let's see... the venue, the band, the photographer, the flowers, the invites. What else can there possibly be?"

He scratched his jaw in thought and ignored her pink little tongue darting out to capture a crumb off one of the fork tines. "Cake, obviously," he said. "Honeymoon. Rehearsal dinner. Gift registry. Guest book. Seating chart. Catering menu. Reception favors. Attendant gifts."

She slapped her forehead. "Duh, attendant gifts. How could I forget after all the engraved flasks I've gotten for bridesmaid duty over the years?" She tapped a note into her phone and then cut her eyes over to him. "Hey, you're good at this. Are you married?"

He almost choked on his herbal tea at her abrupt question. "I bake wedding cakes," he said. "I've picked things up."

"Oh! Of course. Well, thanks. I just added all that to my list." She finished typing as a wide yawn overtook her. "Ugh, sorry. It's been nonstop at work, and I'm wiped out. Things start slowing down for me by the end of the week, thank God."

She paused and looked at him expectantly, although

Erik had no idea what she wanted. After a moment, she rolled her eyes. "*Since you asked*, I'm in marketing."

He winced. Right, back and forth. Give and take. The thing he'd always been bad at.

"You're so lucky that I talk enough for three people." She snagged another forkful of cake. "We're a match made in heaven actually. You, strong and silent. A Great Pyrenees. Me, little and yappy. A Chihuahua."

She batted her long lashes at him, and he bit his lip to hide a smile. This was the strangest business meeting of his life, and he wasn't supposed to be *enjoying* it. She was a client, and he had a career to get back on track. It was definitely time to stop lingering.

"I should go." He lurched to his feet, and she looked up at him in surprise.

"Oh, okay. Sure." She frowned and started to replace the lids on the cake containers, but now that he was standing, he wanted to get gone. Being with her unsettled him, and he no longer had an orderly kitchen where he could retreat to find his center.

"Just keep them," he said. "Too complicated." Unwilling to consider whether he meant the GladWare or her, he turned on his heel and left her sitting alone at the table with some of the finest cake he'd ever baked.

SIX

"Are you kidding me?"

Josie let out a frustrated scream and slammed her laptop shut on the email that had just landed in her inbox.

That *harpy*. That *fucking harpy*.

All those hours she'd spent on the proposal for the clothing boutique opening in Streeterville, and Valerie had swooped in and snagged it. Valerie, who hadn't had an original idea in two decades, would be the one overseeing the new business rollout from the ground up, likely with the launch plan that Josie herself had created. Good ol' team player Josie, who'd shown her brilliant ideas to Val when she'd expressed an interest.

She squeezed her eyes shut to banish the burn of tears. What an idiot, thinking she'd finally get the chance to lead a project of that size. And she'd been so well suited to it too. Who better to launch a business devoted to fashion than someone who'd devoted herself to mastery of the topic out of necessity since she was a tween?

Only one thing might ease the bad feelings. Josie left her bedroom and shuffled to the kitchen, where she stopped short at the ghastly scene she encountered. "Finn! You didn't!"

Josie's roommate muted the old episode of *Barbarian Time Brigands* she was watching and twisted around on the couch to face the kitchen. "Didn't what?"

Josie brandished the empty, unwashed cake container she'd found on the counter. "Did you or did you not finish the last of the peach goodness?"

"Umm," a disembodied voice said, "was I not supposed to?" Finn's boyfriend Tom popped up from where he'd been reclining with his head in Finn's lap, his brown hair mussed.

Josie leveled a flat look at him. "I don't know, were you *supposed* to eat the last piece of the best cake I've ever had in my mouth? The piece I was saving for breakfast before I lost all self-control ten seconds ago, only to be disappointed?"

He offered a *my bad* grimace and disappeared behind the couch again. Seconds later, his words floated back to reach her ears. "Worth it!" he called as Finn twisted around again to mouth an apology.

Josie flounced to the sink, where she looked longingly at the sad little icing smear that was all that remained of Erik's magnificent dessert. With a sigh she pulled from the soles of her feet, she turned on the water and scrubbed the empty container, leaving it next to the counter to dry.

Then she flopped onto the chair next to the cuddled-up couple. "Is it not enough punishment that Tom fell in love with my roommate the day after I went to all the trouble of picking him out and bringing him home for myself—"

"Not quite how that happened," Finn objected, a blush spreading across her face.

Josie eyed the way her prim-and-proper roommate's fingers tangled in Tom's curls. "Oh, I'm sorry, are you *not* in love?"

"We are." Tom cracked one eye open and slid his free hand under the hem of Finn's shirt. "Disgustingly so. Right, Huck?"

Finn's blush deepened, but Josie ignored all the lovey-doveyness to vent about her latest disappointment. "So get this: my nemesis snaked the lead on the boutique project I thought I had in the bag."

"Val." Finn hissed the woman's name with all the venom a best friend should.

"Val," Josie agreed gloomily. "Bright side, I'll have tons more free time over the next few months since I won't have my own team to manage, which is good because Richard just texted this morning that their florist had to cancel."

"Bad luck," Finn said.

"Yeah. Something about a date mix-up and a conflict with the mayor's nephew's college graduation party. So yay," she said flatly. "Now I just need to find somebody who's magically free on the last Saturday in June."

Tom's wandering hand paused in its exploration of the hidden mysteries of Finn's stomach. "Why not just skip the flowers?"

"Ugh, you're such a *man*," Josie grumbled.

Finn flicked his ear lightly. "Not a romantic bone in your body."

"Oh, you want a romantic bone in your body?" he replied, catching Finn's teasing fingers. "I'm on it."

In a flash, Tom rolled off the couch, tossed his squealing girlfriend over his shoulder, and carried her off to their bedroom.

"That's gross, you guys! And you still owe me cake!" Josie shouted at Finn's closed door. Then, to herself, she said, "I have *got* to get my own place."

Rather than hanging around stewing in the dangerous mixture of jealousy and frustration that threatened to engulf her, she slid on her shoes, grabbed her jacket, and let herself out of the apartment.

She trudged down three flights of stairs and crossed the checkered floor of the lobby, exploding through the heavy entrance door. She halted just outside the building and filled her lungs with the early-evening air, uncertain of where to head. She'd been joking just now—well, mostly joking anyway—but in truth, she *had* spotted Tom from across the bar in February and she *had* brought him home, hoping that she'd finally found a good guy. Turned out she had... just not for her. Tom chose Josie's roommate, just like Josie's mom chose her work and Josie's boss chose Val. It was enough to give her a massive rejection complex.

Oh wait, she already had one.

She jolted herself into motion and walked briskly down the sidewalk as if speed would let her escape the excess of emotions buzzing in her skull. After a block, she realized she was headed in the direction of the neighborhood bar, Jeb's Tap, which seemed as good a place as any to spend an hour or so feeling sorry for herself. As she approached the squat pub, her phone vibrated. She slid it out of her jacket pocket and read the message Richard had sent her, then tapped to enlarge the accompanying photo.

"What in the...?" She zoomed in closer and forgot all about her earlier agitation. Instead of entering Jeb's Tap, she leaned against the brick wall near the door and selected a number from her contacts.

"What did you do?" she demanded.

She felt the sigh Erik heaved all the way across the line and pictured those huge shoulders rising and falling in exasperation. "You sure like talking on the phone."

"I sure do!" she chirped, only because he so obviously hated it and rattling his chain was fun. "But seriously, did you send Richard and Byron cake samples at the hospital?" Her amazed question was met with silence, so she snapped her fingers near the speaker. "Hello? Tall, blond, and beautiful, are you still with me?"

She heard rustling and a sharp creak on the other end of the line before he spoke again. "Yeah."

His unexpected thoughtfulness pricked her heart like a needle. "That was so sweet of you."

"I'm not sweet." He sounded a little alarmed by the suggestion, so she amended it.

"Fine, then it was crafty of you to track them down." She tipped her head back against the still-warm wall of the pub and looked up at the sky, which was streaked with the pink of the setting sun above the tops of the brick buildings lining the street.

"Not that either," he said. "I had a name and a hospital, and they needed to finalize the flavors."

Good grief, it must've taken so much work to verify the location, make and package the samples, and see them mailed safely, and here he was downplaying it. He might grump and grumble and act all uninterested, but underneath it, he was turning out be a bit of a softy.

"Well, they loved it. Richard had to feed Byron because he's still pretty immobile with his injuries. Isn't that romantic?"

He grunted. "I thought they should enjoy the only fun part of wedding planning."

And there it was. Long live the grump. Still, talking with Erik was helping ease the pressure that had built up in her chest from her professional disappointment and the image of Finn and Tom wrapped together in a shared happiness she'd never experienced. But she'd bet her favorite Coach bag that if she came even close to explaining all that to him, he'd hang up without a word, so she kept her reply light. "You're awesome. But do you know what's not awesome?"

Silence from his end. She sighed. "*Since you asked*, it's not awesome that my roommate's boyfriend ate the last of the peach cake. I was saving that for breakfast." She shifted down the brick wall to make extra room for a cluster of boisterous men who came pouring out of Jeb's, jostling and shouting from a *very* happy hour by the looks of it. She plugged her finger in her ear in time to hear Erik cluck his tongue like a disapproving grandmother.

"Cake isn't for breakfast."

"Cake isn't for..." She gasped and held her hand over her heart, too outraged to finish the thought. "You're a baker! You should be drowning in cake! You should be gorging on your own exquisite creations morning, noon, and night!"

Silence on his end, which she was only able to hear because the gaggle of men had staggered off down the street, bellowing a Journey song as they went.

"No," she groaned. "You're not one of those bakers who doesn't eat his own product, are you?" A horrible thought struck her. "You're not... *anti-dessert?*"

Another creak from his end, this time accompanied by the ghost of a chuckle that sent a thrill down her spine.

Getting this guy to laugh was turning into her favorite challenge.

"I like dessert fine. In moderation."

Oh, he was too much. She'd never last a day with as much stoic self-denial as he seemed to carry around with him. "Bah. Moderation, schmoderation. I'm currently loitering outside my neighborhood bar because not only did my roommate's boyfriend eat the last of the cake, but he hauled my roommate off to ravish her, and now I'm going to drink alone because I'm feeling sorry for myself. How's that for moderation?"

The sky was shifting to a dark velvety blue now, approaching true night, and she willed him to say something, anything, to distract her from the gnawing emptiness in her chest. It was the same reckless feeling that had driven her to pick fight after fight with her mom during her terrible teenage years, the same feeling that pushed her to go home with wholly unsuitable men and to yell at assholes on the L. But today it felt like an itch she didn't know how to scratch. None of the dudes who'd come boiling out of the bar had caught her eye. Her mom hadn't concerned herself with a single decision Josie had made since the instant she'd turned eighteen. And she wasn't about to shout at Finn and Tom for daring to be happy. So what to do with the buzzing that was getting louder in her skull, urging her to *move, shout, do something?*

Then, almost without her willing it, the itch took over her vocal cords and scratched itself. "What are you doing right now? Want to join me?"

She grimaced as silence vibrated down the line. She barely knew this guy, and she wasn't even sure he liked her all that much, but as soon as the words crossed her lips, the buzzing noise quieted a fraction, dimming its cry for chaos. Question was, had she just scared him off?

"Come on," she wheedled. "Do you live near your old bakery? I'm not too far from there. Keep me company. I swear I won't start any fights while you're with me tonight."

Oh, she'd bet he was good in a bar fight. His broad shoulders and thick chest, those legs like concrete pylons, the huge fists at the end of the world's most perfectly formed arms. All that power and focus, intent on defending her honor. She shivered, her thoughts twisting toward something more intimate, and she had a flash of him turning all that power and focus on *her*. Those big hands at her waist. Those big thighs under her—

She bit her lip and slammed the door shut on that little scenario. It was Finn and Tom's fault for getting their sex vibes all over the apartment. But she was suddenly unsure if she wanted this quiet, confounding man to sit next to her at the bar while she tried to shush her demons. Since those demons were whispering for her to try picturing him naked, it might be best to stay far, far away from him tonight.

Then his deep voice cut through her thoughts.

"What the hell. Give me the address."

SEVEN

Erik wasn't sure who was at the wheel anymore. Certainly not his brain; that organ would tell him that securing his next job was his only priority. Not his dick either; as much trouble as *that* copilot had been over the years, even it would think twice about messing around with Josie Redhead, who shouted more than she whispered, wore shoes that cost more than his first car, and used fifty words when five would do.

Yet here he was, taking the stairs from the L two at a time and heading toward a bar that wasn't actually that close to his apartment to meet an excitable, unpredictable woman who wasn't a friend or even a fuck buddy. He was at the precipice of fear and opportunity in his career, and he was going out of his way to intentionally hold his hand over an open flame for fun.

Nevertheless, he lengthened his stride so he'd reach the address she'd given him as quickly as possible, and before he knew it, he was pulling open the door to Jed's and stepping inside. He tugged out his earbuds and pocketed them, scanning the dim, low-ceilinged room until he spotted the woman he was there for. She was perched on a stool, her elbows resting on the bar and the tips of her toes brushing the brass railing running near the floor. She'd set her purse on the seat next to her, and the sight ignited a flicker of pleasure. When was the last time his arrival had been expected? Anticipated even? Fuck, he'd been alone in this city for too long.

He crossed the boisterous room to claim the seat next to her, and she greeted him with a smile that radiated such ferocity that he cast an assessing glance at the other patrons in the long, narrow space before claiming his seat.

"Looking for someone?" Her brow creased as she followed his gaze around the room.

He turned back to the bar and gestured to the bartender for another of whatever Josie was drinking. "Wondering who I might have to fight later. You've got a look in your eye."

She threw her head back and laughed, freeing a long spiral of hair to brush against his shoulder. He itched to hold it between his thumb and forefinger to see if it was as hot to the touch as its color promised.

"I told you I'd be on my best behavior." Her face was the picture of wide-eyed innocence, and he didn't buy it for a second.

Forcing his tempted fingers away from the red strands, he lifted his chin toward a table in the back. "Just promise you won't toss a chair at any of them."

She turned to look at the three leather-clad, chrome-domed biker types plowing through a platter of chicken wings. One glanced up, met Erik's eye for the briefest moment, and quickly returned his attention to the pile of meat on his plate.

Josie scoffed. "Please. You could take those guys easy."

Her eyes cut to his chest, then to his face, then darted back down to her drink as the blood pumped harder in his veins. He was aware that his size had its own intimidation factor, and he didn't particularly enjoy being the cause of someone else's fear. But Josie had looked at him in appreciation rather than apprehension. In fact, if he didn't know better, he'd think he'd just been properly ogled.

Another wave of emotion took him by surprise, this one a fair bit sharper than pleasure. For a brief, vain moment, he flexed the muscles that a lifetime of physical labor and a regular workout regimen had given him. Then embarrassment swamped him, and he released the tension he was holding in his body. He shook his head and reached for the glass the bartender set in front of him.

The first sip had him sputtering. "What *is* this?"

Josie grinned and clinked her glass against his. "A greyhound. Grapefruit juice and gin." His answering grimace prompted another wild laugh from her. "I take it you're not a fan?"

He steeled himself and tossed the rest of the drink back, barely controlling a shudder. "Beer," he told the bartender, who complied with a knowing smirk. Erik probably wasn't the first guy to choke down something awful to impress a woman, nor would he be the last. Except he wasn't there to impress Josie. So what, exactly, was he doing at this bar?

She rolled her glass of disgusting drink between her palms and said dreamily, "Greyhounds must be the coldest dogs, don't you think?"

That. That's what he was doing here. He forgot about

his own shit while he waited for the next geyser of words to spill from her tart mouth.

"Why's that?"

"Oh my God, you *can* carry a conversation!" She beamed up at him, and he drank in the amusement playing across her face. "They just always look like they're freezing, don't they? All skinny and lean? I always want to dress them in sweaters. Or let them cuddle with a Saint Bernard. Did you have dogs growing up? Do you have one now?"

"Yes. And no." He sipped his beer and changed the subject. "How's the wedding planning?"

She groaned and dropped her head to the bar top. "The florist just canceled. Kill me now. How's the job hunt?"

He resisted the urge to mimic her action and settled for lifting his beer in a salute instead. "Nobody's hiring. Kill me now."

She smiled wanly at him, and they drank in unison.

"I know a florist who might help." The offer was out of his mouth almost before he realized he was making it, and when Josie looked up at him, the assessing look in her eye gave him pause.

She straightened and turned on her stool so she was facing him fully. "I have a proposal."

Nope. He didn't care for that. As a preemptive defense against her words, he reached behind his head and yanked out the band holding back his hair, sliding his fingers through the mess of it and shaking it forward until it obscured his features. Natural camouflage, Gina had once called it, and he'd liked the idea of having a shield against the world when necessary.

The abnormal silence from the stool next to him drew

his attention, and when he turned his head, he found Josie staring avidly at the hair falling across his cheek. He froze under her transfixed gaze until she jolted out of her stupor and cut her eyes back to her wretched drink, at which point he hastily bundled up his hair again. *Christ, talk about epic camouflage fail.*

A trio of middle-aged women crowded up next to Josie at the bar, forcing her to lean closer until her knee pressed against his thigh. "So, uh. My proposal." She downed a slug of her drink as he struggled to ignore that single point of contact. "Wedding planning sucks. Job hunting sucks. Let's join forces, Man Bun."

He shifted to put some distance between them. "Pass."

"Pass? Just like that?"

Did she sound a tiny bit hurt? Unlikely; it would take more than a single word to wound someone as bulletproof as she was. "Just like that," he said. "And my name's Erik." He didn't even stop to consider the pros and cons. Some things were an easy no, and he didn't need… all *this* in his life.

She huffed. "Oh my God, *Erik,* your wolf-pack-of-one attitude is exhausting. Look, I could use somebody who's been around the wedding biz more than I have to give suggestions and keep me company."

"I'm lousy company." True, although it didn't feel good to say it out loud.

"Says you. I think you're fun."

"Fun." He repeated the word flatly, and she bit her lip and nodded. *She thought he was fun?* She had to be messing with him. Still, he was curious how far she'd take the joke. He leaned an elbow on the bar. "What do I get out of it?"

She mimicked his posture, crossing one denim-clad leg over the other and propping herself on her own elbow. "What do you want?"

The question burrowed into his brain. What did he want?

A secure workplace.

A predictable future.

A drama-free life.

"Stability," he finally said.

Her eyes didn't move from his face for a long moment before she returned to her drink. "Nah. You want to take a risk."

He laughed. "I promise you, I don't." And it was true. His early childhood had been nothing *but* risk as his mother dragged him from city to city and scheme to scheme, seeking whatever new vision of fame she'd dreamed up that week. He'd spent every moment since then running away from that life. But his heart sped up at Josie's words anyway.

The white-wine-spritzer trio had moved on, giving his companion room to lean lazily against the bar and study him. "Blondie Bakes."

He blinked, concerned that he'd missed a step, and she read the question on his face.

"For your new bakery," she said. "The new bakery that I'm going to help you open in exchange for your coming along to pick out wedding flowers with me. You didn't like Hot Buns, so what about Blondie Bakes?"

"Ridiculous," he muttered, staring hard at his half-empty glass and ignoring the rush of blood in his ears at the merest suggestion of his own bakery.

"The name or the idea?"

"Both." The word burst out of him, sharper than he

intended, and her tiny flinch made *him* flinch. He sighed. "It's impossible. A new business takes way more than baking skills."

"So let me help."

"Why would you want to?"

"Because I *can*." Her mood shifted in an instant, some unexplained turmoil brewing behind that beautiful face, and he couldn't pull his eyes away from her savage gaze. She was burning, and the longer she stared at him, that fire threatened to consume him too, trapping the breath in his lungs and making sweat gather at his hairline.

"I *can*," she repeated, breaking the spell. Then she planted her feet on the bottom rungs of her stool and leaned forward to rummage behind the bar until she found a stack of napkins, leaving him to glare around the room at anyone who might be tempted to perv on her denim-covered ass while it hovered in the air. Once she was safely seated again, she fished a pen out of her purse and popped the tip of her tongue between her lips. She sketched a flurry of sharp strokes across one of the squares and slapped it in front of him on the scarred wood. He looked down to see the words Blondie Bakes emblazoned on the thin material in bold block letters, accompanied by a rough but recognizable sketch of his profile, his jaw a squared-off block and his hair pulled to the back of his head in a bun. He immediately smacked his hand over the caricature.

"No." As well executed as it was, over his dead body would his face appear in a logo. He hastily shoved the napkin into his pocket and out of sight.

She ignored his definitive tone and hit him with a challenging gaze. "What's stopping you?"

What was stopping him? More like what *wasn't* stopping him. He ticked off the obstacles on his fingers. "Let's see... location. Equipment. Staff. Marketing. A customer base." Each word weighed him down, dragging him farther away from the glimmering dream she was spinning. But she just waved a breezy hand to dismiss his concerns.

"So start small. Put up a website, work out of your kitchen, and build up a clientele. Or let me help you look for a location."

"What is it that you do again?"

A laugh burst out of her. "Meddle mostly." She sipped from her glass. "I work for Dynamic Marketing. We're not massive, so I do a mix of PR, event planning, and advertising." Her voice turned coaxing. "I do this for a living, and I suddenly have some extra time on my hands. I could make you huge!"

Her hopeful face glowed up at him, and it was impossible not to bask in the warmth of it. Still, his voice was gruff even to his own ears when he asked, "Who said I wanted your help?"

Her smile dimmed, and he immediately wished he could call the words back. But she was making him wish for things he couldn't have. Business things. Redhead things.

"I got carried away again, didn't I?" She jammed her straw into her drink. "Sorry. It's a bad habit." Two seconds later, she was smiling again, although a little less broadly this time. He hadn't known mercurial before he'd met this woman.

"I just figured we could, you know, suffer together, with the job hunt and the wedding planning. But if you don't want to, it's fine." She dragged a finger through the moisture rings on the wooden surface in front of her. "So does Chicago's hottest baker really have no leads on any employment options?"

Unease marched down his spine, pushing away the absurd pleasure he felt at being labeled the hottest anything. She took in his silence and tilted her head in sympathy. "Oof, really? It's been, what, close to two weeks? I figured somebody'd be dying to get you in their kitchen."

"Not so much," he mumbled.

"For real?" The outrage in her voice should've encouraged him.

He scrubbed a hand through the whiskers covering his jaw. "Nobody's looking for anything more than a glorified kitchen runner." For all her flaws—her many, many flaws—Dora had given him a chance to graduate from kitchen grunt work, and the thought of going back to an underling role after having the run of the ovens was too depressing to contemplate. But he was out of other options, which meant he'd either have to swallow his pride or move back to the farm with nothing to his name but a few months of mild success. And he wouldn't do that. *Couldn't* do that. Besides, Gina was getting ready to move here. The timing was awful all the way around.

"Hmm." Josie clicked her tongue in thought. "Have you tried at Lutz? Sweet Mandy B's? Bang Bang?"

"Yes. All of them."

She blew out a breath. "Well, that sucks. I guess we'll just have to build you a website then."

"Oh, it's that simple?" His sarcasm hid the interest sparking to life in his belly.

She flicked a hand through the air. "Sure. I do it all the time. Plus you'll need a social media campaign. You should be on Facebook, of course, but you'd kill on Insta."

Her eyes traveled down his body again, and he could've sworn a soft purr rattled in her throat for a moment. He shifted on the stool, the weight of her eyes like a physical caress across his skin. Then she tucked a red curl behind her ear and continued in an all-business tone.

"We could maybe book you a segment on one of the local news shows if I pulled a few strings. It'll be great exposure for your up-and-coming business. And I'll keep my ears open for any events that need dessert catering. *Paying gigs*."

She tossed back the dregs of her drink and slammed her empty glass triumphantly onto the bar.

"What just happened?" he asked, bewildered.

"You, my friend, just became my next project."

EIGHT

"What are you working on?"

The question pulled Josie out of her Monday-afternoon work trance, but she was too slow to minimize the screen, which allowed her worst coworker to get an eyeful.

"Oh, you're trying to design a logo! That's adorable." Valerie Jones sniffed and leaned closer to the screen as Josie twitched in annoyance.

"Thanks," she said flatly. And fuck Val very much for slipping in "trying."

The older woman touched the ostentatious strand of pearls around her neck as she peered at the caricature Josie was tweaking on-screen, as close a re-creation as she could make of the napkin sketch that had disappeared under Erik's big paw Friday night.

"This isn't bad, actually. Are you drafting something for a new client?"

The woman's tiny, grudging compliment scraped along Josie's nerves like coarse sand. "He's not officially a client yet, but I'm trying to convince him to use me."

Use me. Heat flooded her cheeks at her choice of words. Erik had spent his time at Jed's, watching her with the horrified fascination of someone who'd discovered a snake coiled in his bathtub, yet all she'd been able to think about was how his big would mesh with her small. How he'd be able to *use her.* And then he'd gone and unleashed all that thick, wavy hair, and she'd almost melted into her stool from the sheer Nordic hotness of him. She squirmed in her seat and thanked her maker that Vile Val was engrossed in the face she'd sketched on the screen.

"Handsome." The older woman leaned closer to the caricature, which Josie had to admit was as flattering as it was accurate, capturing the strength of Erik's nose and cheekbones, the swoop of his hair, the jut of his jaw. "It's so hard to believe you're not formally trained."

Aaaaand there it was. With anyone else, Josie's instinct would be to lash back, but something about Val's brittle haughtiness shut down her fight instinct and left her meek as an amoeba every time. She hated it, but then again, avoiding open warfare with a coworker might be the only reason she was still employed at Dynamic Marketing.

Lowering the temperature in her voice by a few dozen degrees, she asked, "Did you need something, Val?" She might not be able to snap at the woman, but she could call her by the nickname she hated.

Valerie straightened, her fake friendliness dropping away. "Yes. Just making sure there are no hard feelings that I'm heading up the Streeterville boutique project. Between you and me, I think Gil wanted someone with a college degree to go along with the years of experience. But I am grateful for all your little suggestions."

Josie rolled her lips inward and said nothing. Her lack

of a degree was a sore spot, which Val knew and used to her advantage. "I'm sure you'll find all my *little* suggestions extremely helpful," she finally managed.

Valerie's lips pinched together. "Anyway, I also wanted to ask you about Fielder Shoe. They're opening a second location in North Chicago, and they want us to host an open house next Saturday."

"Next Saturday? Yikes. That's soon." She reached for her phone, already plotting event strategies that would fit the family-owned business's vibe in the high-end comfort-shoe market. "I'll give them a call right now to set up—"

"No need. They're already here."

"What?"

Valerie's voice turned impatient. "Yes, they're waiting in the conference room right now, so I want to have a few ideas to present to them."

Blood pounded in Josie's temples. "Why am I not part of this meeting?"

"Why would you be?"

She clenched and unclenched her jaw. "Because they're my account. Remember that promotion I got last year? I have a caseload I manage now, and it's my job to lead these meetings." Her temper threatened to spike, so she dug her nails into her palm and held herself in check. Work wasn't the place to lose her shit, particularly at a woman who'd gladly see her out on her ass with unemployment paperwork stapled to her lapel. But someday she and Val were going to have words, and it was *not* going to be pretty.

Valerie gave a forced laugh. "Oh, but the Fielders are such good friends of mine. I wanted to put our best team together to meet them. And you're so busy with... whatever *this* is." She glanced pointedly at Erik's caricature on Josie's screen.

She surged to her feet and put her body between Val and the computer, silently counting to three before speaking through gritted teeth. "When Gil chose me to handle the Fielder account, he said he wanted me to be involved in these conversations from the beginning." She hated using the big boss's name to fight this battle, but she was out of options. Gil hadn't cared about Josie's one semester of college when she'd applied for the lowest-level assistant job six years ago, and he'd come to value the creative, high-concept events she put together for their clients, both big and small. *Too bad, so sad, Val.*

"Give me five minutes to jot down some ideas, and I'll join you in the conference room."

She took Valerie's glare to mean "Yes of course, Josie, I would appreciate that." As the woman flounced away, Josie's eyes fell on her nemesis's sensible pair of flesh-colored comfort shoes, which she'd no doubt only worn to suck up to the Fielders. Then she looked down in dismay at the expanse of skin visible above the neckline of her grasshopper-green sheath dress. If she'd known she was meeting with the stuffy shoe people today, she would've dressed a tad more conservatively.

With a grumble, she tugged her hem down as close as possible to her knees and tip-tapped down the hallway in her decidedly *comfortless* shoes to join a meeting she was spectacularly unprepared for.

FOUR HOURS LATER, Josie was thoroughly frazzled. The Fielder meeting could've been worse, but she loathed presenting anything less than a polished plan, and she would've felt more in command of the situation in one of her power suits. Damn Val forever.

And now she was late to meet Erik at the florist he'd suggested. The shop had seemed like a reasonable distance from her office when they'd agreed on the time via text that morning, but the Fielder assignment had ballooned to fill her afternoon, leaving her to all but sprint down the sidewalk in her heels for fear of making him wait.

Rounding the corner at seven minutes after their agreed five o'clock meeting time, she spotted a black awning over the sidewalk, displaying the words Love in Bloom Flowers in an elegant script. She paused at the entryway to catch her breath just as Erik strolled up the sidewalk. His hair was down again, which really ought to be illegal. Honestly, that messy mix of waves and curls was a public nuisance, tempting women to grab onto it and not let go.

Woof. She fanned herself and hoped he'd chalk her heated cheeks up to the Chicago humidity, then cocked her hip and gave her best impression of a responsible person who was always on time. "Running a little late, huh?"

He joined her at the door, looking unruffled as usual. "Sorry."

That was it. No flurry of apologetic words, no attempt at an explanation. She could learn a thing or two from his reserved "take me or leave me" demeanor. He held open the door, and when she stepped inside, she was enveloped by an explosion of colors and fragrances courtesy of the cascade of flowers packed into coolers and arranged in vases and baskets and sprays.

"I don't spend enough time in flower shops." She inhaled, filling her lungs as full as possible. "Heaven. This is what heaven smells like. Well, this and your cakes."

She grinned at him, and he offered the flick of a smile in return as a tall, dark-haired woman came around the counter to greet them.

"Erik! I was surprised to hear from you this weekend."

"Lil."

Ah, yes, there was her new partner in crime. Embarrassingly effusive in his greetings. This Lil must know him pretty well though, because his abruptness didn't faze her. She extended her hand to Josie. "I'm Lily Castillo Franklin. What can I do for you today?"

The woman's strong, callused fingers completely enveloped Josie's, and she did her best to return the enthusiastic shake.

"Hi, I'm Josie Ryan. We're here to talk about flowers for a June wedding."

Lily's thin, tan face broke into a smile, and she moved to the cooler and plucked a long-stemmed pink rose from a container. "Congratulations! Erik, I had no idea."

Josie, who'd reached out on autopilot to accept the flower, immediately realized the woman's mistake and rushed to clarify. "Oh no. No, no, *we're* not engaged." She shot a glance at Erik, afraid she'd find horror painted on his face, but he was as stoic as ever. Still, she pointed between herself and the mountain man. "It's for friends of mine who are out of town. I offered to get things going for them. Erik suggested I talk to you."

"Ah, I see." Lily's surprised expression cleared, and Josie had to agree. She and Erik were as mismatched as two people could be.

Lily gestured for Josie to keep the rose, which she

brought to her nose for a grateful sniff as the woman rounded the counter to snag a battered notebook. "Okay, hit me with the details. When, where, all of it. Let's see what we can come up with."

An hour later, thanks to Lily's no-nonsense approach, Josie had recorded a handful of possible budgets, flower choices, color stories, and arrangements to share with the grooms-to-be, and she'd secured Lily's promise that the wedding date would work with her schedule. As Josie was jotting down the last of her notes, Lily and Erik's conversation drifted to industry talk.

"How are things at the Cake Shoppe?"

Erik shifted in his seat. "I'm not there anymore."

Lily's mouth dropped, but she recovered quickly, her brown eyes narrowed in thought. "Let me guess. Dora showed you her true colors?"

Josie leaned forward. "Oh, so he was the only clueless one?"

Lily tossed her long brown ponytail over her shoulder and turned her back to Erik for a little girl talk. "Honestly, I wondered how he stayed with her as long as he did. Then again, as little as he actually interacts with people, is it any surprise he had no idea?"

"I'm not an idiot," Erik interjected, exasperation coloring his voice. "I knew she was bad, just not *how* bad. And I did quit when I figured it out."

"A shame." Lily closed one of the binders of arrangement options. "You do such beautiful wedding cakes."

Erik inclined his head but said nothing, and Josie rolled her eyes. "Oh, for God's sake. He's going to open his own bakery." She turned to him. "You've got to get better at this."

"Really?" Lily clapped her hands. "That's fantastic!

In fact, I've got a couple who just hired me but haven't found their baker yet. Can I give them your card?"

Erik shot Josie a glare. "No, because I'm not opening my own bakery."

Oh *hell* no. She wasn't losing a second opportunity to launch a damn business. Getting him to agree to her plan had been the only bright spot in her weekend after the loss of the boutique account. "We agreed on this! What, you decided you want to be perpetually unemployed? Just hanging around Chicago being sad and broke?"

His jaw worked, but no words escaped his lips.

Josie turned back to Lily, whose interested eyes bounced between the two of them. "I *thought* I'd convinced him to build a website and social media following while we're looking for a storefront for him."

"Smart. And if you need a place to meet prospective clients until then, you can always do it here." Lily gestured around her colorful, sunny shop. "Oh, let me grab the information for that couple I told you about. Be right back." She disappeared through a door behind the counter.

"See? People want to help you." She elbowed Erik's side, digging into the warm, solid muscle and bone that made up the infuriating man.

"I'm not opening a bakery. It's ridiculous." Every part of his body looked carved from stone, but he couldn't hide a there-and-gone flicker that doused her irritation at his change of mind.

He was scared. She should've realized. Of course this quiet, contained man was reluctant to push his name and his face and his work out in front of the public. She'd worked with people in the past who weren't shameless self-promoters, and it always required extra hand-holding.

Thankfully, she was cool with shameless self-promotion. She swiveled on her stool so her knees brushed his, and once again she was reminded of how much *man* was sitting next to her. "Well, bad news. I already got you your first job."

His blue eyes brightened, telling her she was doing the right thing by pushing him a little. "How?"

"I had to suck up to my worst coworker to do it. Think you can rustle up a dessert buffet for 150 of Chicago's older, wealthier shoe-shopping citizenry by next week?"

She watched his baker brain engage. Was he mentally sifting through possible recipes like he sifted through flour? Measuring his remaining sugar supply in that inscrutable head?

"Sure, I could—"

"Here we go!" Lily was back, brandishing a binder. "I really need to work on my organizational systems. Anyway, their wedding's August twelfth, and I'm expecting to meet with them this weekend to finalize their choices. Want me to pass along your info?"

Josie didn't rush to answer this time, curious if Erik wanted this as badly as she thought he did. Finally, after an eternity of silence, his massive shoulders lifted in a sigh. "Yes. Thank you."

"My pleasure! I owe you after you saved my wedding." Lily shifted to face Josie. "My husband Grant's grandmother turned out to be allergic to the dahlias in her corsage, and I was too much of a bride to have extra supplies on hand, so Erik let me raid his cake-table decor to make her a new one."

He brushed it aside. "It was nothing."

"It was plenty. Grant and I are still grateful." She turned to Josie again. "Please tell me you're running all his marketing. This shy-guy routine isn't going to make him the success he deserves to be."

Lily's support of Erik reinforced Josie's instincts about the whole proposition, and she leaned back on her stool to eye him lazily. "Oh yes. I'll make sure the world hears all about him."

He sighed. "So you weren't joking? You actually want to help me start a bakery?"

"More than anything." She bit her lip and fluttered her lashes at him. "I'm *really good* at branding and advertising and social media."

Lily jumped in. "And we all know that's the stuff that'll either bore or confuse you."

An ally. Excellent. The two women shared a quick, conspiratorial glance as Erik scrubbed a hand along his scruff and then sighed. "Let's at least come up with a better name than Blondie Bakes."

Josie didn't bother to hide her triumphant fist pump. She was damn well going to show Vile Val that she was good enough to will a new business into existence even if it happened during her spare time and on a volunteer basis. Good thing for Erik that he'd gotten on board.

NINE

Erik kept his eyes on Josie's highly ogle-able ass in that tight green dress as they climbed three flights of stairs to her apartment, letting her chatter flow over his skin like water. By his estimate, she'd said more words to him in the two weeks that he'd known her than he'd exchanged with any other human being over the past year.

"So it's a couple of ideas I pulled together on my laptop, just to see what you think," she was saying. "No big deal. It's the kind of thing I do for clients all the time. But we need to decide soon so you can get business cards and whatnot."

He grunted and followed her down the hall to her door.

"If it's clean, that's only because of my roommate," she said as she jiggled the key in the lock. "On my own, I'd be buried in laundry and take-out containers in a week."

She ushered him into the standard-issue "Chicago apartment with a roommate" setup: kitchen on the right, living room on the left, bedrooms to the back. Unlike his own place, it had enough square footage for some breathing room, even for someone his size. She gestured to the kitchen table, and he took a seat while she fetched her laptop.

"Here we go." After a flurry of taps, she turned the screen toward him, and he was hit with his own face staring back at him. It was the caricature she'd drawn on the napkin at the bar, but perfected. The strokes were bold and spare, yet it was clearly him. Him on his best day, looking confident and approachable and cartoonishly appealing in logo form. Next to it were the words HAVE YOUR CAKE in a clean, modern font.

He swallowed. Swallowed again. "That's..."

She clicked to enlarge it. "The name's pretty great, right?"

"Yeah. Yes." His voice sounded hoarse, and for the life of him, Erik couldn't figure out why a lump had settled in his throat. It was just that... she believed in him. So many people had questioned his plan to devote his life to making beautiful creations, and when he wasn't in her presence, it was easy to talk himself out of this crazy plan. But her faith in him was like oxygen to a dying fire. This gorgeous chaos agent had looked at him and seen *everything*. Everything he was scared to want.

"The name's perfect," he said roughly. And it was. Clever, memorable, and far better than anything he'd have come up with.

"Thanks." She grinned before turning all business again. "So I was thinking your website should have a slider that flips through shots of your best cake designs and then a page for different flavors and decoration options. Information about you, of course, and a contact page. We'll try to answer all the basic questions but still encourage them to reach out personally."

The website formed in his imagination, simple and informative. He could see it. He *wanted* it.

"Birthdays," he said.

Josie nodded, getting the gist. "Good idea. Non-wedding items to bring in more cash. Special-occasions cakes. Anniversaries, graduations, things like that?"

He nodded. "All that." His heartbeat picked up. Was he doing this? Was he really going to do this?

"Cookies?" she asked, but his answering grimace spoke volumes. "Okay, no cookies."

"I'll do it for the catering job, but it's not my thing."

"Sure." She nodded once decisively. "And if you just do cakes, it streamlines the marketing message. So we'll need you to make some samples to be photographed. The prettiest cakes, the smoothest icing, the plumpest flowers. Nothing but money shots."

Erik gripped the edge of the table. His poor brain. First there was his bakery dream coming true before his eyes. Then there was this fuck-hot woman, dripping with the kind of breezy confidence that had always left him tongue-tied, shaping her lips around words like "money shot" and "plump." And she just kept blithely talking.

"Oh! Speaking of cakes, did you want to see Richard and Byron's color scheme? It might help with your cake ideas for them. Hang on."

She darted from the kitchen and returned with a wisp of bright blue fabric on a hanger. "Here's my best-maid dress. They're doing cerulean as the main color—not blue, mind you, but *cerulean*—with white and gold accents."

She dragged a chair around and hooked the hanger over the back, and Erik leaned forward to poke gingerly at the fluffy fabric. There didn't seem to be very much of it, and *now* his synapses were firing with questions about just how low that neckline actually went.

"It's... nice." He grabbed his phone to snap a shot of the hue for later reference, hoping she wouldn't notice him wincing over his inane comment. *Nice.*

"So, like, what do we need to do legally to make you a baker?" She tossed the question over her shoulder as she whisked the dress off the chair and walked back to her room, giving him a chance to pull his mind back up from his groin to answer. Seriously, was that strip of fabric the only thing that was going to cover her tits? He'd short-circuit if he kept thinking about it.

He shifted in his chair and cleared his throat. "I've got my food-handling certificate with the state." Licensing. Certifications. Legalities. They were better than a cold shower. "Now I need to register a cottage food operation with Cook County. Could take a couple of weeks."

She sauntered back into the kitchen and reclaimed her seat in front of the laptop. "So do you have the cash and the kitchen to get some things baked? The wedding cake and some samples for website photos?" She smiled approvingly at his nod. A born leader. "Cool. Let me know when, and I'll get a photographer lined up. Next, the bio." She clarified when he looked at her in confusion. "Your life story. Tell it to me for the website. And yes, this is mandatory."

Damn. She'd anticipated his objection. Her fingers hovered over her keyboard, and he almost told her not to bother, to let him write it. But he'd never had a way with words, and he trusted this babbling brook to get the job done for him.

With a grimace, he offered up the pertinent details. "From outside Liberty Valley, Iowa. Twenty-eight years old. Attended the Culinary Institute of America. Worked under pastry chef Philippe Bernaert for a year. Moved to Chicago last summer. Good baker."

The last fact earned him a snort. "Good baker. That's helpful. The people coming to your page will be relieved to hear that." Her fingers danced across the keys, and she spoke without looking up. "Iowa, huh?"

"Yeah. Raised by my grandfather on a farm." Erik had no idea why he was volunteering information that she wasn't even asking for. The click of her keyboard filled the room, and suddenly he was talking again. "My mom left me with him when I was eleven."

She looked up with a sympathetic frown, and he said, "No, it was good. Life with Mom was chaos. Fun at first to try a new town every six months, but... eventually the stability of the farm was a relief."

God. Why was he still talking? He'd caught her mutant strain of chattiness.

She lifted her fingers from the keys, and he forced himself not to squirm while she looked him over. If he saw a trace of pity on her face, he'd dissolve into a puddle of shame.

"A farm boy," she finally said. "Did you get that body from baling hay?"

His eyebrows met over the bridge of his nose, and she rolled her eyes.

"Oh, come on." One burgundy-tipped fingernail waved in his direction. "The shoulders? The chest? The thighs? I told you on the train that first night, you're basically a mythical Viking warrior."

He felt like prize livestock at a cattle auction being sized up by her assessing eyes. "Dairy cows," he finally said as blood rushed to his cheeks. "Feeding them, watering them. Yes, baling hay."

"Milk does a body good apparently." Her lips twitched as she typed.

"That and a gym membership."

She paused over the keyboard and cocked her head. "I was scared of you that first day. Just for a second."

"Sorry." God, he hated that. Hated that he'd frightened her the first time he touched her. "I would never hurt you or—"

"Oh, I know that now. You make me feel safe." She held his eyes for a moment before turning abruptly back to her computer. "So. Are you in touch with your mom?"

That was a hell of a subject change, and he was off-kilter enough to answer honestly. "Last I heard, she was in Reno. But that was two years ago, so she could be living on a Peruvian beach by now for all I know."

Josie looked up, and the softness of her eyes kept his words flowing. Looked like he was really doing this.

"All she ever wanted was to be famous. A singer, an actress, a model. Lots of gambles that never paid off." And nights sleeping on a stranger's couch or hanging around outside clubs, handing out black-and-white headshots that nobody wanted.

"Your dad?" Her soft voice pulled him back into the present, and her guarded expression told him she already knew the answer.

"Not in the picture. Never met him." And wasn't he

describing a perfectly fucked-up family scene for her? Then she surprised him.

"Hey, me too! My mom wanted a kid without the complications of a man, and then in the end, she didn't even want the kid."

He watched as her Josie Ryan light dimmed right in front of his eyes. Her mouth turned down, and she curled in on herself ever so slightly, as if recalling moments that made her feel small. He clenched his hands into fists to keep from reaching for her hand. His brash new business partner didn't need him pawing at her.

And it turned out she didn't need comforting from him anyway. When she looked up from her laptop, her smile was back, if a little more brittle than before. "Lucky you, to have a good grandpa."

True. Pops had been stern, but he'd also been the bedrock of Erik's life, and it made him wonder who'd been Josie's foundation growing up.

"So!" His interviewer was clearly ready to move on to the next topic. "Why wedding cakes?"

Safer ground, thank God. "Grandma was the woman who made the cakes for basically everybody getting married in the Liberty Valley Episcopal Church. She died when I was a baby, but I found her recipes when I was twelve and..." He made a small motion with his hand, hoping she'd get the gist. His attempts to cheer up Pops with his late wife's desserts had grown into a profession that Pops had never fully embraced. Maybe not such safe ground after all.

"Adorable." Josie grinned. "Got any happy customers who'd be willing to talk you up? Not happy with the Cake Shoppe, but with you?"

"Maybe." In truth, he'd rather saw off his own finger

than go begging for help, but he got what she was driving at. As a stall, he tugged the band from his wrist and gripped it between his teeth, twisting his hair high up on the back of his head. Josie made a tiny strangled sound, and he dropped his chin to look at her.

"What?"

"Nothing," she said faintly. "You just... you make that look so easy."

"Years of practice." What had started as a dumb stunt in high school to piss off Pops had become part of his routine over the years: up for work, down for social situations, and kept under control by extravagant doses of conditioner that never quite saved it from getting fuzzy at the height of summer humidity. As a bonus, it was available as a distraction technique when he needed it. Like now.

Her eyes followed his hands through their task of wrapping the band twice around his hair. "Nice. Show off those ears."

It was a normal smart-ass Josie remark, but the tone was off. Breathy. *Did* he have nice ears? He resisted the urge to touch the lobe closest to her.

"So anyway, about those happy customers?"

He grimaced, prepared to offer his blood type and bank account instead, when the apartment door burst open to admit a man and a woman, laughing and laden with carryout bags.

"Jos! You're home!" The black-haired woman deposited the bags of food on the kitchen countertop, then paused when she caught sight of Erik. "And you have company."

Josie was already on her feet. "Oh my God, you brought home Ming's. Please tell me you ordered too much so I can steal some." She glanced up from the bag she was investigating to make introductions. "Oh yeah, this is Erik. He's doing Richard's wedding cake. Erik, this is my roommate Finn and her boyfriend Tom, even though I saw him first."

"Not true. I've been Finn's for years," Tom told Josie before turning his smile on Erik. "Welcome to the madhouse. How'd Josie manage to lure you to her lair?"

Finn smacked Tom's shoulder. "Knock it off. Obviously Josie doesn't lure anybody anywhere."

"And yet that's how I found you again," he said, loosening his tie and pressing a kiss to her hair.

Josie walked around them with a roll of her eyes to grab glasses from the cabinet.

He watched the three of them move around the kitchen with smooth efficiency, sharing details of their respective days as they gathered plates and silverware and spread the containers of food across the table. If they thought having the wedding-cake baker in their midst was strange, they didn't say so. He clearly wasn't the first stray Josie had brought home.

In fact, it sounded like that's exactly what had happened with Tom. Tom, who grinned while Erik grimaced and chatted with ease while Erik stayed mute. Were cocky men in business suits Josie's type? That fit with everything he knew about her, which meant he was fucked.

He lurched to his feet. He wasn't fucked, he didn't *want* to be fucked, and where had that thought even come from? He wasn't in competition with Tom, and the fact that his brain had wandered in that direction meant it was time for him to get the hell out of there. Just as he was about to force out a goodbye, Finn set a plate on the table in front of him. "I assume you're staying for dinner?"

"No, I should—"

"He's staying." Josie's command took the air out of his protest. She wanted him to stay, so he'd stay. Just like that. Plus he didn't relish the thought of going back to his empty apartment; after years of quiet, he was slowly warming to the idea of noise.

"Okay. Thanks." He sat back down and accepted the container that Tom handed to him.

"No, no, thank *you*. Finn and I are still raving about the cake that Josie brought home the other day," he said, looking hopefully around the kitchen. "I don't suppose you brought any more with you today?"

Josie gave his arm a good poke as she walked to her seat. "He's not your personal pastry mule. Besides, any baking he does over the next week is either for his first official job or for website pictures. Ideally both."

His first official job. What a marvelous thought.

"So we need a photographer," Josie said as she reached for the carton of garlic chicken. "Finnigan, who's that guy you used for the product brochure you put together last year?"

"He moved back to New York, I think." Finn paused with an egg roll halfway to her mouth. "You could always call—"

"Absolutely not," Josie snapped, and for the first time since Erik had met her, she didn't have a follow-up comment. No jokes, no smart retorts, no random remarks. Only a harsh expression that didn't sit easily on her usually sunny features.

Finn raised her hands in surrender before picking up

her fork again. "It was just a suggestion. You don't have to do it."

That brought the fight back into Josie's face. "As if anybody makes me do anything I don't want to do. Poor Erik's just now learning that."

She jerked her head in his direction, and his answering grimace prompted laughter around the table. He turned his attention back to the plate, uncharacteristically pleased to be part of a group.

TEN

Josie staggered down the sidewalk and tried to count her blessings.

One: early May in Chicago was only a little humid, which meant her hair was only a little frizzy.

Two: Byron was feeling better every day and wanted to participate in wedding prep by hand-embossing the wedding programs that had been sitting in his apartment for a month.

Three: the box she was hauling to the post office could be filled with lead weights instead of the aforementioned wedding programs and embosser, which were only *slightly* less heavy than actual lead weights would be.

Four: she was in her third-most comfortable high heels for this mad trot to the post office.

Five: her mom still hadn't called her back.

Wait. That last one wasn't a blessing. Or was it? She pondered the question as she entered the post office and took her place at the back of the line of the damned, resting the cumbersome box on her hip and trying to stay balanced as she inched forward.

A blessing. Mostly. And that led her to the final item on her list.

Six: she'd get to see Erik in four days.

It had been close to a week and a half since he'd stayed for dinner and charmed Finn and Tom with his "aww shucks, who, me?" quiet broody guy act. Since then he'd gotten to work on baking and brainstorming items for the website, taking a break to text her work-in-progress photos and wedding-planner suggestions. She... liked it. Liked him. Which was surprising since she usually hung with witty young urbanites who knew all the hot new bars in town and regularly turned a three-minute anecdote into a thirty-minute epic tale.

But the thought of seeing the shy, salty-sweet Erik at Saturday's grand-opening bash for the new Fielder Shoe store got her blood pumping. Not only could she get some shots of his goodies for the website, but she'd get to see *his* goodies. If she could convince him to let her slap photos of his strong brow, sharp eyes, and broad shoulders prominently on the website, he'd generate amazing buzz. Just her luck she got stuck with a client who was equal parts hot and humble.

Got stuck with. Ha. Like she hadn't bullied him every step of the way. Good thing he loved it though. Okay, not love, exactly, but she was starting to think that part of him craved it. He needed somebody to force him to take this opportunity, and she needed someone to build into a towering success. Win, win. Now if she could talk him into taking his hair down for the website photos...

Nope. Hair-down Erik was certainly not appropriate standing-in-line daydream material, particularly not when the air-conditioning in this ancient government building already wasn't up to the task of cooling down the mass of humanity surrounding her. Her loins would generate a mini-heatwave from which no one in the vicinity would recover if she thought too long about that tousled hair skating along his cheeks to kiss the tops of his shoulders.

The buzzing of her phone startled her out of the dirty fantasy that was starting to formulate in her mind, and she blushed to see a text from the man himself. Thank God he wasn't a mind reader. Before she could juggle the box to text a "Call you in a sec" reply, the next available clerk summoned her forward, and she dropped her burden on the counter with a huge exhale.

"Wow, what do we have here?" the clerk chirped, her purple acrylic nails sliding across the box surface.

"The intestines of my enemies."

The younger woman snatched her hands away, and Josie rushed to erase the horrified look on her face. "Ha! Um, no, just some wedding stuff. For my friend who's getting married." She added the last bit because the clerk looked ready to offer congratulations. She'd already had to correct Lily at the flower shop; was she really expected to wander the whole of Chicago, announcing her single status to every person she met?

Her joke was rewarded with a suspicious round of "Anything liquid, fragile, or perishable?" before she was able to swipe her credit card and escape government-office purgatory. Her phone buzzed again when she hit the sidewalk, and she answered without looking.

"You're calling me for a change, Man Bun? I'm touched."

"Josephine."

The cool voice startled her so much that she froze midstep, forcing the man walking behind her to veer sharply. His briefcase clipped her on the way by, and she sucked in a gasp at the stinging pain. "Mom. I didn't—"

"So you need photos taken?" Josie's mother never had time for pleasantries, not even with her only child.

"I-I do, yes." Josie gripped the phone with one hand, cradled her bumped elbow with the other, and tried to ignore the pathetic swell of happiness that enveloped her to be hearing from her mother after so many months of silence. "It's for—"

"I got your message. A bakery website you're launching. I'm in town early next month, so I could squeeze you in on the weekend. Maybe a Sunday."

"That would be great. Thank you. How've you be—"

"I need to run, but text me the location."

With a click, nationally renowned photographer Pamela Ryan ended the call, leaving her daughter with a throbbing elbow and a blank phone screen. She stared down at it as if it would flare to life with a follow-up message. *I love you. I can't wait to see you. Sorry I suck so much as a mother. Sorry I turned my daughter into a bottomless hole of neediness, willing to accept any scrap of affection that lands like soft rain on her parched heart, forever chasing relationships with unworthy men, doomed to be alone forever, yearning for a connection that never comes.* Hell, she'd even accept a winky emoji.

When her phone buzzed again, she almost fumbled it out of her hands, and this time she checked the caller ID before answering. "Man Bun. Calling me for a change. Wow." The same joke but delivered in such a subdued tone that Erik paused before speaking.

"Uh. Everything okay?"

Well, shit, the man with no emotions was alarmed by her existential despair. She must be in a bad way. She pursed her lips and exhaled on a slow five count, reaching inside herself for the fire she'd learned to nurture and feed as a child. "Good. It's all good. What's up?" There, she sounded more like her perky ol' self.

"Just checking in. You worked out the transportation?"

"Yep. It's handled." This was her zone. She launched into motion again, rejoining the flow of foot traffic on the sidewalk as she filled him in on the details she'd arranged. "I asked my friend with a Jeep if we could borrow it for the open house. We should be able to load up all the containers in the back. You're all set there?"

His answering grunt sounded affirmative, so she assumed he'd acquired the containers and other serving supplies he'd need.

"I was thinking I'd be at your place around eleven on Saturday. The open house runs from two to five, so that should give us plenty of time to get things loaded and set up at the store."

"You're going to help?"

"Don't sound so surprised. I'm not useless." *Snippy, Josie. Don't take your bad day out on the innocent man.*

"Didn't say you were," he replied levelly. "I appreciate it."

Of course he wasn't saying that, and of course he was appreciative. He had good manners when he actually chose to speak to people, and she was a touchy bitch. Regardless, time to change the subject. "I found you a photographer. My mom. I've set it up so she'll do the photo shoot at your place when she's in town in a few weeks."

That prompted a trace of surprise from him. "Your mom's a photographer?"

"A good one. Look her up: Pam Ryan." Pride mixed with bitterness in her mouth as she said it.

"Cool. Oh, did you talk with Lily about the centerpiece-arrangement idea I had for Richard and Byron?"

She reached her train stop and climbed the steps to the platform, stepping around a cluster of men in jeans and work boots, presumably headed home for the day. Lucky bastards. She had a corporate dinner to swing by to see for herself that the room had been arranged to the company's directions.

"Yeah, I did. She loved the feather idea. I'll run it by the boys next."

The testosterone-y group all climbed onto the red line as it slowed to a stop, leaving her alone on the platform.

She dropped onto a bench and flexed her feet in their pointy heels. "I love that you're better at this wedding stuff than I am." A grunt was Erik's only answer, and she had to laugh. "At least we know you're not better at this talking stuff than I am."

"Yeah, you're the talking champ." She heard a soft noise that could almost be a chuckle, then he ended the call with "See you Saturday."

When her train arrived, she was still thinking about that small sound, wondering if that really was a twinge of affection she'd heard or if she had only imagined it.

ELEVEN

"We're here!"

Josie's bright voice crackled over Erik's ancient apartment intercom as he was snapping a shot of the bounty he'd assembled for the Fielder open house that afternoon.

He pressed Send to text the pic to Gina, then hit the button to let Josie up, wondering who "we" was. Ninety seconds later, he had his answer when Josie appeared in his doorway dressed in a twinset and loafers like a modern Mrs. Brady, a man by her side.

A tall man. A tall, handsome man.

Erik crammed his phone in his pocket and stepped back to let them into the apartment, an irrational part of him taking pleasure in the fact that he had a couple of inches on the guy following at Josie's dainty heels. Of course, since he was six foot five, that meant the stranger was over six feet tall himself. But still.

"So this is your place, huh?" Josie swept her curious eyes over the small space. "Is this where you come to do all the talking you don't do with other people? Does it know all your secrets?"

He *hmmmed* and moved to lean against the countertop, imagining what she was seeing as she looked around. A couch. A kitchen table and two chairs. Unadorned walls. A closed door leading to the equally unadorned bedroom.

"Wow. We definitely can't have you meet clients here."

"Obviously." Like he'd want anybody to be in here. He was jumpy having *her* invade his space, let alone her friend, who looked utterly out of place in an expensive suit and tie. These weren't people who should fit into his life.

"Hi. Jake Carey. You must be Erik." The black-haired man moved toward him with his hand extended and a confident smile on his face. Erik performed the obligatory shake and hated him the whole time, this good-looking guy who'd arrived with Josie. Guys who wore suits for a living rarely ruffled his own sense of self-worth, but he was suddenly aware of the frayed hem of his jeans and the lack of a collar on his gray T-shirt.

"Oh, sorry. Jake, this is Erik Andersson, my pet baker."

Erik cut his eyes to her, surprised at the title. He was nobody's pet and never had been. Then again, if he belonged to anybody at this point in his life, it was her. What a thought.

"This is Finn's brother," she said. "We're borrowing his Jeep for the night."

"And Finn's brother needs to get back to the office." Jake checked the time on his phone. "You'll text me when you're done so I can come get my baby?"

Josie slapped her hands over her heart, the polish on her short nails bright against the yellow of her cardigan. "I get to interrupt Chicago's most successful accountant twice on a Saturday? My horoscope *did* say I'd have a lucky week."

"Ha." He slid his phone back into his pocket. "Remind me why Finn keeps you around?"

"My restful presence?" She fluttered her lashes at Jake, who scoffed in disbelief. Erik tended to agree but kept his input nonverbal.

"Anyway," Jake said, "I'm here now. Do you need help before I head back to my spreadsheets?"

Erik pushed off the countertop, relieved to have an excuse to cut their banter short. He positioned himself between Josie and the guy she'd brought into his home and pointed to the rows of containers stacked on the counters. "It all goes."

"Okay. I'm not sure how legal my parking job is, so let's get the Jeep loaded."

Twenty minutes later, the three of them had packed every square foot of the vehicle with baked goods and the accessories he'd need to serve them. His bun had gotten scraggly from the effort, and as he pulled out the band to reset it, Erik couldn't help but notice that not a hair on Jake's shiny black head was ruffled even though he'd stormed up and down stairs over and over in a suit. Fucker.

"You'll be careful with her?" Jake rested a hand on the hood, and Josie rolled her eyes.

"Yes, I'll be very careful with your twelve-year-old Jeep."

She extended her hand for the keys, but he paused before relinquishing them.

"Everything's good with Finn? She's all set for rent? She's still happy with that guy?"

"You know she makes bank at her job, and I'm slapped in the face with her happiness on a daily basis." She snatched the keys from him, but her face softened as he continued to frown. "Hey, she's good. She's really good. If you came around more, you'd be able to see for yourself. She doesn't want your money. She wants your time."

Jake pinched the bridge of his nose and exhaled hard. "I know. It's just crazy right now at work."

"Yeah, yeah. Like always. If that ever changes, you know where we live."

Erik listened with interest to see if he'd promise to visit, but Jake settled for patting his Jeep one more time and climbing into his waiting Uber, heading for whatever fancy skyscraper held his office.

"Shall we?" She jingled the keys at him and hopped into the driver's seat.

"I still need to change into service clothes." And wouldn't that be quite the contrast to the man who'd just left?

"Well, hurry up! Your new business can't afford a parking ticket."

He suppressed a smile and took the stairs up to his apartment two at a time, where he threw on a pair of black pants and a polo and slung his apron over his shoulder. Back on the street, he slid into the passenger side, grateful to be riding in a tall man's vehicle with ample room for his legs. Josie fired up the engine and pulled away from their definitely illegal parking spot, and Erik found himself uncharacteristically curious.

"So, uh."

He didn't have to say any more; Josie laughed as she

navigated lanes of traffic toward Lake Shore Drive. "Let me guess. What's the deal with Jake?"

He shrugged, knowing full well that whatever it was he was doing, no part of it was playing it cool. How long had she known the guy? Was there any chance he was actually a married father of five or moonlighting as a Catholic priest? Was it true that Josie only turned those flirty eyes on men in suits?

"That was Finn's stupidly hot, perpetually single, all-work-no-play brother. He's a kick-ass accountant at the best firm in town." The admiration in her voice dissolved into a theatrically over-the-top sigh. "I've known him for basically the entire six years I've known Finn, and tragically, he's never once considered marrying me and making Finn and me sisters for real, no matter how hard I've tried."

An unexpected rush of disappointment clogged his throat, and then she surprised him by laughing ruefully.

"Alas, Jake and I have zero chemistry. You can imagine how frustrating that is since hot, übersuccessful businessmen are exactly my type."

Erik said nothing but filed away yet another piece of evidence that Josie preferred fancy men. Outgoing men. Not-him men.

"Eh, it's just as well," she said easily. "He's better off as a friend. Most of the guys I date don't stick around past a week or two anyway."

Idiots. What would it be like to be the person she wanted? Just imagining it made his skin heat. Sure, she assessed him all the time with a professional eye, but to have her look at him with desire? To have her use that persuasive charm to get him to put his hands where she wanted, and then his mouth and his tongue—

He dragged his eyes away from her pert profile and forced his mind elsewhere. They were speeding past the familiar Chicago skyline. Somewhere in all that chrome and steel, the type of guy she actually wanted was toiling away at a computer, not worrying about napkin counts and whether he'd made enough pear tarts.

The reminder tossed cold water on his thoughts, and he let her chatter wash over him as they drove. Her words stopped when the car did, and before they exited the Jeep to start setup, she turned to face him.

"Nervous?"

"No. Maybe."

"Don't be." She dropped the keys in her purse and grinned at him. "I snuck a few samples as we were carrying everything down. It's all delicious. People are gonna go nuts."

And they did. Five hours later, he and Josie were left with mostly crumbs and empty platters among the racks and racks of sturdy-soled shoes on display. The raspberry-lemon cake that had been the centerpiece of his service had been consumed down to the last crumb, and the supplementary pear tarts and snickerdoodles were nothing but picked-over remnants.

"It couldn't have been better!" she crowed. "The Fielders are thrilled. And I gave out so many of your business cards."

"I have business cards?"

She reached into her pocket and handed him a small square with a flourish. "This isn't amateur hour, my friend. Of course you do." The card was emblazoned with the logo and sketch of him that he was trying very hard not to warm up to, along with his brand-new web address and his cell phone number. At the bottom in a simple font, she'd had printed Delicious Outside, Delicious Inside.

He curled his fingers around the thick paper, thrilled at how official this made things and a little touched that she'd remembered the tagline they'd joked about weeks ago. "Thank you."

She leaned around him to snag the last tart from the tray. "Just keep doing what you do best, and I'll keep doing what I do best." With a wink, she darted off to talk with Mr. and Mrs. Fielder, and *damn* she was cute when she talked with her mouth full.

He squashed that thought, shoved the card into his back pocket, and started carrying empty trays to the back. On his second trip, voices just outside the stockroom door had him pausing with his fingers on the handle.

"I wonder where she found the unbelievably hot baker."

"Right? I couldn't stop *looking* at him."

He was the subject of this conversation? Erik peeked through the crack and confirmed that it was the pair of young Fielder Shoe employees who'd been on hand for crowd control.

"Those forearms!" the woman with braids crooned.

"Those *forearms*," the short-haired woman agreed. "That guy's a snack."

"Girl, that guy's a whole five-course meal."

His ears burned as they snickered, and then a familiar voice joined the conversation.

"Yes, yes, congratulations on having working sets of eyes. When you're done drooling over my hot baker's incredible arms, could one of you help me shift this table?"

Erik felt nailed to the spot, Josie's words zinging

through his brain like an electric current. Did that mean...?

Surely not. The first time they'd met, she'd recoiled from him, and the second time they'd met, she'd done nothing but yell. Sure, she'd looked at his body once or twice, but she'd also just told him that her type of guy was his night-and-day opposite.

Without warning, she materialized by his side, having burst through the doors with an empty tray under her arm. She took one look at his face and grimaced. "Oh no. Did you overhear that?" With her free hand, she patted his chest. "Don't worry, big guy. You're more than a piece of meat to me."

She flitted away, leaving him to study his forearms: thick, wrapped in muscle and veins, too broad to be elegant, too thick to be stuffed into a suit jacket. But if Josie liked looking at them, he'd throw away every long-sleeved shirt he owned and risk death by freezing in the Chicago winters.

"Erik! You with me?" She dropped the tray with a clatter and startled him out of his reverie. "I swear to God, I'm going to start setting fire to things if we don't get away from all these comfort support insoles soon."

Brisk tone. Comical grimace. Not a single glance at any part of his body.

Yeah. He'd misunderstood what had clearly been a joke. Pretty little show ponies didn't fall for Clydesdales. He pushed through the door with a sigh, leaving his foolish fantasies behind him in the stockroom.

TWELVE

"Put your pants on."

Erik's answering grunt was exactly what Josie had been fishing for when she'd called, and she uncorked a delighted giggle before returning to business.

"Why am I requiring you to clad your magnificence in lowly denim this early in the morning, you might be wondering?" She paused for another grunt and was richly rewarded. Her baker was grumpy in the morning. "*Since you asked*, I've found you a delivery van."

"You what?"

"Ah, he speaks!" Yep, grumpy. Maybe even still partially asleep if the lovely, gravelly rasp in his voice was any indication. "It was obvious last weekend that you need something reliable to move your creations around in, so I've been trolling for options online. I found something promising, but it's first come, first served, which is why I called you at this unholy hour. So put your pants on and meet me at the address I'm texting you now before somebody buys it out from under us."

Another grunt and he disconnected, leaving her laughing as she slid on her shoes.

Thirty minutes later, he joined her in an alley in Avondale, north of the Loop, and passed her one of the Dunkin coffees he was holding. "Three sugars, no cream," he said, tugging out his earbuds with his newly free hand.

"Thanks!" She accepted it and took a sip, the coffee warming her insides almost as much as the knowledge that somewhere along the line, he'd made note of her usual order. She gestured to the white van parked behind a two-story brick building. "Isn't it perfect?"

"For me to abduct children?"

His grumbled joke made her laugh.

"Yeah, it's a little... windowless. But it's got fold-up racks inside for cake transport." She sipped her coffee as he scratched his jaw in thought. "Just picture it with your logo on the side. That handsome mug of yours advertising your bakery all over town."

His lips tightened. "Absolutely not."

"It's your logo, Erik." Was he trying to kill her with his bashfulness?

"My face is not going on a van."

"We'll see."

His hair was down that morning, more waves than curls when he came straight from bed apparently. It was all she could do not to reach up and pet that tempting tumble around his shoulders. Maybe it would soothe that forbidding look off his face.

She distracted herself with another sip of coffee as a shiny black car screeched to a halt in the parking spot next to the van and a fortysomething man slid out of the vehicle, wearing a suit and tie and a stressed expression at odds with it being seven thirty on a Sunday morning.

"You're Josie?" The balding man checked his watch and then his phone, barely pausing to meet her eyes.

"Yes, we're here about the v—"

"So here's the deal," he barked. "My great-uncle Al died last month, and I'm the only family member left to clean this all up."

He retrieved a set of keys from his pocket and clicked a button to unlock the van. "I'm due back in Denver this afternoon for a meeting I cannot miss. If you can pay me cash now for the van, it's yours."

Erik stepped forward and opened the van's back door, his voice muffled as he peered inside. "It runs?"

The man handed a piece of paper to Josie, who scanned it. "This is a clean bill of health from Sterling Auto Repair."

"Nice racks." Erik's voice floated from the back, and Josie bit back a laugh and a dirty joke for fear of jeopardizing the sale. He emerged and walked to the front to climb behind the wheel. When Philip handed him the keys, he fired up the engine, raising his voice above the rumble. "Was your uncle a baker? Sorry, I didn't catch your name."

"Philip Jones." Another glance at his watch. "And yes, he was. I don't suppose you want to buy his bakery too? That's the next thing I need to unload."

Philip jerked his thumb toward the building they were standing behind. When Erik's eyes found hers, a current sparked between them, an invisible wavelength that carried a jumble of messages: *Is he serious? Could this be the answer? Is this an actual miracle? Be cool be cool be cool.*

"Bakery?" she finally asked, aiming for polite reserve as Erik turned off the van and stepped out, handing the keys to Philip, who jingled them as he stalked to the building's back door.

"Bakery downstairs, apartment upstairs. Al got sick a few years ago and had to close it down, so it's mostly junk storage now. I have neither the interest nor the time to clean it up myself." As he spoke, he inserted the key and pushed the door open. "Help yourselves. I have to make some calls."

She and Erik exchanged another wide-eyed, *is this really happening* glance, and then she followed him inside the dark building. He felt along the wall for a light switch and flicked it on, bathing the stuffy space in weak yellow light. While Josie's eyes adjusted, Erik made a beeline to the massive oven taking up one wall.

"It's a Doyon," he breathed, and she felt an irrational spurt of jealousy toward the big, boxy appliance. Why had no man ever regarded her with that amount of reverential awe?

"That's good?"

"It's beautiful." He ran his hand over dusty glass to reveal the dull silver interior.

Oh. Hi again, jealousy. Over an *oven*.

She pushed her weirdness aside and scanned the rest of the room. "It's the only part of this place that is." Pans, bowls, and countless cardboard boxes were stacked haphazardly on every available stainless steel surface, and the fuzzy blanket of dust they'd disturbed drifted through the air and stung her nose.

Erik looked up from where he was fiddling with the oven's settings. "No. Look at the bones." He walked over to her, absentmindedly squeezing her shoulder as he went past to run water in the huge sink. "Countertops. Prep stations. Industrial mixers. It's perfect."

The skin where he'd briefly rested his hand tingled, and Josie set her own hand where his had just been. He hadn't touched her on purpose since he'd placed a comforting hand on her back in the coffee shop that awful afternoon they'd learned about Byron's car accident. And maybe that was smart of him because damn, one glancing touch had left her nerves on high alert, just like they'd been after she'd rested her hand on his chest during the Fielder open house. But tingles weren't welcome here. They were working together. And he wasn't her type.

She thrust her wayward thoughts aside and glanced around at the *Hoarders*-level clutter, willing herself to see what he saw. "Okay. Lots of room. You could work back here with a few helpers for sure."

But he'd already moved into the front of the building where she found him standing in the center of a small open space, hands on his hips. She joined him and looked around skeptically at the jumble of chairs and tables shoved to one side. This was clearly where customers could sit and enjoy a slice of cake and some coffee while they decided on flavors and layers and whatever else happened in the wedding-cake biz. Still, talk about a fixer-upper.

"It'll need lots of work. Scrubbing. Paint. Maybe a new floor." She stamped a foot on the faded linoleum. "This building has to be at least eighty years old. The plumbing might—"

"My own bakery." He spoke the words experimentally, as if trying them on for size, and she shut down her litany of concerns at the wonder she saw in his usually stoic expression.

The morning sun pouring through the front windows embraced him in a bright halo, turning his dark blond hair golden, and she caught her breath. Something was happening in his brain, and she wasn't sure if it was her job to encourage it or to slam on the brakes.

"Hey, I'm usually the full-speed-ahead one here, but you look ready to jump." She nudged his arm. "Are you sure? I mean, we *could* keep borrowing Jake's Jeep while we—"

"I'm sure." His decisive words echoed around the space as he walked to the front door and stepped outside. She joined him and looked up and down the street. It was quiet this early on a Sunday, but the row of businesses—a deli, a dry cleaner, an insurance agency—promised plenty of traffic once the block woke up.

"I'm sure," he said again.

Without another word, he turned and walked back to the kitchen, where a door opened to reveal a wooden staircase. Erik started to climb, and Josie trailed behind him like a tugboat in the wake of a steamer. The stale heat intensified as they neared the top, and when they stepped into a large open space, they were again greeted with an incomprehensible jumble of *stuff*, all bathed in early-morning sunlight pouring through large windows. Boxes mostly, and stacks of newspapers and magazines in towering piles. In one corner, a stained dressmaker's dummy stood watch over the clutter, and Josie could make out the corner of a chest of drawers against one wall, buried under a pile of ratty blankets.

"My God. How much to rent a dumpster?" She sneezed as Erik lifted a drop cloth and disturbed a few years' worth of dust to reveal a china cabinet crammed with dishes. Then again... "How much to rent this out?" An apartment in an up-and-coming Chicago neighborhood was a smart way to generate a second income stream.

"Or I could move in. Sublet my place." He turned in a slow circle, his eyes traveling the length of the open space, which included a small sink and oven positioned between two large windows, clearly intended for the occupant's personal use.

"I don't know how you'd ever leave your current mansion." She slapped an overly dramatic hand to her chest, but he didn't acknowledge the joke. Instead, he reached for his phone and selected a number.

"It's Erik Andersson," he said into the speaker. "I'm willing to sell if you're still willing to buy." The words emerged even more clipped than usual, and when he ended the call, he stared at the black screen for a few moments before he pocketed the phone. When he looked at her, there was a tightness to his expression that she hadn't seen before.

He produced an elastic from the front pocket of his jeans. "Go ahead. Ask."

She almost forgot her question as he lifted his hair up and off his neck and secured it in quick, sure motions. Why, why, *why* did she find something that simple to be so damn sexy?

She realized she was staring when he looked at her with raised eyebrows, and she swiftly averted her gaze. "Um. Did you just agree to sell your supply of black-tar heroin or something?" Teasing him left fewer brain cells available to obsess over his hair.

He *humphed* and turned to clomp back down the stairs, leaving her to yet again trot after him. She'd been the one prodding him to do the bakery thing all along, and now suddenly he'd grabbed the reins. She... didn't hate it. Take-charge looked good on him.

"Look," she said when she rejoined him in the bakery kitchen downstairs, "I'm a nosy bitch, okay?"

"I noticed." Over the past few minutes, the clear blue of his eyes had clouded. At first she thought he wasn't going to answer her question despite his invitation that she ask it. Then he leaned against a free section of counter and crossed his arms over his chest, eyes pinned to the floor. She ignored the flex of his muscly forearms to focus on the words emerging from his throat in a low rumble.

"My grandfather died last year."

"Oh, Erik." Her first instinct was to soothe him, to stroke a hand down the tense line of his arm, but his body language screamed *hands off*, so she settled for a simple "I'm so sorry."

"He left me farmland. Valuable farmland."

His jaw worked back and forth, but he said nothing more, leaving her to connect the dots on what he was saying and what he *wasn't* saying. "And you didn't want to sell it until now?"

He nodded shortly, and again, she made an intuitive leap. "I don't have much experience with good parental figures, but have you not wanted to lose that link to him?"

He dragged his eyes up to hers and nodded once.

"But he'd be proud of you for pursuing your dreams, right?"

More bunching of that incredible jaw. "I disappointed him by walking away from farming. I disappointed him by..." He shifted restlessly, more ill at ease than she'd ever seen him. "I don't know what he'd think."

Well, *now* she wanted to wrap her arms around his

waist and squeeze this man who was radiating loneliness, but she remembered the sparks from the shoulder squeeze and didn't dare risk more contact. She settled for a small, encouraging smile. "*I'm* proud of you. Does that count for anything?"

"Yes, actually." He raised his brows, looking so surprised that she had to laugh.

"So who wants to buy your land?"

"Guy who owns the neighboring acres. He's been asking me about it for a year."

She blinked and looked around the shambles of a kitchen once more as she absorbed what this all meant for their bakery-opening plans. It accelerated everything beyond where she'd been thinking of positioning him. A physical space meant different marketing, different cash flow, different priorities. Her mental gymnastics must've shown on her face because Erik sighed and scrubbed his hands down his face.

"You think I'm being hasty."

Yes. She opened her mouth, then shut it. Apparently today was Opposite Day because he was the one to fill the silence with words.

"I'm really not. Been thinking about it for months. Years, actually. Equipment. Possible locations." He pushed himself away from the counter and walked to the oven, tracing the nearest edge with the tip of his finger. "This place has everything I dreamed of," he said, passion thrumming in his voice.

She willed herself to see what he was seeing. Erik, presiding over his own kitchen. Bashfully greeting customers. Moving that big, strong body up and down the stairs that bisected his personal space and his professional one. Reclining on a couch under the upstairs windows.

Dropping to sleep in a bed above his workspace. Her baker had spent his free time imagining this kitchen, this life, and if *she* could see it after only a few minutes, my God, how much more tangible was that dream to him?

Warmth sparked in her chest at the idea that she was helping make this a reality for him. But it went beyond the professional satisfaction she'd expected to find by building his business into a success. No, this was something far more intimate, and it scared the hell out of her. So she cocked a sassy hip in his direction and pursed her lips. "Did that dream of yours include a van for abducting children to fatten up in your gingerbread house?"

To her utter delight, he threw back his head and laughed. "Come on. Let's go negotiate."

THIRTEEN

"Erik?"

Josie's voice floating up from the back entrance had him straightening so fast he cracked his head against the wall behind him. "Up here," he called, rubbing the back of his skull and tracking her progress by the progressively louder creaks on the stairs. Another thing to add to the repair list.

Her bright hair appeared first, tied up with a bandanna, and he braced himself for her unique invasion of color and noise as the rest of her followed.

"I'm here, chief!" she chirped. "You ready to paint?"

Chief. He kind of liked that. Then he caught sight of her clothes and bit back a groan. She was in her favorite work shirt again, and he jerked his eyes to the ceiling, narrowly avoiding another smack to the head. More cranial trauma would serve him right for straining to catch a better glimpse of the black bra that was clearly visible under the threadbare T-shirt she seemed to favor during their cleanup days.

That fucking shirt would be the death of him. He'd

seen it way too many times for comfort in the three weeks since he'd summoned the strength to hand Pops's land over to the Mathison family and Philip the Impatient had pulled some rich-guy miracle and expedited the sale of the building and van at a price that still left Erik breathless. Breathless at the amount of money he'd forked over but also breathless at what a bargain he'd gotten. The man had been too impatient to get back to his Colorado dispensary fiefdom to dicker over the price of a brick building full of junk in Illinois, which left Erik the owner of a well-stocked, if cluttered, bakery. He might actually be the luckiest man in the state.

Next to him, Josie looked around the increasingly organized living space. "You're getting things done up here!"

He grunted. "The kitchen's what matters."

"One-track mind." She grinned, settling her hands on her hips and arching her back in a stretch. It strained the already thin fabric even tighter over her tits and eliminated any doubt in his mind: he truly *was* the luckiest man in the state, and she had no idea what track his mind was *really* on.

Then again, he had a secret weapon of his own. He'd pulled his hair back that morning, but it had slipped out of its band during the hours of work he'd already put in. No time like the present to fix it.

Purposely not glancing at Josie, he pulled the band free and gripped it in his teeth as his hair spilled around his shoulders. He tilted his head and massaged his scalp, working out the tension that came from pulling the heavy strands up and off his neck. Then he scraped his fingers along his skull to gather it up again, bundling it in place with his left hand and reaching for the band with his right. As he did, he looked up and found her standing stock-still, watching him with an almost feral gaze. He took his time securing the mass behind his head, prolonging the seconds that she'd spend watching him with those ravenous eyes. She didn't blink once.

When his hair was safely tucked away again, her lids fluttered shut and she blurted, "Anyway. Yeah. Can you come to the kitchen? I've got something to show you."

He hid his smile at her flushed cheeks and followed her down the creaky steps, eyes carefully at shoulder level. In the now immaculate kitchen, she gestured proudly to a stack of big, flat cardboard containers on the center island.

"We just spent a week hauling old boxes out." He raised an eyebrow.

"I can't believe you don't think you're funny." She flashed him a wrinkled-nosed grin, then pointed at the pile. "Open."

He did as commanded because that's how their relationship worked these days. She gave a command, and he picked up or put down or shifted whatever she required. He slid open the lid on the topmost skinny box and was greeted by the words Have Your Cake Bakery looking back at him in the logo's clean, modern font.

"Window decals!" she chirped. "We can save a little money installing them ourselves. I've done tons of these over the years for other businesses, so I'll put them up once the painting's done. I was just too excited for you to see them."

He ran a hand over his mouth and looked at the large piece of vinyl. His shop name. His brand. His dream, right there in a box. It was all happening, better and faster than he'd ever imagined. He let the box top fall shut, and the motion disturbed a sheet of paper tucked inside. When he retrieved it from the floor, a quick scan revealed it to be a printout of Josie's emails between her and the vendor. He squinted at it, uncertain of what he was seeing.

"This date."

She slid the top box aside to work on opening the next one. "What about it?"

He looked down at the paper again, which was clearly dated April twenty-ninth. Almost a month and a half ago. "I wasn't even sure I was going to work with you then."

She waved a dismissive hand. "I knew you would. You were too good not to be in business for yourself. I just got a jump on lining up vendors for the future. Whatever it takes to make you a success."

The return of her quick grin had him rocking back on his heels while he gripped the paper in one hand and squeezed the back of his neck with the other. That long ago? She'd believed in him that much, without any actual proof that he could pull all this off? Something warm ignited in his chest, and he opened his mouth, unsure of what was going to come out but afraid it would be drowning in earnest sentiment.

And then the back door slammed open and a voice called, "Your work crew's here!"

Josie tossed a guilty look his way as Finn and Tom tromped into the kitchen with their arms full of painting supplies. "I invited some helpers. Hope that's okay. Hey, guys!"

And just like that, Erik found himself enveloped in the happy chaos of Josie and her friends as they placed drop cloths and distributed cans of paint in the front room. Not the ideal scenario for a man used to solitude, but before long he found his groove, rolling paint onto his portion of the side wall and letting their conversation wash over him in waves. A TV premiere that weekend. A new restaurant to try. Mutual friend gossip. Job complaints. Everyday life in Chicago that actually sounded like something Erik wouldn't mind exploring. Under the right circumstances. With the right people.

"I hear my control-freak brother let you borrow his baby."

The question pulled Erik out of the trance he'd fallen into as he applied strokes of bright yellow paint to the wall in front of him, and he looked left to see that Finn had progressed on her area so much that they were working side by side.

"Yep." He kept the answer short so Finn wouldn't guess that if he hadn't lucked into his own van, he would've strapped cakes on his back like a packhorse rather than ask her brother for his Jeep again. Anything to avoid giving Josie another reason to look at that fucking guy with admiration shining in her big brown eyes.

"Pretty gorgeous, right?"

Erik's paint roller stuttered to a halt as he frantically wondered how she'd known he'd been thinking about her roommate's eyes.

A denial formed on his lips, but she kept talking. "I assume Josie chose it? Everything she does is so bold." She gestured to the now-yellow walls, and Erik's shoulders relaxed.

"Oh, the paint. Yeah, that was all her."

If it were up to him, the walls would be some shade of bone or ecru or eggshell, but Josie had insisted on something sunny and optimistic to reflect the excitement of the couples who'd be picking out their wedding cakes there.

He hadn't had the heart to stand in the middle of the hardware store and tell her that not every engaged couple was as starry-eyed about marriage as she seemed to be. Instead, he'd handed over his credit card and mentally calculated what fraction of the farmland he'd sold was covering this purchase. That's how he was thinking about all his expenses now: how pinched would Pops's expression have gotten to know that his beloved land was paying for a new pack of aprons or light fixtures for the public area? Would he begrudge Erik the rented sander to refinish the wide hardwood beams they'd uncovered underneath the old linoleum?

The thought had him dropping his roller into the pan and muttering an excuse to Finn as he pivoted and walked to the kitchen, hoping it would help him locate the heart of his mission again. Once there, he opened the refrigerator and peered at the empty shelves waiting for the eggs and butter and cream he'd stock them with soon. He cracked the oven door to look again at the interior he'd scoured to a shine the previous weekend, working so vigorously that his arms had ached the following day. Then he braced his hands on the kitchen island and sucked in a steadying breath. His domain. He was in control here. Hopefully someday soon he'd need to hire assistants to help keep up with the order volume.

Of course, that wouldn't happen if they didn't finish painting and get his signage up. The thought had him running his hands over the boxes Josie had delivered, pausing over the final unopened one. When he broke through the tape securing the lid and saw what was inside, his jaw clenched too tight for words.

Too bad that's when Josie sauntered into the kitchen.

"Hey, did you want us to—?"

"What's this?"

Her eyes widened a fraction at his clipped tone, but her voice stayed chipper as ever. "For the van. Cool, right?"

He held up the huge magnet. "I said no."

"It's your logo, Erik. It belongs on your delivery van."

He ignored the exasperation in her voice. "My face is the size of the sun. No."

She narrowed her eyes and planted her hands on her hips.

"It's also on the window decals."

"That's different."

"How?"

"I don't drive the shop around. It's just..." He shook his head, frustrated at being unable to articulate the horror that flooded every cell in his body at the thought of that fucking magnet. Putting it on the van felt desperate. Felt like his mom making the round of casting agents and nightclub operators. Felt like begging people to love *him* when he only wanted to be known for his cake.

"Putting it on the van is flashy," he finally said.

"Opening your own business is flashy!" she shot back.

He huffed and swung away from her to lean against the countertop behind him, discomfort crawling over his skin.

Josie was silent for a moment, and when she spoke, her voice was calm and low. "Do you trust me?" She sounded as if she were soothing an animal caught in a snare. And honestly, maybe she was.

"Obviously I do." He wouldn't be standing in his own kitchen right now if he didn't. He turned back around to face her but kept his lips pressed tight.

She slid the magnet back into the box and leaned it

against the back wall. When she opened her mouth again, he braced himself for more questions about trust, but instead she asked, "What was your grandfather like?"

The subject change rattled him—the man had been on his mind almost constantly for the past few weeks. Not since the days following Pops's death had Erik felt his loss so keenly. The weight of the memories drove him to answer honestly. "Quiet. Frugal."

"Frugal with money or with praise?"

Erik tucked his chin, never having considered it like that before. "Both."

She nodded slowly. "And did he love you?"

Christ. This was hell. "Yes," he muttered. "In his own way. We didn't discuss our feelings."

"Wow. How weird that his grandson turned out the way he did." Josie's flat voice held a trace of amusement, and he shifted from foot to foot as her steady gaze kept him pinned. "And is that the reason part of you thinks you don't deserve to have all this?"

She waved a hand around his kitchen as a peal of Finn's laughter drifted over the music from the wireless speakers set up in the front room, the happy sound incongruous with the tension in the kitchen.

"That's ridiculous." He crossed his arms over his chest and studied the tile between his feet. Still, the idea took hold. Pops had hated the way his daughter chased even the tiniest promise of fame from town to town, and he'd wanted Erik to instead find joy in a small, self-contained life on the farm. Was it any wonder that using his larger-than-life face to hawk his business felt like a betrayal of Pops's wishes?

Josie sighed into the silence. "I'm no shrink, but I've had to drag you along at several points even though you clearly want to do this, and I don't think it's only because you don't understand marketing. I'm just trying to figure out whether your 'aw-shucks shy guy' deal is nature or nurture."

His head snapped up. "Look, I just don't want my fucking face on a van."

"Fine!" She tossed her arms in the air in exasperation. "It's just that your handsome fucking face is a great selling point, and people are going to love seeing you drive around town with it! But whatever. Run all over Chicago in your unmarked windowless van like a creeper and never become as successful as you could be." Her words hung in the kitchen for a beat before she dissolved into laughter. "Wow. You really know how to push my buttons."

"What buttons?" He spread his hands wide, genuinely baffled by how they'd ended up squaring off over a kitchen island.

She jabbed a thumb at her solar plexus. "The fear-of-rejection button. The anger-when-people-don't-appreciate-the-things-I-do-for-them button. You can hit that one even when you haven't actually asked me to do those things for you, by the way." She blew out a breath. "Mostly though it's the mommy-issues button."

"Ah, that button." He was familiar with that one himself.

She slanted a smile at him. "Well, you'll see soon enough. My mom's going to be here next week to shoot photos for the website. This mess"—she gestured down at herself, at that goddamn tissue-thin shirt—"will make a ton more sense."

A month ago, he'd have taken her self-deprecation at

its surface, but he'd spent enough time with her to catch the vulnerability in the words. "You're not a mess."

She laughed softly, a little sadly. "It's nice of you to say so. But I'm mostly bad decisions and an even worse temper."

"Don't forget bossy." He shot her a quick smile, hoping to tease her quicksilver mood into a happier place. He wasn't disappointed.

"Bossy to the bone." She ran a tongue over her lower lip and adjusted the bandanna holding back her hair. "Hey, I'm sorry I pushed you on the van magnet thing. I truly didn't think it would bother you that much."

He couldn't help but return her contrite smile. She'd come a long way from her grudging apology on the L that first night. Then her lips twisted to one side. "But I still think you'll come around to it someday."

"Never."

"We'll see." Josie blew him a kiss and whirled to head back to the front room, leaving him to stare at the magnet box.

She was right, of course. The logo was a solid, memorable brand, and putting it on the van was smart. But the memory of his mother's obsession with fame dug its claws into his chest and chased away all rational thoughts.

With a sigh, he followed her out of the kitchen. Maybe he actually would come around to it someday. It was becoming obvious that he should never bet against Josie Ryan.

FOURTEEN

"I'm sure she'll be here. Any minute now." Josie took another turn around Erik's tiny apartment and paused to look out the window. No fine-boned, pinched-mouthed woman hurried down the sidewalk, burdened by photography bags. The street was quiet, and Josie was furious.

Her mother was almost an hour late despite a short text the day before, confirming their Sunday appointment. But that's not what was making her angry. No, she was good and pissed at herself for thinking Pam Ryan would make her daughter a priority for a change.

"Dammit." The buzzing was back, the itchiness under her skin. She'd controlled her most impulsive urges fairly well over the past month, but all it took was the familiar burn of Mom-based disappointment to have her on the brink of running, shouting, fighting.

She pushed the destructive urges down and stepped away from the window, taking another lap while Erik reclined on the couch, legs stretched in front of him, an oasis of calm in the middle of her frenzy.

"Maybe she's at the bakery?"

"No. I texted her this address last night." Between the sanding and staining of the wooden floors upstairs, the building was safe for neither humans nor cakes this weekend, so Erik had prepped for the shoot in his apartment. "I'm sorry," she spat out, her frustration bleeding through into her voice.

His own phone vibrated, but he ignored it to focus on her. "For what?"

The question surprised her. It even quieted the buzzing for a moment. She gestured around his apartment, empty but for the two of them and the platters and platters of gorgeous carbohydrates. "For making promises I couldn't deliver on." Didn't he know by now how much she hated letting people down?

He heaved himself to his feet, causing the ugly orange-flowered couch to groan in protest, and moved to stand in front of her. God, he was big, and she wanted to sink into him, to allow those long, strong bones to hold her up so she could let go of the tense energy that propelled her forward from minute to minute.

But he didn't touch her. He just stood inches away and hit her with his clear blue gaze. "You've delivered plenty for me. And I still don't quite know why."

"Because..." Her eyes drifted down as she tried to articulate a reason he'd understand. "Well, for one thing, I wanted to prove that I could do it." She brushed her hands down the front of the cashmere sweater and expensive jeans she'd carefully selected that morning to present her most polished/casual/professional self for her mother's inevitable judgment. Then she glanced up at him. "And for another thing, I like you."

She had to smile at the confusion on his face. "Is that so surprising?"

He jammed his hands into his pockets. "Yes, actually."

Making Erik blush was the best distraction. "I don't understand who you were hanging out with before you met me. Do your friends not see how clever you are? How thoughtful?"

His gaze dropped to the floor. "Not many, no."

His bashful confusion was adorable. So adorable, in fact, that she should move away, put some distance between them. She didn't take a step back though. "Well, they're idiots. You make me calm. You quiet things for me." Like now. Exactly like he was doing now.

His brows snapped together, and she had to laugh. "I'm not saying it makes *me* quiet. Nothing does that. But you soothe what's restless in me."

She pressed a hand over her heart, and his gaze followed the motion. Realizing she'd just drawn his attention to her breasts, she held her breath, aware of a strange tension vibrating between them. Did he feel it too? Was he—

Her phone chimed, shattering the mood, and she moved to rummage through the bags she'd brought with her.

"Dammit!" Every part of her sagged in defeat. Pam had decided that getting drinks with some local patron of the arts was more important than her daughter's passion project. Josie already knew all about her mother's priorities, but it still had the power to wound her.

The floor creaked behind her, likely Erik preparing to flee before her inevitable shouting tantrum. But she didn't *want* to be the hotheaded brat her mother thought she was. With effort, she heaved a shuddery breath and dashed the tears from her eyes. "It's cool," she forced herself to say brightly. "I brought my camera stuff." She reached for the closest bag and started mechanically unpacking the contents. Keeping her hands busy should prevent her from calling back and unloading twenty-six years of resentment onto her mother's voicemail. "I don't have a fine arts degree or anything, but I'm not bad."

She snapped together her umbrella light kit with stiff movements and waited for him to argue against using her amateur photography skills, but he didn't, of course. He just regarded her with the same trusting gaze he'd been turning her way since she'd parachuted into his life.

Trust. He was trusting his business to her. She couldn't let him down.

"My mom started training me as soon as I could hold a camera." As she talked, she set out foam core pieces that she clipped together to form three sides of a box where she'd place his beautiful creations. "I wasn't the prodigy she was hoping for, so she lost interest pretty fast. But I still enjoy it as a hobby."

Next she moved the lights into place to provide the most flattering illumination. The kit wasn't as fancy as anything her mother had, but it would certainly work for product shots for the time being.

"Okay, Man Bun. Let's see your goodies."

He rolled his eyes—He actually rolled his eyes! She was teaching him sass!—and handed her the first of the items he'd assembled to show off his handiwork. She positioned the cake with the most intricate marble ripples facing out and fired off a flurry of shots before moving on to the next one, and then the next, falling into a soothing routine of decadent treats and shutter snaps. More than half of Erik's cakes were actually rounds of Styrofoam covered in his unique icing techniques. All the height and drama and bold colors he executed so well but at a fraction of the effort and cost and with no one looking at the pictures any wiser.

Once she'd gotten all the exterior shots, she straightened to stretch out the kink in her back. "Okay, time for the good stuff. Start slicing."

Erik's only response was to salute her with his silver cake server, and she indulged in the luxury of simply *watching* him. His brow creased in concentration as he eased the sharp edge of the server through the pink-veined cake on the counter in front of him, and she stealthily lifted her camera to fire off a few shots of the artist at work before turning her attention to the slices themselves.

She moved them to her makeshift light box and started clicking. "It all smells so good. How do you keep from eating everything all the time? Other than the chance that it might be foam, of course."

She was surprised when he actually answered.

"I don't."

The curl of amusement in his voice had her looking his way.

"I taste everything. Why do you think I wanted to find a gym close to the bakery?" He looked down at his forearms—his strong, corded, deliciously muscled forearms, and she lifted the camera in a flash, firing off several quick shots. When he realized what she was doing, his expression shifted to pained.

"Oh, don't do that!" she cried. "Those were getting good."

"You don't need any of me," he muttered, swiping a hand across his mouth.

Good thing she'd just shot the last of the gorgeous

sample cakes because she was ready to launch into a new fight. "I really do. You're..." She sighed. "You're magnificent, frankly. You're as delicious as the things you make. If we don't put that on your website, we're idiots."

He started shaking his head as she spoke, his movements becoming more decisive with each word.

"Erik." His name, spoken in her gentlest tone, stilled him. "Trust me."

She held her breath, wondering if they'd be in for a repeat of last week's disagreement in the kitchen, but he froze, a giant of a man enthralled by the force of her stare.

Then his shoulders shifted downward a fraction of an inch. "I hate this."

"I know, baby," she crooned, working quickly to move things into place. His apartment was shabby as hell, but that just might work. She turned her lights to face the wall, then put her palm to his chest and walked him backward until he bumped against the crumbling plaster over the brick. For the first time in their acquaintance, he looked startled. At her touch? Was the press of her fingers causing the unflappable man to flap? Without stopping to think, she smoothed her hand along his collarbones, hoping the gesture would soothe him. But she'd miscalculated; his breath caught as her fingers traveled along those dips and curves.

She took a step back, not wanting to fluster him more than she already had, and raised her camera. It clicked as she captured his unguarded expression. "Just pretend I'm not here."

She watched through the viewfinder as he looked directly at her. "Teach me how to do that." His voice darkened on the last words, and she almost dropped her camera.

With effort, she forced a light laugh. "Come on. You had no problem ignoring me on the train that first night after I insulted you and then you fell asleep."

His lips twitched, and her camera captured it all. With the soft lighting falling on his face, his battered apartment wall served as a compelling backdrop for his square jaw, his sharp eyes, his impossible cheekbones.

"That night on the L."

She kept clicking, too absorbed in the planes of his face to respond, and her not speaking for a change seemed to encourage him to fill the empty space hanging between them.

"That night on the L," he repeated, "you looked ready to pull every rivet and bolt out of the train car with your teeth."

She lowered her camera to study his expression without any equipment in the way.

His blue eyes held her in place. "You were all I could see. The only thing."

The strength drained from her arms as she absorbed his meaning. He was telling her that he'd seen *her* that night, not Pam Ryan's underachieving daughter or Finn's funny, disposable roommate. *Her.*

She carefully set the camera on the counter, avoiding the stacks of tempting desserts piled all around. Right now the biggest temptation in the room was the man who'd made them with his big, capable hands.

Not sure what she was expecting to happen, she walked toward him, her gaze locked on his, and when she was standing a hairbreadth from his chest, she reached up to run the pads of her fingers gently along his jaw. "What if—?" She swallowed, her mouth suddenly dry. "Turn your head this way."

His eyes never leaving hers, he allowed her to shift the angle of his jaw a fraction, toward the window. But instead of fetching her camera, she lingered over the scratch of his stubble against her skin and his hot breath as he exhaled once, hard.

"A-and I'd like..." Earlier, her greedy little eyes had followed every economical movement as he'd bundled his lion's mane into a bun and, after not finding an elastic, impatiently secured it with a pencil he grabbed from the table. She was dying to reach up now and pluck it out, but she was afraid freeing his hair might break the spell. She was close enough to feel his chest rise and fall as he breathed, and her eyes fluttered shut at the warm vanilla smell of his skin. The buzzing was back, although this time it wasn't in her brain. It was in her chest, the tips of her breasts, between her thighs. *This* buzzing was going to make her do something stupid, but a very different kind of stupid than picking a fight on a train or counting on her mother to come through for her.

His sharp inhale made her eyes spring open, and she found his burning gaze fixed on her mouth. His lips parted, and she waited for him to say something, to tell her to quit pawing him or to go pick up her camera, but this was Erik. He never used words when he could communicate in other ways, and right now the heat in his eyes told her not to stop touching him.

So she moved her hands up to brush her thumbs over the crests of his cheeks and pulled him downward, closer to her, until those blue eyes filled her vision. His mouth hovered over hers, his breath a whisper across her lips, and oh God, then she was kissing him. He was so tall that he had to duck his head, and she took advantage of his position to step closer and press herself against him. Every part of him was strong: his hands, his shoulders, his thigh when she twined her leg around his. She wanted to climb him like an oak, to find shelter in the branches of his arms, to use him to shut out the realities of her life for a while.

As if he'd read her thoughts, he wrapped his hands around her waist and lifted her up without breaking their kiss so she was closer to all the parts of him she wanted to be closer to.

"You're the only thing I can see." He pulled away to rasp his confession in her ear. "Ever since that first night on the train."

She shivered and twined her fingers behind his neck, chasing his tongue with her own while he pulled her down to grind against him.

She'd die if he kept kissing her like this.

Then again, she might die if he didn't keep kissing her like this forever.

The urge for more overwhelmed any other concerns. She took the hand that was gripping her hip and slid it up and over her rib cage. She felt the strength in his arm, pulsing under his skin, and knew he was allowing her to guide him. She reveled in it, the power he gave over to her, the sheer width of his wrist as her fingers strained to circle it. She dragged his hand closer and closer to where she needed it, until it brushed the underside of her breast. He shuddered, and she pressed against him harder, and then—

His door buzzer screamed through the apartment.

They broke apart, both breathing hard, and he dropped his hand.

"Ignore it," she whispered, seeking his lips again.

Before he could respond, the buzzer sounded again, this time followed by a voice on the crackly intercom.

"Erik? It's Gina. Are you home?"

"Fuck," he breathed, dropping his head against the wall. At the clear shift in his mood, she pushed herself away and slid down his body. When she stepped back, her heart dropped. He'd just had his hands all over her and his tongue in her mouth, but his face was as impassive as ever. How did none of that have any effect on him?

Well. Not *all* of him was unaffected. Her eyes swung to the front of his jeans, and she forced herself to look away as words like "massive" and "girthy" spun through her fevered brain.

"Who's Gina?"

Her hushed question was uncharacteristically meek, and he closed his eyes, the lines bracketing his mouth making him look ten years older.

"My fiancée."

FIFTEEN

"Your *what?*"

She recoiled as if he'd slapped her, and part of him felt like he actually had. He willed his dick to calm the fuck down so he could think. *Goddammit.* Two hastily spoken words could've just fucked up everything.

"No, I didn't mean... It's not as bad as it sounds."

"Not as bad as it *sounds?*"

He felt her sense of betrayal, felt it down to his marrow, and he scrubbed his hands over his face. He was such an idiot. He'd been wondering all afternoon if Josie's tits were as soft as they looked under the pink sweater—hell, all afternoon? Touching Josie had been the primary refrain in his brain for quite some time now—and when she'd stretched up to press her lips to his, everything in his body had turned staticky, hot, and hard.

Then he'd heard Gina's voice, and it all came rushing back: who he was, who Josie was, how impossible it was for the two of them to be together like this. And his brain had thrown the emergency brake in the worst way possible.

What a shame it worked so damn well.

"How is my putting my tongue into someone else's fiancé's mouth 'not as bad as it sounds'?" Her incredulous tone lacerated, and she backed into the living room, putting the length of his apartment between them. "Why didn't you ever tell me?"

He opened his mouth helplessly, but before he could figure out how to unfuck what he'd just fucked, there was a knock at the door. Josie stomped to the door and yanked it open.

"Hi. Gina, is it?" Her aggressively perky greeting caused Erik's lifelong friend to pause uncertainly in the doorway, as anybody would when faced with a seething redheaded stranger.

"Um, hi?" Gina's broad forehead creased in confusion, and her eyes found him where he was slumped against the far wall. "Is this a bad time? I tried texting."

He forced himself to stand up straight and own this mess as best as he could. "Josie, this is Gina Trendall. My fiancée."

The lines on Gina's forehead deepened. "What? No I'm not." She stepped into the apartment, lugging a suitcase almost as tall as she was, and said to the grim-faced Josie, "I'm really not."

"Okay, cool. That's nice. You two obviously have things to work out."

Erik winced at the thick sarcasm in Josie's voice. He hadn't heard that level of venom from her since their earliest encounters.

She walked briskly to the corner where they'd set up the makeshift photo studio and started cramming equipment into the various bags she'd brought with her. "You have Richard's cell phone number, right?" Her tone was coolly polite as she settled the camera into its padded container.

"Yes," he said, wary about her change of subject and demeanor as she folded up the last of the lights.

Gina ruffled a hand through her short brown hair and shot him a *what's happening here?* glance, but he held up a finger to hold off her questions.

Josie slung the various equipment over her shoulders until she had a hoop skirt of black vinyl bags surrounding her. "Okay. Tell you what, why don't you talk directly to him about the last of the wedding-cake details? Cut out the middleman. I'll email you when I get these pictures uploaded to your website."

He followed helplessly in her wake as she stalked toward the door. "Wait."

"For what?" She paused at the threshold, and when she swung around, he was startled to see not anger on her face but bleakness.

His words failed him, as they always did when it mattered the most, and she turned toward Gina. "He never said anything about a fiancée, so that's on me for assuming. Sorry I—" She shook her head, then looked his way with glassy eyes. "Sorry I forced you into all this, I guess."

Without another word, she was gone, leaving behind a phalanx of unspoken words, an apartment full of cake, and the woman Erik had once promised to marry.

"Can I have some?" Gina asked, gesturing toward the pile of baked goods.

Same old Gina. Leading with her stomach. "Sure. Whatever. Eat everything in the apartment."

"Challenge accepted." She grabbed one of the slices

and settled onto the couch, kicking off her orange Chuck Taylors. "So what did I just interrupt?"

He plopped onto the couch next to her. "Nothing." Everything.

She shrugged and speared a chunk of cake. "Fine, don't tell me," she said around a mouthful of chocolate raspberry. She looked around the apartment as she chewed. "You haven't changed a thing since I was here for Thanksgiving."

"Why would I?" he asked irritably. "I've been busy."

"With what? You quit the bakery. Unless Fancy's making you jump through hoops."

"She doesn't make me do anything." He glared at his best friend, who smiled broadly in return. Everything about Gina was agreeable: her voice, her body, her demeanor. She'd been the nicest girl in school when they were kids, and he'd made a long-ago promise to keep her safe from the world in any way he could. He still wanted to protect her, but he'd handled it all wrong today. Blame whatever was happening with Josie for twisting up his feelings.

She crossed her legs and settled her plate on her lap. "Of course not. Nobody makes you do anything you don't want to do." When he didn't respond, she leaned forward to pat his knee fondly. "So what does she think she talked you into doing that you really wanted to do anyway? And what does it have to do with finally selling Pops's land?"

He sagged back against the couch, reminded of the twin comfort and irritation of someone who knew you better than you knew yourself.

When he didn't respond, her next pat to his knee was a little sharper. "You okay?"

What a question. He was a mess. He was upside

down and inside out. He was doing things and saying things and dreaming things he'd never considered before. Yet all he was able to muster was a short, "I'm fine."

"Pretty sure you're not fine. Who was she?"

"A friend." He kept his voice flat and might have pulled it off if Gina hadn't leaned forward to study him as closely as she'd just studied the selection of cake slices.

She reached down and ran her thumb along the side of his mouth, then held it up to show him a smear of pink before rubbing the lipstick off on her jeans. "Want to try that again?"

That got him up and off the couch. Unlike Josie, Gina's touch didn't jangle his nerves, but he couldn't keep sitting there like everything was normal. An hour ago, he'd watched Josie prowl around the room, upset about her mother. Now it was his turn to feel so agitated about his own shitty decisions that he was ready to explode out of his skin.

"I'm sorry, Gina."

"For what?" She licked a smear of icing off her fork. "I never wanted to marry you."

"I know."

"And you never wanted to marry me."

Unlike Josie, he wasn't compelled to pace, but he couldn't look at Gina's sweet, familiar face while they had this conversation. He walked to the window and stared unseeing at the sidewalk two stories below.

"No." He sighed. "I didn't."

"So why'd you tell the fancy redhead that?"

He laced his hands around the back of his neck and forced himself to be honest. "Because I'm a fucking coward."

"Ah. You like her."

He nodded without turning around.

"And you're feeling guilty because you know how much Pops wanted us to get married." He heard the couch creak as she stood. "So you told Fancy we were engaged because once upon a time you told *Pops* we were engaged, and it was the easiest way you could think of to put up a wall."

"Fuck," he said softly.

"You sure do love your walls." She set her empty plate down and joined him at the window. "Erik, Pops is gone. I miss him like crazy, and I know you feel that times a million, but he wouldn't want you to stick with a promise that makes us both unhappy. Just like he wouldn't have wanted you to hold on to that land forever. He'd be glad you were putting those resources to better use."

He stuffed his hands in his pockets, wishing he could accept what she was saying.

"You're not honoring him by holding on to the past or by telling people we're something we're not," she said. "Especially not someone you were just kissing."

Memories of Josie's lips on his came flooding back, and he had to bite his cheek to keep his body in check. "She's not who I should be with."

"Says who?" Gina asked.

"She's... well, you said it. She's fancy."

"Mmm-hmm."

"And she talks. Constantly."

"Heaven forbid you spend time with a well-dressed woman who forces you to use your vocal cords," she said wryly.

He huffed and leaned his back against the wall, crossing his arms. Gina didn't understand the cavern that stretched between him and Josie. If he walked into her fire, what would be left of him when their time together was over and she moved on?

"What are you even doing here?" he grumbled.

His abrupt question didn't faze her; she'd been tolerating his communication style all her life. Instead of sniping back at him, she said placidly, "Moving to Chicago."

"That's not until August." She'd accepted a new IT job near Schaumburg, and he'd been planning to help her pack up her life in Iowa when the time came.

"You haven't been picking up your phone," she chided.

"Sorry." Guilt over his selfishness pulled at him, particularly when he noticed discomfort on her face for the first time since her surprise arrival. "What's going on?"

She turned her gaze toward the window as a vehicle in need of a new muffler rumbled down the street. "I decided to move that timeline up a little." Her ruddy cheeks flushed even redder. "I had a, um, a pregnancy scare."

That got him up off the wall. "A *what*? But you were..."

"Dating Christine?" Her soft mouth drooped downward. "Yeah, well she and I broke up."

The back-to-back revelations knocked him sideways. "What happened?"

Gina's whole body deflated, and he cringed to think that he'd been such a shitty friend when she'd needed him the most.

"I brought up marriage." She trembled and pressed the heels of her hands against her eyes before continuing. "Christine freaked out. I took it badly, and unfortunately that included an unwise rebound decision at the bar at closing time and..."

He couldn't pull his eyes off her abdomen, which didn't look any different than the last time he'd seen her. "So, um?" He gestured tentatively.

"Nope." She brushed a hand over her stomach and shot him a relieved smile. "Despite a broken condom and a period of intense panic, there's no need for Uncle Erik to report for duty, thank God. But it seemed smart to make the move sooner rather than later. You know how gossipy Liberty Valley is."

"Sure do." And if any of those small-minded assholes gave her an instant of trouble, he'd find them and make them wish they hadn't. Gina's business was nobody's but Gina's. "I can't believe you stuck around there as long as you did."

"Oh, you mean after I caused the biggest scandal in town history by bringing Mary Beth Phillips to the prom?" She leaned against the window frame and smugly crossed her arms over her chest.

The memory of fierce-faced Gina in her boxy tuxedo pulled a smile from him. "That, or when you calmly recited anti-discrimination laws in the middle of Main Street Café until they gave you a waitress job."

"Yeah. I'm pretty badass." She nonchalantly buffed her blunt nails against the sleeve of her shirt.

Familiar shame moved through his stomach, and he said quietly, "I can't believe I worked for Dora as long as I did. I'm sorry."

She lifted one shoulder and let it fall. "Like I told you, what matters is that you quit when you finally realized how bad it was. Do I wish you'd pulled those headphones off sooner and figured out what was up? Sure. Should you have taken a page from my book and recited nondiscriminatory legal statutes out loud until that bitch begged you to stop? Undoubtedly. But you handled it your way. And hey, you're in a better place now, yeah?"

"Yeah," he said distractedly. "Or I was, anyway." When was the last time he'd plugged his earbuds in to block out all other distractions? Not for weeks and weeks. Not since he started craving Josie's voice more than any other sound in the world. *Christ*, he'd fucked things up.

"So, uh." Gina interrupted the churn of his thoughts, her round face creased into a frown. "Can I stay here until I figure out a housing solution? Or I can go to a hotel if that would be better. I don't want to cause a problem with you and Fancy."

"Josie," he corrected. "And it's fine. I'm glad you're here." And he meant it, despite it all. Living in the same town as Gina again would be good for both of them.

"Thanks." She wandered back to the kitchen island and surveyed the remaining cake slices. "So you finally sold the land."

"I did." The thought still made his blood pound in his ears, but she just smiled.

"I'm so proud of you. Chase those dreams." With a smack of her lips, she chose a piece of lemon curd layer cake and settled back into the couch with a grimace. "My God, this is worse than I remembered. I can't believe a woman wearing designer jeans let you feel her up on this ugly thing."

"It was actually against the wall," he admitted before his usual don't-kiss-and-tell filters kicked in.

Gina's face lit up with an unasked question, but he silenced her with a look.

"Shut up and eat your cake."

SIXTEEN

Hot. Loud. Crowded.

Ordinarily, Josie would consider all three qualities hallmarks of a successful club opening, and she'd be sweaty and happy in the middle of it all on the dance floor. But tonight it was all too much for her. The throbbing bass booming through the packed room rattled her teeth, and she'd given up on getting any bar service an hour ago. Just as well since this was a working Friday for her.

Well, this *had* been a working Friday anyway. Club Diego was officially open to the public, with all the pretty young things in Chicago decked out, gyrating, and throwing back drinks thanks to Dynamic Marketing's promotional campaign. Her job for the night was done, and she'd never been more grateful to leave a party.

"Need anything else from me?" She had to shout over the crowd noise.

Diego Vasquez shook his head and blew her a kiss. She returned it with a saucy wink, faking enthusiasm she didn't feel. Thankfully, the handsy nightclub magnate had been too busy overseeing the launch of his namesake nightspot, the new jewel in his Chicago-area entertainment empire, to sling a heavy arm over her shoulders as he had at every step in the planning stages leading up to tonight. Small mercies.

With one last overly enthusiastic thumbs-up, she slipped out the back entrance, praying to the god of new nightclubs that nothing dire happened to summon her back. Once she hit the sidewalk, her body rejoiced at the slight breeze in the mid-June air. Was she getting too old for the club scene? Surely not. Yet her feet hurt, her eardrums throbbed, and she was dying to get home to free herself from her bra and brew a cup of tea. Granny Ryan, in the hizzy.

She might be achieving senior-citizen status in her nighttime tastes, but the thought of stuffing her overheated body into a train car held no appeal, so she secured her purse across her body and prepared to hoof it home in her going-out shoes.

One block into her trip, she realized her fatal error: she was now alone with her thoughts.

Fucking. Engaged.

No matter how loudly her high heels clicked on the pavement, it wasn't enough to drown out those two little words.

Erik was fucking engaged.

God, she was an idiot. He'd told her he wasn't married, and that had been good enough for her. She'd thought it was weird that he knew as much as he did about fancy folded napkins and had chalked it up to his job, but maybe it was because he'd been intimately involved in planning his own nuptials.

She reached the intersection where a cluster of pedestrians waited for the WALK sign to illuminate, but her feet refused to carry her into the middle of that laughing, jostling throng. Instead, she stepped off the curb and jogged through a break in traffic, ignoring a trailing honk from an irate cabbie. If she didn't keep moving, she might collapse.

How had she blundered into yet another unwinnable romantic situation? Find a guy unlike anybody you've ever dated—hell, unlike anybody you've ever *known*. Slowly allow yourself to enjoy the subtle nuances of his humor, his facial expressions, his way of communicating. Run headfirst into the extremely obvious pleasure of his big, strong body and too-good-to-be-true lips. Get stomped on anyway. Har. Joke's on Josie.

Good thing they'd only been palling around for a month or so and her feelings weren't engaged. Just her brain and her body and her pheromones and her taste buds and...

Shit.

She'd fished around in her purse, popped in her AirPods, and was searching for her loudest, most thought-drowning-out-est playlist when the phone buzzed in her hand.

"Hey, doll."

"Richard!" Oh, she was glad to hear his voice, even if he sounded slurry from fatigue and the beeping, squawking, and intercom noises she associated with hospitals were blaring in the background.

"How's Byron?" she asked, pausing under the awning of a pizza joint that was still swarming with customers despite the late hour. Her mouth watered at the lingering scent of tomato sauce. If only Richard were in town, she'd grab some takeout and divert to his place for a nightcap of deep-dish and wine.

Instead, her friend yawned so loudly she heard his jaw crack. "I'm hiding out in Byron's bathroom so I don't wake him up, but he's doing lots better. Hating physical therapy and missing Chicago."

"That's amazing. I'm so glad!" She stepped aside to give a hand-in-hand couple access to the menu affixed to the restaurant wall, and their lovey-dovey smiles were enough to send her on her way again. "Are you still on track to be home before the wedding?" Part of her question was selfish; she missed her friend and wanted him back in town ASAP. But mostly she hoped the guys could follow through on the celebration they'd been looking forward to for months.

"Yep. He should be discharged tomorrow, so that gives us two weeks to clean up whatever fires you've left burning before the big day."

"Ha." The only one she could think of was the dumpster fire she'd ignited with the wedding-cake baker. Not that she wanted to talk about that.

"Hey, what did you do to the wedding-cake baker?"

Her feet stuttered to a stop at Richard's words. "Why?"

He chuckled softly. "Lordy, don't you sound guilty. He's just been texting me directly is all."

"Oh. Well," she said, dawdling under a streetlight, "it turns out he's, um, engaged. Or something. I met his fiancée last weekend."

"Reeeeeally," Richard drawled.

"We, uh. We kissed." Huh. Maybe she wanted to talk about it after all. She ignored Richard's theatrical gasp and continued. "And then this woman showed up at his door and he told me he was engaged. And then his fiancée told me they *weren't* engaged. And then I stormed out. And it's been six days, and all I've gotten is one text from him saying, 'I'm not engaged. Sorry.'"

Silence reigned on the other end of the line.

"Hello?" she asked. "Did you flatline?"

"Girl. Are you telling me that you kissed Man Bun's man buns and then ran away, and he texted to tell you he's single—"

"After telling me he's not!" she interjected, the irritation propelling her into motion again.

"—and you haven't called him to sort things out?"

"No! Why would I?"

"Because he's incredibly attractive? And he bakes? And he's tidy and polite and thoughtful and spells everything correctly in his texts?"

She scoffed. "Is that how low our standards are?"

Richard scoffed back. "Excuse me, Your Highness, but those are not low standards. Remember a few years ago when we both spent a month crushing on that coffee-cart guy with the bad posture and no eyebrows because he gave us free shots of espresso once?"

"Point taken," she muttered, slapping the soles of her shoes against the pavement harder than was strictly necessary. "But you're supposed to be on my side!"

"I am on your side, sugar bum. I want you to have good sex with the god of thunder and bear his large Nordic babies. Is that so much to ask?"

It was on the tip of her tongue to tell him that's what she wanted too, but she shut that down. Nobody was bearing Erik's big blond babies, least of all her. Instead, she replied, "Just... can you deal directly with him for the rest of the cake planning? And then you and I will never speak of this again." She was too hurt and embarrassed to be anything remotely resembling professional around Erik's carefully neutral face.

"Fine. If that's what you want." Richard's voice conveyed an unspoken "you weirdo," which she was grateful he didn't actually vocalize.

"It is." She swallowed. "I miss you."

"Miss you too. I'll call you once we're back home."

"You'd better," she said, hanging up as she approached her building.

She climbed the three flights and let herself into her apartment, where she found no Finn but a huge cellophane-wrapped basket of fruit on the kitchen table. She crossed the room and scanned the attached card with a disbelieving laugh. Her mother thought she could make up for the previous weekend's disappointment with glossy apples and some aggressively suggestive bananas? Hardly.

"'Sorry we missed each other,'" she read aloud, mimicking her mother's clipped tones. "'Have you thought any more about the photography program at the Art Institute?'" With a strangled shriek, she ripped the card in half and tossed the pieces to the floor. "Guess what, Mom. I haven't, and you'd know that if you'd call me once in a while."

Great. She was ranting out loud in her kitchen. After a beat, she forced her hands to unclench, stretching her fingers out straight and closing her eyes to breathe out on a slow five count. Once she was centered again, she bent to pick up the mangled card halves and jammed them into the trash. Then she eyeballed the unwanted basket of nature's candy.

What she really wanted was cake. Erik's cake. The slightly bruised pears staring back at her from under the shiny plastic wrap were no substitute for a single bite of any of the delicacies she'd fondled in his apartment on Sunday.

She groaned and kicked off her heels. Erik. Fondled. *Not* words she needed to be thinking about in her current self-pitying mood. After all, she'd been the one who'd attacked him with her mouth last week. Knowing Erik, he'd probably been politely waiting for her to let up so he could tell her he wasn't interested. She was such an idiot.

An idiot who still had work to do. With a sigh, she trudged to her bedroom and shimmied out of her electric-blue club dress and into sleep shorts and a tank top. She piled her hair on top of her head and plodded back to the kitchen with her laptop, where she settled at the table for the sweet torture of choosing the best shots of Erik for his website. Once she'd finished the setup and gotten it launched alongside his social media accounts, she could wish him good luck and sail out of his life. More importantly, she could do it all over email without needing to actually spend time with him again.

But that Erik-avoidance plan didn't allow her to escape one last, excruciating task: sorting through dozens of pictures of his annoyingly handsome face to choose the best shots for the website and, as a side effect, reliving the moment the heat of his gaze had driven her to touch him and lose her mind. With a grumble, she ripped a hole in the cellophane and grabbed the first cake substitute her fingers touched.

It was a banana. Of course. She barked a laugh over the on-the-nose absurdity of the situation, then peeled the damn thing and bit into it as she clicked on the first photo of a face that had become surprisingly dear to her.

SEVENTEEN

"Sí, sí. Claro que sí."

Lily shrugged helplessly at Erik and held the phone away from her ear as a stream of Spanish poured from the other end. "De veras, Mamá, pero tengo un cliente ahora." She paused for another burst of words before ringing off with "Te amo, mi corazón."

She disconnected with a sigh. "Family crisis. My sister's stylist gave her lilac highlights, and my mother's threatening to disown her."

Erik paused with his coffee halfway to his mouth. "The sister or the stylist?"

"Whoever she bumps into first, I think. So what time do your clients get here?"

"Any minute," he said, checking his phone. "And thanks again. Kitchen's operational, but I'm still waiting on a few permits."

Lily breezed by to collect a bundle of pink tulips from the cooler against the wall. "My pleasure. I'm so proud to be here for this moment." She smiled at him fondly. "Baby's first clients!"

Erik couldn't muster more than a scowl even in the face of Lily's cheerfulness. The last person who'd called him baby had ended up kissing him until his brain shut down, and the white-hot memories of his hands on her body hadn't receded a week and a half later.

"Where's your partner in crime today?"

Damn. Was Lily a flower whisperer *and* a mind reader?

"She's not my partner," he grumbled. "And she has her own job."

Lily's eyes widened at his forbidding tone, but she didn't pursue it further, instead turning to the back counter to begin arranging the tulips in a smoked-glass vase. That left him free to ignore her, chew over his own dark thoughts, and critically examine yet again the small sample cake he'd brought for Richard and Byron's approval. He rotated the plate to scrutinize it from every angle. Yep, he could say without hesitation that it was some of his best work. He'd poured all of his focus into this project in an effort to keep his mind off Josie. Now he just needed the grooms' seal of approval.

Just then, the bell on the shop door jangled to admit the man he'd met with Josie in April. Richard held the door open for a short, slender man who followed behind, dressed in dark jeans and a navy suit jacket and leaning heavily on a cane. Once they were both inside, Richard took the other man's free hand and held it to his mouth, kissing his knuckles so gently that Erik looked down, not wanting to intrude on such an intimate moment.

"Hello! Good to see you again!" Richard called to him as he took the other man's free arm and they made their way slowly toward the high counter where Erik was seated. "This is my fiancé, Byron Cutter."

"Hello." Erik stood to shake Byron's hand.

"So nice to meet you." Byron slowly climbed onto the stool opposite him, leaned an elbow against the countertop, and dragged a slim hand over his perspiring brow and through his short-cropped sandy hair. Once he'd caught his breath, he told Erik with a shaky laugh, "It takes a little more effort to get around at the moment."

Erik started to nod in sympathy but froze when he realized that Byron was giving him a thorough once-over from underneath his pale eyelashes.

After a long moment, one corner of his mouth curled upward, and he cut his eyes to Richard, who'd just sat down next to him. "Oh honey, I see what you mean. Sky-high standards."

Erik furrowed his brow as the two men shared a moment he didn't understand but that left the two of them looking amused. Whatever. He didn't have the extra emotional energy to unravel mysteries. Time to get this meeting started.

"Cake, for your approval."

He pushed the plate toward the grooms, who *ooooh*ed in unison—as they should. He'd trimmed various sections of cake into a hexagon shape, fitted it together, crumb-coated it, and applied his marble frosting technique so the ivory base color was shot through with swirls of palest blue and brassy gold for contrast. The delicate filigree topper he'd made of spun sugar added height and drama, and when he'd stepped back to check out the full effect in the bakery kitchen before he left, he'd performed an embarrassing little victory dance on the spot.

"This size is a middle layer. We'll do a smaller cake on top and two larger ones on the bottom. The shape was just a suggestion."

"I love it," Byron breathed, excitement suffusing his thin, drawn face for the first time since he'd walked into Love in Bloom Flowers. "It's perfect."

"Just wait till you taste it," Erik said.

Richard laughed. "Damn, fella, that's some swagger."

He shrugged and picked up the onyx cake cutter. No false modesty here; cake he was good at. He made the first cut and held back a smile when a tiny squeak emerged from Byron's throat as the blade traveled through the pristine iced surface.

He plated the first pieces and set them in front of the two men, who gave identical moans of approval after their first bites of the hazelnut. Erik folded his arms and took it all in. This was his favorite part. No huge reception hall full of guests losing their minds over his creations was as satisfying as watching the two people at the center of the day enjoying the first taste of their wedding cake.

"It tastes even better when I'm not eating it in a hospital room," Byron said.

"Everything tastes better outside a hospital." Erik picked up the cutter again. "Peach-pecan next."

The men watched in surprise as he produced a new variety from a different side of the cake. He'd baked all their flavor choices and cobbled them together into a Frankenstein's monster cake that he'd iced, both to show off the technique and to make sure everyone was on board with the final choices.

After the first bite of the peach, Richard sighed and said, "Tastes like home," which was the exact response Erik wanted.

Once they'd approved of the pistachio crunch and the cardamom, Richard leaned back and patted his stomach.

"That was the best thing we've eaten in weeks. Right, sweetie?"

Byron nodded at Erik. "Thank you so much. Truly. The samples you mailed were incredibly thoughtful, but seeing it all put together like this..." He swallowed convulsively, and Richard caught his hand again.

"It may not be exactly the wedding we thought we'd have"—Richard glanced at the cane resting against Byron's stool—"but we're so damn lucky we're still having it."

The palpable emotion running between the two men made Erik's throat tighten. Since when did the whole wedding scene fill him with longing for what he didn't have?

The answer was obvious, of course. Josie was the invisible presence in this meeting, the redhead who linked them all. And he'd been too much of a chickenshit to do more than text her once and hope she'd forgive or forget or... fuck, he didn't know. Leave him be? Vanish from his memory so he could move on with his quiet, lonely life?

He grunted and pushed the thought away. "Want to take the leftovers home?"

"Oh, of course," Richard said. "It may be all we eat between now and next Saturday. Nuptial nerves and all that. And I'm hoping we can take some with us on our honeymoon."

Lily joined the conversation then. "Oh, where are you headed?"

"Camping at Big Sur," Byron said.

Erik flicked a glance at Richard's slim-fit suit and shined-up shoes, and the man raised a brow. "Don't let my fine exterior fool you. This Georgia boy can hunt."

"Oh boy, here we go." Byron sighed. "And we made those plans before my new lack of mobility."

"Then we'll just have to get a hotel room and spend all our time in bed," Richard murmured, and once again Erik was reminded of what it looked like when two people were truly in love.

Once the kissing had died down, Lily asked, "Can I steal them now to finalize the flowers?"

"Sure. I'll start boxing." Erik stacked their empty plates and moved his portion of the show-and-tell off the countertop, carrying it all into the back room where he rinsed the plates and set about transferring the remains of the cake to the glossy box he'd brought with him for that purpose. Before their... whatever... Josie had ordered large stickers with his logo and contact information on them, and as he'd stuck them on a few boxes that morning, he'd wondered if she'd be pleased he was bowing to her branding efforts and plastering his face on something.

His hands stilled as he closed up the box. He was a baker with his own bakery. It was real, thanks to her. And Josie had vanished from his life, a little sooner than expected, but better now than later, after he'd gotten *really* attached, right? The past week had only felt a little bit like torture.

He dawdled in the back as long as he could before pushing through the swinging door to face Josie's friends once again. He set the box in front of Richard and, transaction concluded, prepared to gather his things and depart.

"Hey, Man Bun."

He turned slowly, frowning to mask the pang in his heart at hearing Josie's pet name for him. Richard tapped a finger to his lips and studied him for a long moment.

"You're the one setting up the cake next week, right?"

Erik nodded, already dreading whom he might bump into there. Okay, dreading bumping into Josie. It would probably be smart to set it all up early and get the hell out.

"Have you got plans afterward?"

"I— No. Why?" he asked suspiciously.

Richard glanced at his fiancé, who inclined his head.

"Consider yourself invited to the wedding," Byron said. "Set up the cake and stay for the whole thing."

Erik opened his mouth to decline, but Richard jumped in. "Please. We had a few last-minute cancellations, and you've been so kind to us. Just come and watch us say a few vows. Then you can enjoy the sight of everyone demolishing all your hard work."

"We promise not to smash any cake into each other's faces," Byron said with a delicate shudder.

"Thanks, but—"

"Oh, come on. Live a little." That last voice belonged to Lily, and he turned to her in surprise. She shrugged. "They just invited me and Grant too. We can sit together at the oddballs table."

"No oddballs at our wedding," Richard said. "Just old friends and new ones. We're grateful to you both, and we have a few empty seats to fill. No pressure. And it would mean so much to us."

No. Say no. For God's sake, man, open your mouth and say no. But one thought strangled his vocal cords: filmy blue fabric. He hadn't been able to forget the dress Josie would wear as Richard's attendant during the ceremony. It was soft. It was short. And God, did he want to see her in it even if she spent the night freezing him out, as he deserved. The dress had come to represent everything elegant and untouchable about her since she'd shown it to him when he'd visited her apartment, and it had featured in more than a few of his solo shower fantasies since then. And now he was being offered the chance to see her wearing it in the flesh.

Only an idiot would say no. Only a masochist would say yes.

"Thank you. I'll be there," he said gruffly, and this time Lily joined Richard and Byron in a round of meaningful glances.

Dammit. This was a setup, wasn't it? They were plotting a scenario presumably involving Josie and either his humiliation or his apology. He should tell them all to go to hell.

And yet. This would give him the opportunity to explain things to her in person since she was only communicating with him in terse emails ever since last Sunday. Question was, did he have enough words inside him to do it?

He didn't have an answer by the time he left Lily's shop, rode the train home, and walked the block to his apartment. Well, Gina's apartment now; she was officially his subletter, and he was officially moved into the second floor of the bakery.

He let himself into the transformed space; in less than a week, she'd turned it from a hovel into a home. His feet sank into the jewel-toned rug on the floor, and he set his serving supplies on a coffee table decorated with oversized art books and a decorative bowl of some sort. In the corner, Gina was engrossed in a project on her elaborate computer setup.

"Hi." She swiveled in her chair to face him. "How'd it — Whoa, why do you look shell-shocked?"

He shook his head and crossed to the bedroom

without a word, laser-focused on the contents of one of the clothing boxes he hadn't moved to his new place yet. He found it in the second one he pulled open: his black suit, haphazardly folded halfway down the stack.

"Going somewhere?" Gina asked from behind him.

He hated the material under his fingertips. He hadn't worn it since Pops's funeral, and he'd hoped never to have a reason to put it on again. "A wedding apparently."

"The one that Fancy's in?"

"Josie," he said automatically, noting her amused smile out of the corner of his eye.

She pulled the suit from his hands. "Yeah, I don't think you can go to a swank Chicago wedding in an off-the-rack suit from Liberty Valley, Iowa, especially since it barely fit you the last time you wore it." She turned and eyed him speculatively, tapping a finger to her lips. "As a matter of fact, I need to upgrade my wardrobe a little bit too. A post-breakup, new workplace kind of thing. You know what that means?"

"No way." But his mind got stuck on the memory of Josie's little blue dress and of Jake, the suit-wearing, Jeep-driving, all-smiles accountant. That's the kind of guy she liked, and even if he'd never be that guy, he could maybe, *maybe* dress like it for a night.

Gina must've seen the surrender on his face. "Yesssss," she crowed. "Time to go shopping."

EIGHTEEN

"What's so interesting?"

Josie jumped and almost dropped her phone. "Nothing!"

Richard pursed his lips in amusement. "Oh sure. That's convincing." Then he struck like a snake and plucked the device from her hand. "Today's supposed to be all about me, remember?"

She looked pointedly down at herself, kitted out in the best-maid dress, and then at their surroundings. They were tucked away in one of the dressing rooms at the swank Parker House, where Richard and Byron were set to exchange their vows in less than an hour.

"This hubbub is all for you," she pointed out, but he only had eyes for the images filling her phone screen.

"Aha!"

Good Lord. "Aha what?"

"You're thinking about the delicious baker." He smirked when she snatched her phone back and put her screen to sleep.

"I'm just making sure the website loaded properly! I

put the final images up this morning." She tucked the phone into her pocket—oh yes, her best-maid dress had pockets—and turned to the mirror, trying to approximate nonchalance as she studied her appearance. But she felt Richard's eyes scorching the back of her neck.

"Sure." He moved to stand next to her and adjusted the cuffs of his sleeves under his wedding suit. "You're worried about the website. That's why you had the page open to a close-up of Erik's hot Nordic face."

The only words of defense her scarlet-painted lips were able to conjure were "I like looking at him. Sue me." She lifted her chin and poked at the pile of curls pinned to the top of her head.

Next to her, Richard said nothing, not even a quip or a jokey insult. She didn't trust that silence *at all*.

"What did you do?" She spun to face him, turning so quickly that her chiffon skirt swished through the air before settling back against her thighs.

"Me? Nothing! It's my wedding day. Why would you accuse me of scheming?" His face was all innocence, and she studied it with narrowed eyes.

"I *didn't* accuse you of scheming, which tells me that's exactly what you've been doing. Guilty conscience much?"

"I'm wounded." He pressed a hand to his heart, taking care not to wrinkle his jacket. He'd chosen all white to go with his black tuxedo pants, while in the other dressing room, Byron was in all black and hanging out with his brother until go-time.

Richard's phone vibrated in his pocket, and he fished it out. "Hey, could you run to the entrance and see if they have enough programs? I'm worried we didn't make enough."

"Okaaaay." One didn't argue with the groom on his wedding day, although what did he expect her to do if they *didn't* have enough? She slid into her strappy gold heels and exited the dressing room, crossing the rustic wide-plank flooring of the open room where the ceremony would take place. A smattering of guests had already claimed seats in the rows of white folding chairs, and she waved at a cluster of people she recognized from Byron's office as she breezed past.

Thirty seconds later, she'd confirmed that the program supply was holding up just fine, although Richard's elderly aunt was ever so grateful that she'd checked to be sure. And two seconds after that, she laid eyes on something truly magnificent.

Erik. Andersson. Was in. A suit.

And not just any suit, but a beautifully cut navy-blue suit that accentuated his wide shoulders, his trim waist, his impossibly long legs. She'd deny it if anybody asked her later, but when she caught her first glimpse of him, silhouetted in the entrance to the venue with the late-afternoon sun pouring over his shoulders and his hair tied back in what she could only describe as a formal man bun, well... she might have whimpered a little.

Almost as if he heard her—and please God, don't let him have heard her—his gaze sought her out across the space that separated them. The color of his suit made his eyes glow an even lighter blue, and her legs carried her across the distance before she was consciously aware of what she was doing. She met him just inside the door.

"Hi." She was so overwhelmed by the shock of seeing him in the world's most important formal wear that she completely forgot to be mad at him.

His response came even more slowly than usual as he

dragged his gaze from her meticulously coiffed hair down to her gold-tipped toes and all the way back up again. "Hey." He didn't smile, but the intensity of his eyes told her that *something* was going on behind that calm mask.

"You own a suit, huh?" she said faintly. It was the best banter she could come up with; her higher-order brain functions didn't seem to be working at the moment.

"Yep." Even in the face of her judgmental question, his voice was as neutral as ever, and when he nonchalantly flicked open the button holding his jacket together —*bam,* a few of her wet parts were suddenly dry, and a few of her dry parts were suddenly wet. Mother Mary, have mercy.

"So this is the dress." His eyes seemed to have gotten stuck on the neckline of her bodice.

"Y-yes," she said faintly, the heat of his gaze flustering her almost as much as the sight of his arms in that fitted material.

He quirked his lips and took a step closer to her to avoid a large family that had just entered the hall. He smelled so good. Had he always smelled this good? Josie suddenly realized that this was the longest stretch of days that she'd gone without seeing him since their first meeting on the L.

"So I—" she started to say at the same time that he asked, "Can we—?"

They both broke off with a laugh, although it was slightly strained and nothing at all like their usual "I tease, you brood" vibe. Then she remembered her unwise kiss attack, and the smile dropped from her face. With dread pumping through her veins, she surveyed the entryway, looking for his surprise fiancée. Or not-fiancée. Whatever. But she didn't see any trace of the friendly-faced Iowan whose man she'd accidentally tried to steal. Was he here alone? And why was he here *at all?*

Silence fell during her not-at-all subtle perusal, and she forced a laugh. "I should probably get back to Richard. You'll recognize me during the ceremony. I'll be the one up front in blue."

Something moved behind Erik's eyes when she said the word "blue," and he did another of those long, slow sweeps of her body that should've offended her for the sheer male gazey-ness of it. Instead, it ignited a low, slow burn in her stomach. Unsure of what to say to defuse this strange tension or if she maybe wanted to ratchet it up until they both exploded, she turned on her stiletto heel and sauntered away, her skirt fluttering in her wake.

THE WHOLE CEREMONY seemed to last only a few minutes. Richard and Byron exchanged sweet vows that they'd written in separate corners of the hospital room over the past weeks, after which Josie shed happy tears as she watched them walk down the short aisle as a married couple, hand in hand. Byron, who'd always been slender to start with, had returned from his hospital stay gaunt and a little gray around the gills, but today he was lit from within.

"He looks so much better, don't you think?" she whispered to Byron's brother, Cecil, as they walked arm in arm after the newlyweds on the way to the reception hall.

"Much better. I wish Mom and Dad had come."

She squeezed his arm. At twenty, Cecil was eight years younger than Byron and the only member of his immediate family who'd kept in touch after Byron came out in college.

"Well, he's thrilled *you're* here." She smiled up at him as he escorted her to their assigned table, where she set her small bouquet of ferns and wildflowers down next to her plate. Lily had worked wonders on the rustic arrangement, which matched the naturalistic swags of greenery that decorated the round tables in the intimate reception hall under the tulle-and-twinkle-lights-festooned ceilings.

By now the rest of the guests were trickling in to share their good wishes with the couple before finding their assigned tables, and she watched with a giddy smile as Richard and Byron received hug after hug from the people who loved them. They deserved this beautiful day.

Finn and her two escorts joined the throng of well-wishers, and after they exchanged a few happy words with the grooms, they headed toward Josie's table. Tom, of course, only had eyes for his girlfriend, pulling out her chair and smoothing a hand over her exposed shoulder as he took the seat next to her, while Jake only had eyes for his phone as he took his seat next to Josie. Six years ago, his lack of attention would have been a crushing blow to her ego. Now it was only a mild bummer that she was seated next to a guy who looked good enough to eat, or at least to lick for a few hours, but neither of them was interested.

Then another trio entered the reception room, and this time her jealousy jumped off the charts. Lily floated across the room in a vine-embroidered green dress flanked by a handsome man on each side. The dark-haired man holding her hand was undeniably attractive, but Erik? He was Thor, god of thunder, arriving at Valhalla, if Valhalla had an open bar with a signature cocktail called Love

Always Wins and Tonics. And Thor, god of thunder, was walking straight toward her.

"Um, did the guys change the seating chart last night?" she asked Cecil, fighting to calm her nerves.

"Dunno." He shrugged, apparently unconcerned that the trio of Georgia cousins who were supposed to be at the cool-friends and family table had been replaced by a perfectly nice florist, her (presumably) perfectly nice husband, and a baker who was so much more complex than "nice" could begin to cover.

Still, she was Josie freaking Ryan, and a heaping dose of discomfort mixed with sexual tension wasn't about to keep her from doing her Josie freaking Ryan thing. "Hey, guys! Lily, I'm swooning over how great that dress is. Everybody, Lily took care of all the flowers tonight, and Erik made the cake. We are in the presence of artisans."

Finn, Tom, and Cecil all said hello as Lily settled herself gracefully into her chair, as long and lean as the plumosa ferns she'd placed around the wedding hall. "Hi, everyone. This is my husband, Grant. If you need something to talk with him about, just ask him how the Cubs' free-agent acquisitions are doing in comparison to the Yankees."

Grant groaned and dropped his head into his hands. "Can we not air our bitter rivalry in public, please?"

The rest of the group slid into baseball chatter while Josie grappled with the fact that unfortunately—or fortunately? She wasn't sure anymore—Erik had ended up in the seat directly across from her at the round table. Lily had thoughtfully kept the fern-and-feather table arrangements low enough that nobody's line of sight would be blocked, which meant she'd be spending her evening studying the triangle of exposed skin at the base of Erik's throat where it was bracketed by the open collar of his crisp white dress shirt.

"So!" she said a touch too brightly as the uniformed waitstaff started making the rounds of the room with the plated dinners. "Nobody's throwing any bouquets at this wedding. What a relief to be off the hook for a change, right, Finnie?"

She'd expected minor flushing and stammering from her reserved roommate, but instead Finn and Tom shared a sly glance, and Tom linked his fingers with Finn's, bringing her hand to his mouth to kiss the back of it.

"I don't know about that," she said without shifting her focus from her boyfriend.

It was like that then? Engagement, marriage, happily ever after? Geez, she really *would* need to find her own place. She slid her eyes over to Jake, who looked equally floored by the reveal.

He leaned close to murmur, "Did you know about this?"

She shook her head and glanced across the table to find Erik trying to set her on fire with his gaze. Her skin heated, and she looked down at the bouquet, shocked to find herself the flustered one.

By the time she'd composed herself, the rest of the table had dived into their meals and the conversation had moved on to Lily's flower-wholesaler secrets, which allowed Josie to focus on the honey-glazed salmon on the plate in front of her. It melted into flavorful deliciousness the instant it touched her tongue, sure, but it also kept her from shouting over the table and demanding to know what Erik's deal was already. Where was Gina? Had they ever been engaged? And how dare he show up looking this good?

Soon enough the meal was over, and the deejay handed the microphone off to Richard to start the toasts.

"Friends. Family. Friends who've become family," he began. "Byron and I are so touched that you're here with us on this special day. And I'd like to share a little story that some of you know and many of you don't. It's the story of how I left a pair of pants in an Uber and Byron found a pair of pants in an Uber, and even though it wasn't the same pair of pants, it nevertheless brought us together."

The chuckles that moved through the room turned to full-blown laughter as Richard described his and Byron's modern fairy-tale meeting, which he concluded by turning to his new husband with a soft smile. "Everyone who finds love in this world is lucky, and tonight I feel like the luckiest of them all."

Emotion clogged Josie's throat, and she stared down at the bubbles swirling in her champagne flute, guiltily aware of the twinge of self-pity coloring her joy for the two of them. When she looked up, she found Erik's unreadable gaze on her, and she stared back for a long moment, snared by his blue eyes, before wrenching away at Richard's cry of, "To love!"

After the assembled company cheered and sipped, it was her turn at the microphone. She swept to her feet and walked to stand behind the grooms' table, relieved to be in her comfort zone.

"Let's hear it for finding love in the gig economy, everyone!" She soaked up the laughter and turned up her wattage. "I'm Josie Ryan, Richard's best maid, and I'm here to offer a few more reasons why these two men are perfect for each other."

Give her a crowd and a few prepared jokes, and she'd

rise to the occasion. By the time she'd wrapped up her toast, the newlyweds were gazing at each other in goofy adoration, and the crowd roared when she instructed them to raise their glasses.

The night got even better when Richard and Byron sliced into the cake. Oh, the cake. Although she and Erik had been out of touch while he'd been finishing it up, she'd marveled at the end results earlier in the evening. She had no idea how he'd done it, but the gold-veined blue-and-white marble looked so authentic you'd almost expect to see it in a South Beach villa owned by a cartel kingpin whose decorating aesthetic was juuuust on the right side of gaudy. In other words, it was perfect for the couple whose love it was honoring. And of course it was the best-tasting cake she'd ever had in her mouth.

"Oh my God, each flavor's better than the last one." Finn moaned after she and Tom exchanged bites from each other's plates.

When Josie turned a speculative eye on Jake's half-eaten slice of peach-pecan, he tossed up his hand as a barrier. "You already finished your piece. Live with your choices."

"Food aggression much?" she scoffed. "I was just looking to see what flavor you picked!"

He shifted the plate closer with a dark look, and when she glanced to her right, Cecil edged his plate of chocolate hazelnut farther away from her to continue inhaling it. At her huff of exasperation, Jake laughed. "Just go and get a second piece, devil woman!"

"I will if you'll save me a dance." As this wasn't their first friend-group wedding, Josie knew for a fact that Jake danced the way he performed every other social nicety expected of him: with technical flawlessness and a total lack of zeal. But it was also good for him to remember that life existed outside the walls of his office, and sometimes that life involved a compulsory dance or two with an equally single friend. In fact, he might just be her most frequent wedding dance partner, and wasn't that saying something about her pathetic love life?

"My pleasure," he said, almost managing to sound sincere.

"The awkward platonic tradition continues!" she said with a laugh. But when she glanced across the table, she found a pair of blue eyes glaring at her, so she glared right back. Mister "I'm possibly engaged but maybe not" could go ahead and stare daggers at her until those gorgeous eyes fell right out of his head. What did she care? It's not like he had any right to be jealous.

She hardened her jaw and flounced out of her chair to grab a piece of cardamom before the dancing got underway in earnest.

She might be confused over everything having to do with Erik, but that didn't mean she wouldn't eat every crumb of his cake that she could get her hands on.

NINETEEN

Erik was strapped to a roller coaster, and he hated it.

First was the agony of watching Josie exchange private glances with that good-looking asshole she was sitting next to. Then came the perverse pleasure of watching her bound out of her chair to toast the newlyweds. She spoke for close to six minutes with no notes and, effortlessly and with great charm, had the whole reception hall laughing. How anybody possessed the skill and courage to do that he'd never know, and he hoped never to find out for himself. Then there was the ecstasy of watching her eyes roll back as she wrapped her red lips around that first bite of cake, knowing that *he* was the one who did that to her. And, finally, there was his old friend agony again when she and fucking Jake agreed to a dance.

As the guests flocked to the floor, Erik started eyeing the exit. He'd satisfied his masochistic curiosity about Josie in The Dress—it was even more torturous than he'd expected, showing vast swaths of flawless skin—and now it was time to go. Look-but-don't-touch had been difficult enough before he'd given in and put his hands all over her. But now that he had the memory of her taste on his lips, look-but-don't-touch when she was lit from within and wrapped in filmy blue material might actually kill him.

Before he could make good on his exit strategy, a polite voice yanked his thoughts back into the now. "Excuse me. Are you the baker?"

He turned to see a silver-haired woman from a nearby table hovering at his elbow and nodded.

"The cake was divine! Can I talk with you next week about baking something similar for my fiftieth wedding anniversary party next month?"

"Absolutely." He didn't have to force his smile as he took down her information. Another job meant another small weight lifted from his shoulders.

Across the table, Josie's hand darted into her clutch and emerged with a Have Your Cake business card.

But he raised his brows and produced an identical stack of cards from the inside pocket of his jacket. "Here. I'll call you on Monday to set up a meeting."

"Wonderful!" the woman trilled as she tucked the card into her handbag. "I look forward to it."

When he looked back across the table, Josie was beaming at him like a proud parent.

"They grow up so fast!" She wiped a pretend tear from the corner of her eye. "I'll make a marketing expert out of you yet."

His lips pinched together as he crammed the cards back into his pocket. "It *is* my business, after all." He hated that he sounded testy, but God, how many emotions was he supposed to juggle in one night? Lust, pride, regret, relief. It was too much—and that was before

Finn's handsome fucking brother chose that moment to stand and offer Josie his hand.

"Shall we?" he asked, and she grinned up at him and chirped, "We shall!"

Add murderous jealousy to that list.

His eyes tracked their progress to the floor, and any hope that he'd been at all circumspect about his surveillance was dashed when Lily patted his knee under the table.

"You could ask her to dance next, you know."

"I don't—"

She cut him off. "Oh please, you're not fooling anybody. Just do it."

Ridiculous. Him, dancing? His bulk on the dance floor would have all the grace and charm of a barge.

"Quit tormenting him, sweetheart," Grant said. "Come argue with me on the dance floor."

Every starchy bit of Lily melted as her husband pulled her to her feet and they walked away hand in hand, leaving Erik alone with Byron's brother, who was immersed in God knew what on his phone.

Nothing to do but watch the happy couples swaying to Lady Gaga's cover of "Your Song." He had strong opinions on the topic of wedding songs after lingering around the periphery of countless receptions over the past half a year, and it was usually one of his favorites. But tonight Gaga's singing dragged on and on while his narrowed eyes focused in on the places where Jake's hands made contact with Josie's body: her fingers, her waist, her back where her dress dipped low. He wanted to storm the parquet floor and forcibly separate the pair of them. Then, to his horror, the deejay queued up a second slow song as

Gaga's final notes faded, and Josie and Jake showed no signs of leaving the floor.

He was up and out of his chair without a second thought, striding across the room to the opening notes of "Can't Help Falling in Love." Touching Josie's shoulder took every ounce of courage he could summon, but he did it, forcing his arm up, allowing his fingers to skate along her upper arm. She looked around in surprise.

"Dance with me." Now that the words were out, he was aware of how likely she was to loudly tell him to fuck off. They hadn't exactly had a proper apology session yet, and she could be... impulsive.

After a split second of silence, she cut her glance to Jake and said, "I guess you're off the hook."

His insides eased when Jake turned and left the floor without argument and Josie moved into his waiting arms. It was the two of them now, and the reception hall shrank to the small circle of space that encompassed only them as Elvis's voice crooned through the speakers.

His nerves fled as his fingers took their place at her waist, half on the soft material of that damn dress and half on her warm back. It felt right to be touching her. His skin had been craving hers for two weeks, and if he had to stand in the middle of a group of people to satisfy that need, so be it.

She slid her arm around him and he pulled her closer, only relaxing into the dance when she gave a little sigh and melted into him. While she and Jake had chatted through the entirety of their song—and Erik knew that to be a fact because he'd watched every second of it—all her words dried up once she was in his arms. But her eyes never left his, and they seemed to be asking a question.

He could guess what it was, or at least land in the

ballpark. And he owed her those answers. So as the song came to an end, he dropped one hand from her back but kept hold of her fingers with the other, using that connection to lead her off the floor and out onto one of the balconies overlooking the sleepy street below.

By some miracle, the area was empty of guests, but he still led her through the velvety summer air to a dark corner where the strands of lights twined overhead didn't quite penetrate. She leaned against the metal railing with her back to the street while he leaned against it with his back to the building. It was an apt metaphor for the two of them: in the same spot but facing opposite directions.

"Good cake," she said after a moment.

Small talk? Okay. If that's what she needed. "Thanks. It's what I do. Good speech."

She flashed a cocky smile. "Thanks. It's what I do."

"Are you seriously not into him?" Fuck, that was abrupt, but he had to know.

"Who, Jake?" Her laughter floated over the muffled sounds of the party raging just beyond them. "No. Not for years and years. Now he's just fun to tease."

His fingers tightened around the metal railing. "Like I'm fun to tease?" The words hurt his throat, hurt his heart, but *Christ*, he needed to know. Needed to know if he was just another Jake to her, another man to string along and laugh about.

She studied him in silence for a moment, until he worried that she didn't intend to answer.

"No," she finally said. "I mean, you're fun to tease too, but it's... different."

Different how? He wanted to howl the question, but instead she threw the conversation back at him.

"Erik." Her voice was serious but gentle. "I need you to explain."

He didn't ask her to clarify. Releasing a long breath, he tipped his head to the sky and prepared to mine the most disappointing parts of himself. "I lied to you about being engaged to Gina. But I lied to my grandfather about it first."

Josie said nothing, so he continued.

"I've known her since we were kids. Her parents weren't the best, so she was at our place pretty often." He paused to sort through his memories of the dysfunction that had filled every corner of Gina's unhappy childhood home, particularly after she'd come out to her parents in high school. "Pops loved her. He wanted me to love her. And I do, but not the way he meant. I tried though."

He lapsed into silence as images of his grandfather's strong body wasting away in a hospital bed surfaced. "He spent his last weeks in the Mayo Clinic. Complications from a rare blood cancer."

Josie's head bobbed once as if she'd just slotted a puzzle piece into place. "That's why you knew so much when I was making plans for Richard."

"It's not a great thing to be experienced in, believe me." The sky above them was empty of stars thanks to the city's light pollution. He'd never not find that disorienting. "The only thing he could focus on at the end was me. My future. He wanted me to forget about baking and move back to the farm. Marry Gina. Have a stable life. And never, ever live like my mother, chasing pointless, risky dreams. And I promised him I would."

He clenched the metal railing, welcoming the scrape of rust on the underside against his fingers as remorse clogged his throat. He'd done everything his grandfather had begged him not to do. Sold the farm. Risked it all on a likely-to-fail new business. Set his sights on a woman who was Gina's polar opposite in almost every way.

Josie shifted against the railing. "So you told a kind lie to a dying man you loved very much."

He nodded, unable to speak.

"Has it occurred to you that you eased his final days, and that's no reason to punish yourself for the rest of your life?"

Sure. Because forgiving himself was that easy. He risked a glance at her beautiful face and found her serious and unusually still in the silvery moonlight.

"And that day in your apartment?" she asked.

From one bad memory to another. He peeled his fingers off the railing and shoved them in his pockets. "I'm so sorry. I never meant to make you feel..."

"Unwanted?"

Her bereft tone tore at him. "Never that. Never, ever that." He turned toward her. "You scare the shit out of me, woman."

His honesty startled a laugh out of her. "What? How?"

The suit jacket suddenly felt three sizes too small. Truth telling made him feel even bulkier than usual.

"I've never met anyone like you." He shook his head. "Nobody makes me feel the way you do."

Her breathing quickened. "How, Erik?"

"How am I different than Jake?" He shot the question back, and she laughed softly.

"You make me feel..."

Her words trailed off, and a strange compulsion took over him. Before she could finish her thought, he cupped her jaw as words came spilling from his mouth, each one more revealing than the last. "Do you feel like trailing your lips all over my skin until you've explored every inch of me? Like a circuit will blow in your brain if you can't kiss me again? Like you only spark to life when I'm around? Because that's how you make me feel."

She swallowed, and because he hadn't moved his hand away, he felt every delicate twitch of her throat muscles.

"I didn't think you were capable of speaking that many words in a row," she said with a breathless laugh.

"Only with you," he said. And inexplicably, he had still more words for her. "I want to feast on every word that tumbles from your mouth. I want your smiles all to myself. Your laughter should belong to me." He brushed his thumb along her lower lip and inhaled hard when her tongue darted out to stroke along his skin. "I want to rip apart every man who touches you. Every man who even looks at you."

"Even Jake?" Her breath trembled across his thumb, and he responded instantly.

"*Especially* Jake," he growled, uncaring that his jealousy was oozing through the cracks in his crumbling defenses.

"You..." She brushed a shaky hand over his lapel, and his whole body strained in her direction. "I thought I was the one who took advantage of you that day. I thought afterward that I'd pushed for something you didn't want."

"Didn't want?" He huffed an incredulous laugh. "I'd imagined touching you for so long I could barely believe it was actually happening. God, I'm sorry I made you feel that way. But when Gina showed up, I remembered who I really am. I panicked."

Her eyes rounded. "And who are you really?"

"The guy who doesn't get the girl like you."

His lips hovered above hers, and she didn't push him away. "Look around you, pal. You've got me."

The last of his doubts sloughed away at her words. "I guess I do." He slid his hand behind her head and buried his fingers in her hair, not caring about the fancy arrangement she had it in. He needed to unravel her, to mark her as his. Talking might not come easily to him, but this he could do.

She was practically panting as he held her immobile with a hand in her hair and another at the base of her throat.

"You're who I want, Erik. Nobody else here tonight. Nobody else anywhere in the world. This girl wants *you*."

Well, fuck. How could he not kiss her after that?

TWENTY

Josie's head was spinning, but she hadn't had more than a few sips of alcohol during the toasts.

It was Erik, filling her lungs, bubbling through her blood, giving her goose bumps. His eyes never left hers as he closed the tiny distance between them, his fingers tightening in her hair, and this time there was no mistaking who was going to kiss whom. He wanted her, and he wasn't engaged, and he'd just recited a soliloquy that left her breathless. She needed to put her hands on this good, kind, wonderful man without further delay.

Just as her eyes fluttered shut and his lips brushed against hers, the balcony erupted in a flurry of noise and laughter. A group of wedding guests surged from the reception hall and broke the spell.

She dropped her head against his shoulder with a soft groan. "I don't think the universe wants us to be together."

"Fuck the universe."

His growl made her shiver.

"What are your thoughts on screwing around in a coat closet?"

"Not ideal."

Still, his hand crept up her thigh and under the hem of her dress, and she bet if she pulled him into an empty room, she could change his mind.

Raucous laughter reminded her that they were no longer alone, and exhibitionism wasn't one of her kinks.

"Do you want to come home with me? Or I can come home with you."

He fell silent, his face unreadable in the semidark, and Josie felt a trickle of self-consciousness wiggle down her spine.

"I said 'come' too much, didn't I? You're paralyzed with lust." When in doubt, joke it out.

"Good God," Erik muttered, putting his huge hand on her back and guiding her toward the bright lights of the reception. She chattered nervously the whole time, keenly aware that he hadn't actually answered her question.

"Oh great. I scared you off again. Someday you're going to tell your great-grandchildren about the crazed redhead who kept hitting on you in inappropriate settings and trying to get you into supply closets to—"

Her voice cut off with a squeak when he spun her so her back was pressed against the wall next to the reception hall entrance. Wedding guests milled around the balcony mere feet away, but Josie didn't care. Not when the distant throbbing bass of the music echoed the pounding of her heart and the deejay's strobe light fell through the window and painted Erik's face in streaks of red and purple and blue as he pinned her in place with his hard body.

"We're going to my place tonight, because when I finally get you naked, it's not going to be in a goddamn closet." His hands flirted with the hem of her skirt again, ghosting along the backs of her legs. "It's going to take all night, and you're going to be as loud as you want. Nod your head if that's okay."

She bobbed her head like a newly sprung jack-in-the-box while the rest of her body clenched in anticipation of Erik following through on his promises.

"Okay." He nodded once and bent to give her a fast, firm kiss that ended with the merest brush of his tongue against her lower lip.

"You're exceptionally good at talking when you put your mind to it," she said shakily.

"Oh, I'm just getting started at showing you what I'm good at." The slow, cocksure smile that slid across his face at that moment shocked the hell out of her.

Her head fell back against the wall. That face with that body, in that suit, oozing sexual confidence? It was possible she wouldn't survive the night.

"Where'd all this come from?" She'd only ever seen him this self-assured about his baking, and it was seriously doing things between her thighs.

His smile flashed wickedly in the dim light. "Talking to women has always been hard. Kissing them's a lot easier. No conversation required."

"Take me home. Now," she ordered. Then a dreadful thought struck her. "Wait. Nooooo! I'm supposed to help with the cleanup."

Erik groaned and dropped his forehead against hers. "Presents, flowers, all that?"

"All that," she confirmed, dismay swamping her. "When I offered, it didn't occur to me that I'd have a hot hookup on the line."

His sigh brushed her cheek. "So we stick around to

help out." He dropped a kiss behind her left ear. "And you spend the rest of the reception thinking about all the things you want me to do to you later tonight."

Another kiss, this time on her collarbone, robbed her of her breath.

"Already on it," she managed to gasp as his teeth lightly scraped her skin and gave her full-body shivers.

He took a step back, his fingertips running the length of her bare arms before they finally fell away. But the heat in his eyes remained, and they seared her from behind as he ushered her back inside and to their table. Once he'd delivered her to her chair, he ambled over to the cake table while she willed her nipples back into submission. Of course, watching the big slice of man she'd be going home with did nothing to calm her body down. He circled the remains of his cake like a jungle cat, assessing she knew not what. But that miraculous suit stretched over his body as he made the rounds, and she bit her lip while she openly ogled his ass.

"I guess I really *am* off the hook tonight."

Jake folded himself into the seat next to her, and ordinarily, she'd make some kind of jokey come-on that he'd pointedly ignore. But tonight her eyes bounced right back to where Erik was smiling as he sliced a piece of cake for a little girl in a frilly pink dress whose head barely cleared the table. And just like that, her ovaries exploded.

"Does he know what he's getting into with you?"

Heat rolled through her body for the second time that night, but this time it was the angry variety, which was way less fun than the lusty one. "Excuse me?" She narrowed her eyes at him, but Jake just calmly rattled the ice in his mostly empty highball glass.

"Listen, you toy with me and don't mean any of it. But I think you might mean it with him." He tilted his head toward the Beauty and the Toddler show happening in front of the cake.

"Mean what?" Even as she asked, she knew. She didn't know how *Jake* knew, but somehow the seventy-hour-work-week brother of her best friend had seen past her showy exterior and divined the secrets in her heart.

"You're the most optimistic romantic I've ever met, even though you hide it behind your legendary man-ogling. But every time you take somebody home, you're hoping for forever. It's one of the reasons that you and I haven't ever..." He had the good grace to look a little chagrined as he waved his glass in a vague circle between the two of them.

She tipped her head toward him. "Why, Jake Carey, are you saying you've thought about getting with *all of this*?" She slid a hand down her side with a saucy wink.

"Yes, actually. Once I got to know you, I... thought about it. You mean a lot to me."

Her mouth fell open. In all the time she'd been messing with him, not for a second did she think he'd taken her seriously.

He quirked his perfectly perfect lips at her surprise. "I know. It shocked the hell out of me too. But you're my sister's best friend, and the thought of fucking up that dynamic made it impossible for me to..." He frowned and stared into his glass, suddenly looking tired and more vulnerable than she'd ever seen him. Then he straightened. "Anyway, we both know how busy I am. No first dates and definitely no second dates."

"Sounds lonely," she said softly.

He drained the rest of his drink in one quick motion. "Yeah. But it's who I am." He set the glass down on the table with a thump, then nodded toward the cake table. "That guy though? Is he a second-date kind of guy?"

She frowned. "I'm not sure actually." Erik's explosion of words on the balcony had twisted her insides. He wanted her. That was clear now. But did he want her in a "bang it out and get on with our lives" kind of way or a "let's go on a third and fourth and fifth date" kind of way? She watched him serving a fresh wave of cake-hungry guests, pride flickering in her chest as he sliced up his product and handed out business cards with his *this-is-physically-hurting-me* smile. Wow, did she like him.

"Oh my God, get out of here already," Jake ordered.

Josie groaned, folding her arms on the table and dropping her head. "I told the guys I'd collect their gifts and whatever else so they can go start their honeymoon without a care in the world."

Jake tapped a finger against his empty glass before he spoke. "What if I handle it?"

She lifted her head slowly. "Really?"

"Not like I'm taking anyone home tonight." He nodded toward Finn and Tom swaying together on the dance floor. "I'm sure the lovebirds will help me out."

Pseudo-big-brother to the rescue! She shrieked and threw her arms around his neck in a quick hug, which he accepted with a grimace and a swift pat of her shoulder. "You're the best!"

"I know. Now go forth and have sex." Jake pronounced it like a benediction, but she was already out of her chair and stalking across the room to claim her man.

Erik straightened from the cake table and watched her approach with hooded blue eyes. When she reached him, she hooked a finger through a belt loop on his beautiful suit.

"Let's get out of here."

As she was hoping, he dropped the cake server and followed her out the door without a single word.

TWENTY-ONE

Erik was well on his way to being hard as fucking iron by the time he slotted his key into the back door of the bakery. Josie's body was nothing but curves, and every one of them had been pressed against him from the moment they'd left the reception hall and climbed into the waiting Lyft.

He pushed open the door and waited for her to step inside so he could lose himself in her at last, but she paused in the alley, uncharacteristic hesitation crossing her face.

"Is, uh, is Gina here?"

Like he'd bring her back to his place if they weren't going to have privacy for all the things he had planned. He rested his hands loosely on her waist but restrained himself from slinging her over his shoulder and carrying her to his bedroom. She needed to be the one to make this decision. "Nope. We're all alone." He'd explain about the sublet later, after they finally did this thing.

"In that case," she murmured, turning to smooth her hands along his shoulders, "take me inside. As amazing as you look in this suit, I can't wait to get it the hell off you." She slipped her hand underneath his collar and grazed her nails over the back of his neck.

Had the damn suit felt tight before? Because he was ready to burst out of the expensive material, Hulk-style, so he could absorb every touch she was willing to give him. He swung her into his arms, stepped over the threshold, and kicked the door shut, then took the stairs two at a time. He wasn't able to focus on any details beyond the weight of her in his arms and her good, clean citrusy scent tickling his nose.

He stalked across the room and settled them both on the couch, pulling her onto his lap to straddle him. His sofa screeched in protest, but he was already too busy kissing her to worry about anything else.

She was positioned exactly where he wanted her, and he devoured her mouth, telling her with his actions that he'd be happy to do nothing but this all night long. And then she told him without words that she wanted more, pushing down to grind against his cock. Her gasp of approval at finding him hard and ready acted like a starter's pistol for him, and he dragged his hands down her sides until they tangled in the frothy material of her skirt. The dress was frivolous and feminine and maddening—exactly like Josie herself, and he couldn't get enough.

She broke the kiss and leaned forward to reach for his shirt, and he half expected sparks to trail in the wake of her fingers. Instead, she worked her way down the buttons and untucked the fabric from his suit pants, exposing his chest to her avid eyes.

"Goddamn, Erik, you look good." She reached out to

touch where her eyes had just been, but he grabbed her hand and held it immobile a few inches from his skin.

"Me first." Because if she got anywhere near the vicinity of his belt buckle, he'd be inside her in a matter of seconds, and he needed this to last for her, needed her to remember it. So he swung her around to sit on the couch back, which allowed her to lean against the wall while he knelt between her legs. She reached to unzip her dress, but again he stopped her.

"Leave it on." His voice was rough with need. "I've pictured you like this so many times."

Her head lolled against the wall, and she looked down at him with lust-clouded eyes. "Oh yeah? What did you imagine?" She skimmed a hand over the blue of her skirt as her legs drifted wider to give him better access.

"This." He reached up and tugged her neckline down to expose her breasts. Then he tilted his head to look his fill, his chest heaving at the effort it took to draw enough breath into his lungs at the sight. Everything. She was everything he wanted. Flushed and flustered and his to touch.

"Erik," she breathed, leaning forward to smooth her fingers along his hair, gripping the knot at the back of his head where he'd secured it for the evening. A small little smile ghosted across her face, and he had a pretty good idea of what had just popped into her mind.

"Say it." He surged upward to growl the command into her ear, pressing his chest against hers and reveling in the soft fullness of her breasts and the drag of her hard nipples across his skin. She shifted to quirk a smile at him, as if daring him to guess what was on the tip of her tongue.

"What?" she asked innocently.

"You know," he growled.

"Oh do I, Man Bun?" Her breathy sass ended in a gasp when he bit her ear.

"You should know by now," he said darkly, moving down to capture her exposed nipple with his teeth, "I don't do nicknames."

"I can tell—" She gave a squeak as he bit down gently before moving to her other breast. "T-tell how much you hate it."

"Hate it," he repeated, pausing to lick and tease each of her gorgeous tits before moving down her body. "So much." He knelt between her legs, loving that she was still wearing her fancy shoes, and inched up the blue material of her skirt to reveal ivory lace underwear. Before he touched her again, he glanced up to check that she was still with him.

She was. Her big brown eyes were locked on his hands where they wrapped around the tops of her thighs, her lower lip caught between her teeth. Then one corner of her mouth lifted and she braced her weight on her heels, pushing herself up so he could pull the lace down. He freed one leg, but the material tangled with the buckle on her other shoe. He didn't give a single fuck though, not when the heart of her was exposed for him.

"Please..." She shifted fractionally closer to him.

At that moment he would've done anything she asked, of course, but what she was begging for would be nothing but pleasure for them both. He pushed her legs wider and lowered his mouth to her hot center. At the first swipe of his tongue, her hands flew out to grip the back of the couch, and by the time he'd settled into a rhythm that pulled shuddery breath after shuddery breath from her, she was rocking against him in time to his strokes. The material of her skirt draped around his shoulders, and he lost himself to the blue of her dress and the pink of her pussy, all of it so much hotter than his fantasies over the past weeks.

He followed the cues her body gave him, slowing down when her movements slowed, speeding up when they became frantic, sliding his fingers inside her when she started to whimper. The more she lost her mind, the more he lost his, and before he knew it, his unfiltered thoughts came spilling out of his mouth.

"Like one of my cakes," he said after he'd given her a long, hard suck that practically levitated her off the couch.

"H-how so?" Her eyes had fluttered shut as he worked, but he wanted her to know that *he* was the one doing this to her, so he took his mouth away and replaced it with his fingers, delivering a light spank that made her whole body jolt. She hissed a curse as her eyes flew open, and there was a chance that she'd actually driven one of her pointy heels straight through his couch cushion. She panted out, "Please *please* tell me how I'm like one of your cakes."

Two "pleases." Fuck if a compliant Josie Ryan wasn't the biggest turn-on yet.

"The slogan. The business cards."

She shook her head helplessly, her face a mixture of confusion and arousal, so he took the opportunity to remind her.

"Delicious on the outside." He reached for her hand and pressed a kiss on her palm before twining their fingers together. Then he rewarded her sweet obedience with a long, slow lick down her center that ended with another hard suck where she most wanted it. "Delicious on the inside."

The combination of his talk and his touch pushed her over the edge. She gripped his hand and fell apart against his mouth, and the sight of her, half in and half out of her fancy dress, her hair a vibrant, disheveled mess and her cheeks glowing pink because of him, was too much. With a groan, he gave in to the demands of his straining dick, yanking open his zipper and stroking himself in time to her ragged gasps until his breaths matched hers and he came hard and fast with her name on his lips.

After a few long moments, Josie's eyes fluttered open to survey the mess he'd made, her mouth curving with a lazy, well-pleasured smile. "Delicious," she agreed, and he bit his lip to keep from saying anything more. Because he was starting to wonder about the shape of his life once she'd moved on with hers. Would any future sexual encounters ever live up to what he'd just experienced? Likely not, and for one simple reason: he'd never find another woman like Josie.

TWENTY-TWO

It took a little time for Josie's soul to return to her body after Erik was through with her. Seriously, what woman could be anything but boneless and satisfied after that experience?

"I think we ruined your couch." The words emerged from her mouth slightly slurred, but that was only because their shared marrow-rattling orgasms had temporarily shut down her fine motor control. She'd be okay in a few minutes. Probably.

"No regrets." He was reclined against the arm of the sofa, looking relaxed and maybe even a little smug. He still wore his suit jacket over his unbuttoned shirt, and he'd straightened but not refastened his pants.

She'd never imagined she'd see him looking so undone, and all she wanted to do was drape herself across all those thick muscles and big, heavy bones. Yet when she tried to shift off the back of the couch, she found her right foot stuck.

"Um." She tugged at it, but the heel had actually sunk

into the nubby orange upholstery. "Shit, Erik, I really *did* ruin your couch."

"This couch was ruined long before you stabbed it."

He leaned forward, the muscles in his stomach rippling in intriguing ways, and gently circled his hands around her ankle, tugging until she was free from the predatory furniture. Then his big, blunt fingers fiddled with the straps, loosening first one buckle and then the other. There was nothing overtly erotic about his actions, yet she could barely breathe as he slipped the shoes off her feet and set them to the side. As soon as he straightened, she gave a little growl and launched herself at him, driving him backward. Just as her brain was processing "warm" and "strong" and "man," the sofa gave a loud crack and the bottom hit the floor with a jarring thud.

Erik broke the startled silence first with a burst of laughter that rippled through his body. "Okay, you *definitely* just ruined my couch."

"I'm so sorry!" She rolled off the cushions and onto the floor to see one of the arms sticking out at a crazy angle, a splintered couch leg underneath. She slapped her hands over her eyes and curled into a ball of embarrassment, aware that she was witnessing an unusually literal manifestation of her penchant for chaos. "I'll... buy you a new one?" She cracked open one eye and found his face still alight with laughter.

"This was a one of a kind, babe." His matter-of-fact tone made her giggle, and with a graceful movement he stood and pulled her up alongside him, adjusting her dress so she was fully covered again. Her skin heated as his hands brushed the tops of her breasts. This quiet, self-contained man had just assumed total control of her body and then shamelessly worked himself until he came, his eyes on her the whole time. She'd already known that his everyday stillness hid depths, but she hadn't expected him to be so commanding once he had her naked from the waist down.

She cast a playful glance in his direction, and what she saw hit her like a spray of cold water. The enthralled, passionate man from a few minutes ago was gone, replaced by the stranger she'd met on the train: aloof, bored, indifferent.

She crossed her arms over her chest, the uncertainty from the past two weeks kicking its way into her psyche. With any other guy, she'd either have him in bed already, or she'd be on her way out the door. Of course, most other guys probably wouldn't have bothered moving off the busted couch before doing the not-so-subtle "nudge your head south" move on her for round two. But Erik's whole vibe was screaming that one round was enough and he was ready for her to get gone. He definitely wouldn't be the first guy to hit his limit with the Josie show, but it hurt to think he'd already gotten there so quickly.

"So, um, should we call it a night?" She was aiming for breezy lady-about-town, giving her casual hookup an easy way out. Instead, she remembered the last time she'd stormed out of his apartment, how utterly rejected she'd felt, and it made her voice emerge creaky and small.

He tucked his hands into his pockets. "If that's what you want."

"Is that what *you* want?" she shot back.

When he didn't reply, her heart sank. He *did* want her to leave. Jake's question had an answer: Erik wasn't a second-date guy after all. He looked thoroughly uninterested in the prospect of her coming and then going, and she wanted to sink back onto the floor and howl at the unfairness. But just as the buzzing started to build in the base of her skull, threatening to sweep through her body and propel her out the door in a frenzy of bad feelings, she realized how ridiculous she was being.

"Oh my God, I'm *so* not this girl." When he raised his brows in a question, she clarified. "You know, the girl who doesn't say what she really wants. That's not what I do. That's what *you* do."

He shrugged. "I took your shoes off."

"What does that have to do with anyth—" It took her a second, but once she realized what he meant, it spun her sideways. He *had* told her what he wanted, but he'd done it in his wordless Erik way. She slowly turned to face him.

"Just so we're clear," she said, "you took my shoes off."

"Yes."

"You took my shoes off because you want me to stay."

"Yes."

"For sex."

His throat rippled as he swallowed. "If that's what you want, yes."

His strangled response made her grin. "Okay then. Well, that's awesome because I very much want to do bad things to all *this*." She waved a hand from the top of his dark blond head down to the tips of his cordovan shoes.

"I'm good with that," he deadpanned.

"Well, why didn't you say so?" She grinned saucily at him as the tension drained from her body.

He rewarded her by literally, physically upending her over his shoulder and giving her ass a light slap. "Josie Ryan, I'm taking you to bed so I can fuck you properly, and you don't get to leave until I say you can. How's that for direct?"

She almost burst into flames at his words. "It's good.

It's so good." *Tell me you don't ever want me to leave*, she wanted to add, but even she wasn't *that* honest. Instead, she dug her fingers into his back as he carried her to the bedroom. If she wasn't careful, she'd get addicted to being hauled around like a sack of flour.

When they reached his bed, he tossed her onto the center of it, where she bounced up to a kneeling position.

"Fair warning, I'm planning to destroy this piece of furniture too."

A smile spread across his face as he gazed down at her. "You can certainly try. Take that off." He lifted his chin to her dress.

"So bossy," she murmured, unzipping her dress and pulling it over her head to send it sailing into a corner. It was the kind with a built-in bra, which barely provided enough support for someone with her "ample endowments," as her mother once phrased it. And while she'd been slightly concerned that she might burst through the seams during that afternoon's ceremony, every second of worry was worth it to be instantly naked under Erik's gaze right now. His chest expanded as he sucked in a giant breath, and when she gave a little stretch, causing her breasts to shift, his eyes tracked their movement. To test just how carefully he was watching her, she leaned back on her left arm, her breasts swaying with her. A millisecond later, Erik's eyes followed the same path.

Oh, this was fun. Actually maybe *too* fun. Although she was tempted to abuse her power over the poor boob-drunk male, she redirected his focus. "Man Bun. Off with it," she ordered, twirling a finger in his direction.

And Erik being Erik, he lifted a brow and wordlessly followed her directions. Of course, he did it in his own Erik way, taking his sweet time to peel off the jacket and kick off his shoes before slowly pulling off his shirt. Her eyes followed his hands as they moved to his pants; and the clink of his belt buckle, the rustle of fabric, the slide and tug as he pulled them off launched her anticipation into overdrive. His movements were sure and unhurried, and it was all a special kind of torture that had her running her tongue over her lower lip in her eagerness.

Once he was naked, she leaned back and looked her fill at his body: powerful, tense, seemingly carved of stone. "That's it. You should never be allowed to wear clothes again."

"Health code violation," he replied as he joined her on the bed.

She reached for him with grabby hands and pushed him on his back, following him down to kiss him until they were both gasping for air. Only then did she allow herself to explore the rest of his body with her hands and mouth and tongue, revealing details he'd kept hidden: the freckled skin of his shoulders, the faded scar bisecting his ribs, the lion tattoo on his chest. She wanted to own all his stories, to know what sun under what sky had kissed those tan specks into his skin, to identify the sharp objects that had pierced him and dared to leave their marks on his body. At the reception, he'd promised her time, and she planned to take everything that he'd give her.

She moved lower and ran the tip of her finger down his cock, which she hadn't gotten a satisfying glimpse of before. "Oh, thank God. You're proportionate," she said rapturously.

His hips twitched forward, and he gave a strained laugh.

"What?" she asked. "It's a compliment! Everything

about you is big, and now I know for a fact that it's *ev-uh-ree-thing*."

Then she wiped away his laughter by stroking her hand down the whole glorious length of him, which was hot and hard and ready for her. She punctuated the motion with quick pulses of her fist that had him arching his back with a strained grimace.

When she leaned closer, he spoke through gritted teeth. "Wait. Stop."

She paused with her mouth inches from the tip of his cock, which looked to her like it would welcome the flat of her tongue running across it. "No?" She spoke in a challenging voice but backed away when he shook his head.

"Condoms. In the drawer." He gasped the words, and this time she didn't argue, instead reaching over to fish around in the bedside table drawer until she found a packet.

"Let me guess." She quirked a smile up at him, loving the flush on his cheekbones. "Even though you already got off once, the sight of my mouth on you would've been too much and you would've embarrassed yourself?"

The instant she finished rolling the condom on, he surged up and reversed their positions, rolling her onto her back and using his knee to push her legs apart. "Essentially."

Heat bloomed in her center at his honesty, and she offered the best smug smile she was capable of. Then he reached for her, and all teasing fell away when she realized what was finally happening between them. But there was something else. She needed something else...

"Wait. Stop."

He froze, his forehead knotted in concern.

"This first." She reached up and released his hair

from its elastic. At last. Months of dreaming about those golden-brown curls, and she was finally tangling her fingers in all that softness.

Her fantasies hadn't come close to the real deal. His hair was thick and warm, and her fingers tightened at how *right* it felt to hold him in place like this, his eyes burning into hers. She used her grip to pull him down until his scruff tickled her chin and his hair caressed her cheeks.

"Now you can go," she whispered.

He didn't need to be asked twice, barely even waiting for her to finish her command before he slid into her in one swift motion, stretching her with a sweet burn.

"You," he murmured into her ear. Her hands fell away as he pulled back and surged forward to claim her again. "You're perfect."

"You're pretty okay too," she panted as he started to move even faster.

Her hips rose to meet each of his thrusts. His big body was hot and heavy against her, but instead of feeling crushed, she was consumed, like he'd absorbed her and had taken control of both their bodies. And in a way, he had. He set the pace, and he wrapped his arms around her back to lift her off the mattress, bringing her breasts to his waiting mouth. It thrilled her to let him move her body where he wanted it; each new position brought a new wave of sensation, all of it adding to the growing wave of pleasure building deep inside her. She loved his stubbled jaw scratching against her breasts almost as much as she'd loved it abrading her thighs earlier.

With one last swipe of his tongue across her nipples, he lowered her carefully to the mattress and wrapped his big hands around her thighs, spreading her wider, and just the sight of his blunt fingers digging into her skin almost sent her over the edge completely. Oh, she loved watching this powerful man keep his strength in check, giving her just as much as she could handle.

He must have noticed the stutter in her breathing because he reached down and pressed his thumb just above where they were joined. The thickness of him moving inside her combined with the steady pressure he was applying outside caused white-hot static to crackle through her brain, and before she could process it, she was shuddering and pulsing and grabbing his shoulders.

Then she witnessed something incredible: Erik, the most self-contained person she'd ever met, coming apart molecule by molecule. He buried his hands in her hair and filled her ear with the sound of his broken breaths until he drove into her with final, frantic thrusts, pulling back at the last moment to hold her gaze as he came with a groan. Then he collapsed onto the mattress next to her and dropped his head onto her shoulder until their breathing returned to normal. Afterward he disappeared into the bathroom briefly and returned without the condom, dropping heavily onto the mattress and pulling her against his chest.

"The bed survived," he said into her hair.

"We'll get it next time." She burrowed against him. It had to be well after midnight at the end of a crazy busy day, and she was about to pass out. "You're okay if I stay the night?"

"I didn't say you could leave yet, did I?" He nipped at her ear, and she realized that those tiny bites were his way of disciplining her for minor insubordination. She'd simply have to increase her backtalk a thousandfold, if only to keep the soft little reprimands coming.

"Oh fine," she said on a yawn. "But I'm only staying because I've discovered your twin superpowers."

His arms tightened around her. "Oh yeah? What's that?"

"Making cakes and making women come." She snuggled into his broad chest, which shifted under her cheek as he laughed softly.

"Should've put *that* on my business card."

She placed a kiss over his heart and murmured, "I'll redesign it in the morning."

TWENTY-THREE

Erik woke up braced for a freak-out, although he wasn't sure whose was more likely. Josie was a woman already given to high emotions, and he had no idea how adding sex to the mix would affect her. And then there was him, with his lifetime of keeping his emotions on lockdown. How would mixing in feelings affect *him?* Because he was fairly sure that's what was ricocheting through him as he looked down at Josie's body pressed against him in sleep. Warm feelings. Tender feelings. Feelings that made his chest glow and his lips press against the crown of her head.

"Mmmpf." The woman in question stirred and stretched, then blinked up at him sleepily. "Good morning."

"Morning," he replied, sliding a hand down her exposed shoulder. She wiggled closer and folded her hands on his chest, propping up her chin to look past him to the rest of the room.

"So you moved."

"Yep."

"I love it."

He followed her gaze around the sunlit bedroom and answered honestly. "Me too."

"Uncle Al left all this?"

"He did." During the last of the cleanup, he and Gina had uncovered an old maple wardrobe along with a small chest of drawers, a sturdy wooden armchair and table, and a few framed black-and-white photos of the Chicago skyline from what looked like the sixties. They'd arranged it in a corner of the open space to make a bedroom, and it had instantly felt more like home to him than any other place since the farm.

"Work downstairs, life upstairs. That seems ideal for you."

"Yep."

Josie rolled to her back with a giggle. "So other than wow them with your conversational skills, what do you usually do with your women the morning after?"

He was finally free to give in to the temptation of her hair, and he twirled one red lock around his fingers. Not hot to the touch after all, but so soft he never wanted to let go. "The parade of women? I usually make them cinnamon rolls and then kick them out."

He could see on her face just how badly she wanted to know more; the strain of playing it cool showed in the studied casualness of the hand she used to push her tousled hair back from her face, pulling it out of his grasp.

"Parade?" Her tone was breezy, but the insecurity underneath came through loud and clear.

So he set her straight. "Hookups mostly. Not many, and none recently." He hesitated, then added, "None of them ever got this many words out of me."

A smile bloomed across her face. "And the cinnamon rolls?"

"Coming right up." He placed a kiss on the underside of her jaw and moved to slide out of bed, but she stopped him with a hand on his wrist.

"No. Stay." Pink stained her cheeks, turning her into a riot of color against his white sheets. "I already know you can bake. You don't have to impress me."

He'd been planning to do it as a nice gesture and nothing more, but far be it from him to leave his bed when Josie Ryan was naked and asking for his company. So he stayed. And he kissed. And he touched. And he forgot his own name a few moments later when she returned the favor.

In the end, he did make her cinnamon rolls. And not the no-yeast kind he could simply mix together and slide into the oven. No, he made the kind that had to rise twice. The kind you made when you wanted to extend your lazy Sunday as much as possible because a bright, beautiful woman was chattering away next to you as you whisked icing ingredients.

"Best morning after ever," Josie declared around a mouthful of warm cinnamon roll two hours later.

He leaned against the kitchen counter opposite her and looked his fill over the rim of his coffee mug. It was cliché as hell, but he wanted a mental snapshot of her exactly like this: in his kitchen, wearing his too-big T-shirt, chasing a stray bit of icing with her tongue.

"So I've been thinking," she said once she's licked her lower lip clean. At his silence, she rolled her eyes and stretched to nudge his foot with hers. "*Since you asked*, it occurs to me that I owe you a couch."

He raised his mug in a salute. "Worth it."

She leaned forward to clink hers against his, and he basked in the glow of their shared joke. "So worth it."

"I hated that couch."

She nodded sagely. "Honestly, its destruction was a blessing. Where was it *from*?"

"It belonged to Pops. I brought it with me from the farm."

For a moment he was lost to the past, remembering the couch's place of pride in Pops's front living room, the one they'd reserved for company. The one he'd perched on uncomfortably as his mother begged Pops to just take her son for a few months so she could see about getting that job on a cruise ship. Thank God he'd agreed and that he'd insisted Erik remain with him when Suzanne turned up a few weeks later to take Erik with her to Austin, the location of her next big dream.

When he looked up, he found Josie watching him worriedly, and he offered her a reassuring smile. "No. It's good. Change is good." And to his surprise, the words were true. The changes he'd embraced recently made him happy. Happier than he'd ever been maybe.

"In that case, I have a suggestion." She grinned and drained her mug. "You're gonna hate it."

ERIK STEPPED BACK to survey his handiwork. Well, if he was being honest, to survey the woman who was surveying his handiwork. Said handiwork involved selecting, transporting, and successfully assembling the most basic black couch they could find at IKEA.

"I feel like we've passed an important test in our r-relationship." She gestured broadly at their work, but her cheerful theatrics didn't keep Erik from noticing her tiny hesitation over the last word. In response, he dropped to the couch and tugged her down onto his lap, kissing her until the worried crinkle between her eyes fell away. He didn't want to get ahead of himself, but if they could survive both IKEA on a weekend *and* the mostly useless sheet of assembly instructions, he was pretty sure they could survive anything.

"Seems sturdy," he said when they came up for air.

She laughed and gave a little bounce that traveled straight from his groin to somewhere in the vicinity of his heart. "Yeah, but we'd better do a few tests to be sure."

He wanted nothing more, although for the moment he was content to just hold her close and enjoy the way strands of her hair got hung up on his scruff when she ducked her head to kiss his neck. He'd spent a Sunday furniture shopping with Josie Ryan. None of that sentence computed for him. Not the furniture-shopping part—his new suit notwithstanding, he wasn't a go-out-and-buy-new-things kind of guy—and not the part where he succumbed to laughter in the middle of the IKEA kitchen accessories department when the flirtiest, fanciest woman he'd ever spent time with had tried to provoke him into a spatula duel. Now, in the middle of this new life she'd helped him create, a sense of wonder propelled him to squeeze her tighter and nudge her chin upward for a kiss. He didn't understand how someone so drawn to designer labels and white-collar success could be content snuggling with him in his worn-in jeans on a cheap assembly couch, but he planned to enjoy it while he could.

As if she'd read his thoughts, she shifted her head up

to kiss him, but as their tongues met, his phone buzzed in his pocket.

"Woo!" She wriggled off his lap. "As much as I appreciate the vibration, do you need to grab that?"

"Nope," he said, reaching for her softness again.

But she pointed to his pocket. "It could be a new customer. Grow your business!"

It was, in fact, a new customer, the third one that day. Richard and Byron's wedding had been excellent advertising. He moved to the kitchen table to set up a meeting for an October event while Josie fanned herself and pantomimed overheating, presumably because of his business-phone voice.

He rejoined her on the sofa at the conclusion of the call, and she extended her hand in a fist bump. "Kicking ass! Taking names! I told you I'd make you big!"

He gently knocked his knuckles into hers. "I'm just taking it one cake at a time."

"No! Keep dreaming," she commanded. "We've turned the downstairs into a functional kitchen and customer area, and we've made the upstairs your home. What do we need to do next?"

We. Over and over and over again. He grasped that little word and shoved it into the center of his chest, using it to stoke the fire that she'd kicked to life that first night on the train. What he'd initially seen as volatile and bossy was actually passionate and, well, bossy. And while he hungered for the color she injected into his life, he also feared that she was getting the short end of that bargain. He might crave *her*, but she craved noise, excitement, drama, all things he wasn't equipped to provide. Once she'd built up his business, she'd move on to her next project, and he needed to prepare himself for that.

But that didn't mean they couldn't satisfy a mutual craving right now.

"Next? We break in the couch properly," he told her. "Strip."

Turned out, she followed orders just as well as she gave them.

TWENTY-FOUR

"Success!" Josie clicked the Update button and punched her fists into the air in triumph, then looked guiltily over her shoulder at Finn's closed bedroom door.

She and Erik had spent the night at her apartment, and she didn't want to disturb her roommate any more than she already had the night before. Even in her tamest sexual encounters with Erik, she tended to get a little... vocal.

"Check it out," she said more softly, shifting her cross-legged position to face him on the couch. "Your website is officially finished."

He took the laptop from her, a tiny spark of excitement flashing in his blue eyes. Josie of three months ago would never have recognized it, but at this point she could see how jazzed he was to check out the finished product. She'd launched a bare-bones site during the dark period when she thought he was engaged, and since the wedding, she'd spent all her free time perfecting it.

She held her breath as his gaze flicked across the screen. The homepage slider offered shot after shot of his creations, looking pristine and elegant against the backdrop she'd set up in his old apartment. "Not too shabby, right?"

She drank in the sight of him smiling softly over her work. The past two weeks had been a challenge. Her schedule of evening events hadn't meshed well with his client meetings and the time he'd been spending with Gina on some tech upgrades for the bakery. The two of them always seemed to be on opposite ends of the city, and when they'd managed to get together, it had always been too rushed.

Not only did she miss him, but they'd left their relationship maddeningly undefined, and the limbo was seriously messing with her. Now that they were finally enjoying a leisurely morning together, she wanted to use the opportunity to suss out how he was feeling about the *you, me, we* of it all. Was she just a hookup with an expiration date, or were they something more? What could she possibly expect from a guy who'd invented a fiancée a month ago to keep her at a distance? Why wasn't he dropping any hints, dammit?

"This looks great, babe," he said.

Babe. It was the second time he'd called her that, and although it wasn't terribly creative as far as nicknames went, a non-nickname guy calling her a term of endearment had to mean *something*, right?

She was distracted from the implication of "babe" by the memory of *how* he'd made his no-nickname policy clear. Heat rolled through her body in a slow wave, but before she could wrench the computer from his hands to demand another demonstration, he clicked on the About section and grimaced.

"Stop it," she ordered before he could say a word. "You look magnificent in that picture."

"I look like a smug asshole."

She nudged his shoulder with her own. "You look like the talented artist that you are. And that mysterious little smile you've got going on will be the thing that pays off your mortgage in a few years."

It was true; her light kit and the crumbling plaster in his old apartment had done wonders, but mostly she'd allowed his stark beauty to take center stage. He looked steady and competent, warm and thoughtful.

He looked like a man she could love.

The thought popped unbidden into her brain, stealing her breath. This was new emotional terrain; her previous relationships had been too brief and too shallow to fill the great chasm of need inside her. But here she was wondering if this reserved man could give her what she'd spent a lifetime chasing.

Her jokes, her clever words. All of it crumbled as she turned to study his face. When she first met him, she'd considered him as inscrutable as granite, but she could read him now. The lip twitch. The shift in the muscle near his eye. He was pleased. Hell, he was downright ecstatic. But was it the website or was it her?

His gaze flicked to her, and his mouth curled into that private smile that was hers alone. It made her bold. Maybe he'd *welcome* her feelings. Maybe he'd even return them someday. She opened her mouth to tell him everything, all her fears and her hopes, all the soft yearnings blossoming in her heart.

And then her phone rang and ruined everything.

"Fuck." The word was short but heartfelt, and Erik's soft expression shifted to concern.

"What's up?"

She scrambled to her feet, phone clutched to her chest. "Fuck!"

"Jos? You okay?" The question came from Finn, who'd emerged from her bedroom with a sleepy Tom in tow.

She waved her phone at Finn. "It's Pam."

Finn winced as she gathered her long dark hair into a tail at the nape of her neck. "I should've recognized that 'my mom's in town' panic." She moved to the kitchen and the coffeepot while Tom slumped into a kitchen chair.

Josie's phone buzzed again, and her stomach dropped. "Oh God, she's summoned me. I've got ninety minutes to get cleaned up and present myself at Monteverde for brunch." She paced a circle around the living room, her brain clicking through possible responses.

She should tell Pam to go to hell. That it was a Saturday and she already had plans. That she wasn't a puppet on a maternal string.

But she wouldn't. Her mother snapped her fingers and Josie jumped. That's how it worked.

Erik closed her laptop and set it on the coffee table, his steady eyes tracking her movements. "Do you want me to—?" he started to ask at the same time she turned to him and said, "Would you mind if I—?"

She laughed weakly. "Would you mind if I cut this short? Maybe we can catch up after, either here or at the bakery?" Dammit, she hadn't gotten a fraction of the time she'd been wanting with him.

"Sure," he said. "Text me."

Tom looked up from where he'd propped his head on his hand at the table. "In the meantime, feel free to keep your kitchen skills sharp by making us pancakes."

Josie paused on her way out of the room. "Don't you dare let those jackals take advantage of your good nature," she ordered Erik before diving into the bathroom and resigning herself to a long session with her hair straightener.

After she'd wrestled her naturally bouncy curls into submission, sleek and straight the way her mother preferred it, she rummaged through her closet for her most sedate baby-pink sheath dress and pair of nude slingbacks. Nothing said "relaxed Saturday with Mom" like cosplaying Joan from *Mad Men*.

She emerged from her room as she was securing a pair of pearl studs in her ears, and surprise surprise, there was Erik at the stove with a spatula in his hand.

"Shame on you two!" she chided Finn and Tom, who both grinned back at her, unrepentant.

"I volunteered," Erik said as he flipped a pancake.

She nevertheless hit the freeloaders with a glare. "You did nothing to deserve this generosity."

"Which makes us all the more grateful for it," Tom said after a slurp of coffee.

Josie just shook her head and grabbed her purse, pausing awkwardly at the door. Were she and Erik at the goodbye-kiss stage? And was it weird to leave her business partner/hookup alone with her friends? Another glance at her phone chased every other thought out of her head as her anxiety soared.

"Gotta run. Finn and Tom, if I come home and find out that you made this man bake you anything else, you're both officially cut off."

She had her hand on the doorknob when Erik surprised her by abandoning his pancakes to give her arm a quick squeeze just above the elbow.

"Don't let her push your buttons, okay?"

His brow creased in concern, and the unexpected emotions that had overwhelmed her on the couch came flooding back. God, she just wanted to stay here with him.

"I'll try. But you have no idea what she's capable of." She pushed up on her toes to give him a quick kiss for luck and left to meet her fate.

SUCCESSFUL WOMEN NEVER SLOUCHED.

Pamela Ryan hadn't taught her only daughter a damn thing about unconditional love or placing value on her own self-worth, but she had ensured that Josie could make it through a hellish meal without her spine once touching the back of the chair. Ordinarily Josie lived for seeing and being seen at a posh lunch spot in the Loop, but the ice queen seated across from her in austere black turned every bite into sawdust and every interaction into a verbal land mine.

"How's work? Are you still an intern?"

Josie's knuckles tightened around the heavy fork in her hand.

"I was never an intern there, Mother." She struggled to keep her voice steady. "It's been six years. I have my own accounts that I manage."

"Hmm." Pam gave a noncommittal noise as she lifted her water goblet, and even the click of her fingernails against the glass sounded disapproving.

There it was. Like clockwork, a low buzz had kicked up in her brain, the way it always did after any amount of time with her mother. Would it kill the woman to offer even a shred of support?

"I like my job," Josie said. "It's something different every day."

Pam waved a hand through the air as if she could bat away her daughter's words. "Anybody can order hors d'oeuvres for parties. But you could've had a different career if you'd just let me—"

"If I'd let you bully the Art Institute of Chicago into accepting me?" It was an old fight that neither one of them got tired of having.

"*Bully* is a strong word." Her mother's flat eyes tracked Josie's movements as she reached for a roll in the bread basket. Maybe the carbs would help her channel Erik's eternal chill.

"It's exactly what you would've done." She forced the truth past tight lips. "My photos weren't good enough to get me in on my own."

"You'd have improved." Her mother lifted her hand to smooth it over her immaculate chignon. "Who knows where you'd be by now if you'd have let me help you get in after high school. Such wasted potential."

"That's not how I wanted to get into college," Josie said stiffly.

"So you didn't go to college at all?" Her mother's chunky gold bracelet clicked against the table, and Josie knew better than to bring up the one semester she'd completed before wanderlust carried her into the workplace. Not that it mattered; Pam raised one thin eyebrow, the action radiating more disapproval than a squadron of *Project Runway* judges, and said, "I don't know why you wanted to hurt me like that."

"Believe it or not, my dropping out of college had nothing to do with you. And I'm good at my job, Mom."

"Oh really? And they treat you well there?"

That shut her up. The buzzing got louder as she recalled the last half dozen interactions with Valerie, who never missed a chance to sneak in a dig about being "self-taught" or "operating on instinct." Her mom and Valerie. Different women, same condescending attitude. Neither believed in her, although she'd spent years chasing their approval. And for what? She dropped her half-eaten sourdough roll to her plate, disappointed that it hadn't magically produced any Erik vibes.

Naturally, Pam noticed her silence and pounced. "Have you considered going back to school, darling? You could make art for yourself instead of other people. Just think about it: two Ryan women at the same institution."

For a second, Josie let herself picture it. Studying where her mother had studied, building on her photography skills. Producing work that would win the approval Pamela kept dangling just out of reach. Something in the photos Josie occasionally texted her must've finally hinted at a talent worth nurturing.

And then Pam overplayed her hand, leaning forward to say conspiratorially, "You'd be helping me too, darling. Sending my daughter to my alma mater might be the last thing I need to help me secure my residency."

Josie's runaway thoughts slammed to a halt. "Your what?"

Her mother gave a stilted chuckle and waved a hand. "Oh, just a few conversations I've had with the administration. They're considering naming a new artist in residence, and I'd like it to be me. I'd be in Chicago full time then, and we could have these lunches regularly. Wouldn't that be nice?"

No. God no. But Josie kept a polite smile on her face

while her hands clenched in a death grip on her lap under the table. "What do I have to do with it?"

That fake laugh again. "Well, certainly there's the matter of legacy and loyalty. And just imagine if you took a few seminars with me and I could turn your middling talent into something special."

A bomb detonated in the middle of Josie's chest. *"Middling?"*

Her sharp tone earned what passed for a sympathetic look from her mother. "Come now, Josephine. We both know you have some raw talent. You'll never be a true photographer, but with my help, perhaps you could—"

"What about my wasted potential?"

"Don't be a child." Pam sighed the words, her patient tone in place but a tautness creeping around her eyes and at the corners of her mouth. The cords in her slender neck tensed as she spoke the next words low and hard. "My overseas work opportunities are drying up, and I want to settle in one place. Chicago's as good as anywhere else. Foolish me, I thought you'd be willing to help me look like a team player by bringing in some tuition dollars. Given your underwhelming work situation, I would've thought you'd be grateful for the opportunity to expand your horizons."

She flinched at every word spilling from her mother's mouth. It was one thing to believe something ugly about yourself and quite another to hear your mother casually voice the worst things your brain whispered to you at 3:00 a.m. when you couldn't sleep.

Josie stood abruptly, the chair shooting backward from the force of her motion, and Pam tucked her chin to hiss, "Oh, stop making a scene. Apparently party planning's where you belong after all. Now sit down and finish your meal."

The buzzing was back, but this time it enveloped Josie's whole body and made her vision go hazy at the edges. A sliver of hope had burned in the center of her chest her whole life. It was what compelled her to seek out her mother's approval over and over, and in that moment, she felt it twist into something new, something so sharp it threatened to slice her insides to shreds.

Her body trembling in fury, she regarded her lifelong tormentor through slitted eyes. "Do you want a scene? Because I can make a scene that nobody here will ever forget."

As Josie's chest heaved with each painful breath, Pamela Ryan looked at her and *laughed*.

A scream built inside her, so big it threatened to shake this restaurant to the ground. She had to get out of there. Because the buzzing? Oh, it was still there, hotter and more destructive than ever, but she didn't dare let it out in the middle of this restaurant.

Thankfully, she knew just where to go.

TWENTY-FIVE

"What's Fancy doing in the alley?"

"Hmm?" Erik braced his hand on the ceiling of the dining area as he turned the last of the screws on the security camera he'd just mounted.

Gina pivoted the laptop on the café table to face him. "Fancy. She's fluttering around your van like a malfunctioning car-show booth babe. I saw it on the alley cam."

That was... puzzling. He tucked the screwdriver in his back pocket and descended the ladder to join Gina at the table. Sure enough, her laptop screen showed video of a dervish pacing around the side of his van, her movements agitated.

"What the...?" He squinted as the figure bent to yank something out of a cardboard box at her feet. "Oh fuck."

"Problem?"

"Potentially," he said grimly. "Are we good here?"

"Yep. Your security's up and running, and you'll be able to monitor the feeds on all your devices."

"Thanks. I owe you."

"Yep. That's why I'm swiping your van to get the last of my stuff from Iowa some weekend soon."

"Sure. Pick a day I'm free, and I'll come along to help load it up." He looked at the screen again, where security-cam Josie was now standing with her hands on her hips, pissy defiance evident even on the grainy feed. "I need to go handle this."

Gina grimaced. "Good luck. I think I'll leave through the front door."

Erik opened his mouth to tell her that wasn't necessary, then reconsidered. "I get that."

She smirked up at him. "You know I'm loving this, right? My no-drama llama's got himself a class A drama queen."

"Hilarious," he grumbled.

"I'm just glad it's you and not me for a change."

She grabbed her bag and eased out the front door with a laugh, and once he was alone, he snagged a band from his wrist and yanked his hair back, feeling a little like he was preparing for battle. At the back door, he paused and pulled the screwdriver out of his back pocket, leaving the potential weapon on the counter just to be safe. Then he pushed through the door to confront the pink whirlwind.

"We talked about this, Josie," he said as he approached her.

"And?" She didn't bother turning around.

"And I told you I'm not comfortable with it." The manhole-sized caricature of his face stared idiotically back at him from the side of the van, but he forced himself not to rip the fucking thing down until he figured out what was up.

"And I told *you* it's part of your brand." She slammed

a hand against the metal and spun to face him. "Not putting the logo on your van is fucking stupid."

She crossed her arms under her breasts, and although her clothes and hair screamed uptown class, the *fight me, motherfucker* gleam in her eyes made him rock back on his heels. She reached up and yanked the demure pearl studs out of her ears, dropping them into the purse at her feet. He hadn't seen that combative look on her face in ages, but here it was now, twisting her pretty features into a snarl.

Gina'd been smart to tiptoe out the front. He didn't have that same luxury, so he stroked a hand down his jaw as he considered his approach. He could explain that he wasn't quite ready to drive around in a van with his face plastered to the side, but he was fairly sure she was looking for a different kind of fight.

"Get in the van."

She set her jaw. "No."

"Get. In. The. Van." He walked forward with each word, watching as her breathing accelerated the closer he got.

Their staring contest didn't last long before she rolled her eyes and spat out, "Fine."

She turned and clambered into the back, and he jumped in after her, slamming the door behind them and shutting out the street noises. Bright afternoon sunlight filtered through the windshield and fell across the back, where the delivery racks were folded flat along each wall. The air was still and hot as they eyed each other from opposite sides of the space.

"Well?" Her voice lashed across the distance between them, but he kept his response intentionally calm.

"Well," he replied.

"What do you *want*?" She was shouting now, and fuck, he hoped he was playing this right. He was operating on a hunch based on the hints she'd let drop about her mother, the combative sides of her he'd seen in the past, and the whiteness of her knuckles where they curled into tight fists on her lap.

He went all in, leaning back and crossing one ankle over the other. "You're obviously looking for a fight. So here I am."

She flopped back against the opposite wall, hostility rolling off her in waves. "And what am I supposed to do with that?"

He laced his fingers over his stomach, projecting as much stillness as he could. "Talk to me. Yell at me. Punch the wall. Whatever you need. But I'm here for you, babe."

"Oh, fuck you," she snarled. "You're not better than me because you never get mad about anything ever."

He held his hands out to the sides. "Never said I was better than you or that I never get mad. But you're the one having the bad day, not me. So take what you need."

"What I need?" Her eyes glittered as she rolled her head to the side to study him with predatory interest. "And what if what I need is to fuck you until we're both too tired to move?"

He didn't dare let the hint of a smile slide across his face, even though that was exactly how he was hoping this would play out. *That's* what he could do for his girl: aggression release through orgasm. Her burning gaze followed his hands as he unzipped his jeans, pushing them down far enough to free his dick, which was well on the way to being ready for her.

"If that's what you need, come over here and take it."

He was only able to stroke up and down his length

once before she was on him, her fingers clawing at his hair and her mouth on his. No gentle kisses today; they met with a clash of teeth and breath and lips battling for dominance. As she yanked up her skirt, he groped behind him until he retrieved the wallet that had tumbled from his back pocket, emptying the contents until his fingers touched a condom packet. As soon as he'd rolled it on, Josie impaled herself, sinking down until he was fully seated into the tight heat he'd never get enough of. One set of her nails dug into his shoulder and the other skated along his scalp as she worked herself up and down, those wild eyes never leaving his.

"How?" she panted. "So patient. How do you put up with me?" She gasped the words as she ground herself against him, and he absorbed her meaning and her movements and the rough treatment of his hair in silence, keeping his eyes locked on hers, keeping his hands clamped on her hips, letting her know that she might be the storm, but he'd be the cliff she could crash herself into. He could absorb her fury and stay standing. When her head fell back and her movements turned jerky and uncoordinated, he slid one hand up her back to keep her steady while he pressed the heel of his other hand against her where her body met his. He let her work herself against him until she came apart with a sob, and only then did he drive himself up into her hard and fast, following her over the edge.

Afterward, she slumped forward and draped herself over him, the fight draining from her limbs. But her breathing remained ragged, and it took him a moment to realize she was crying, soft and broken. Helpless in the face of her distress, he did the only thing he could think of and cradled her against his chest.

"I'll get your shirt all wet." She sniffled and tried to pull away, but he held her closer, and soon enough, her heart-wrenching snuffles quieted to nothing while he gently stroked her back.

Once she'd collected herself, she rolled off his lap and reached for her purse, producing tissues for both of them. She mopped her face while he dealt with the condom as best as he could in the back of a bakery delivery van.

After they'd both cleaned up and straightened their clothes, he asked, "Ready to tell me what's going on?"

She shifted to sit next to him and rested her head on his shoulder. He reached down and twined his fingers through hers.

"Mommy issues. So pathetic." She gave a shaky sigh. "I did warn you though."

"Anything specific?"

"No. And yes."

He remained still, giving her space to process whatever she was struggling with while every part of him howled with the need to do violence to anyone who'd ever tried to diminish Josie's vibrancy. Especially her mother.

She shocked the hell out of him by not filling the silence that surrounded them, and the longer she kept her eyes turned downward on their joined hands, the more he chafed at the unnaturalness of her quiet. That was the only possible reason for him to open his mouth and tell her something he'd never shared with anyone before. Not Pops, not Gina. Nobody.

"When I was fifteen, I decided I wanted to live with my mom. Pops was working long hours, trying to get the crops in before the frost hit. We could go full days without seeing each other, and I was..." He sighed. "I was a teenager. Pissed all the time. Hated living on the farm.

So I collected all my cash and got on a bus to Nashville. That was back when my mom still sent birthday cards with return addresses."

Just like that, Josie shifted into comfort mode. "Oh, Erik. Was she not happy to see you?"

Her eyes flew up to his, and the sadness there, sadness for *him*, made it hard to swallow. But he forced himself to continue, to recall the look in a different set of eyes from thirteen years ago. The same blue as his own, but dull and unwelcoming.

"Definitely not. Her new boyfriend didn't know about her teenage son, and she told me she had a big opportunity at the Grand Ole Opry that she didn't want me to ruin." He laughed without humor. "It was an interview to work as a barback at a restaurant nearby. For that, she put me back on a bus. Pops didn't even know I'd been gone."

She stretched up and pressed a kiss just under his ear, and that little movement meant more to him than an encyclopedia's worth of words. "Are you still in touch with her?"

"I didn't see her again until last year."

"For your grandfather's funeral," Josie guessed, and he nodded. He'd been too wrung out from grief to feel anything at all when he'd encountered his mother at the graveside.

"I've made my peace with it mostly. I wish things were different, but when I lost Pops, I lost my true parent. After all this time, I don't want or expect anything from her."

Josie's mouth hardened. "Well, fuck her very much. She doesn't know what she's missing with you."

Her ferocity tugged a bark of laughter from him.

"What's so funny?" she asked indignantly.

"You are. My warrior." He reached out to cradle her head in his hands and kissed her softly, wondering the whole time why she'd sought him out this afternoon. Was it just to pick a fight she knew he'd give her? Or was she after something else from him, some comfort that only he could offer her? That thought wasn't as ludicrous as it would have been a few months ago, but then again, in his experience, fashionable, vivacious women didn't choose him. And Josie was the most vivacious woman he'd ever known, which meant he'd never be a permanent part of her life.

But God, he wanted to try.

She shifted. "Can we go inside now? Van sex is incredibly undignified."

He wasn't quite ready to let go, but in the end he pulled his hands away from her sweet face. "It was hot though."

"With us, it's always hot." Then she ran a thumb along his damp hairline. "It's also literally hot in here. Let's get inside. Avoid heat stroke. Have some dignified indoor sex."

He couldn't argue with that, so he popped open the door, stepped out, and extended his hand to help her down.

TWENTY-SIX

Josie snuggled deeper into Erik's new couch and silently listed the things that made her feel calmer: Erik's smile. Erik's baking. Erik's confidence in her. The glass of wine Erik had just handed her.

Just... Erik. Seriously, did he even drink wine? It was possible that he only had it on hand for her. The thought warmed her almost as much as the Malbec did.

He joined her on the couch, and she shifted to lean against the arm and stretched her legs across his lap. Sure enough, he was holding a beer.

He took a sip and rested his free hand on her shin. "You ready to tell me specifics?" When she hesitated, he offered her that rare, beautiful Erik smile and said, "You know you want to."

She sighed. Sipped her wine. Considered deflecting with sarcasm. Decided to rip off the Band-Aid. "I'm middling."

Erik said nothing, just stroked a hand down her leg, and now that she'd started talking, the words came pouring out.

"She started trying to turn me into a photographer from the time I was little, but it was super obvious from early on that I might understand the technical side of things, but I'd never be able to find the soul in my photographs." She idly swirled the wine in her glass as she relived the dawning realization that had disappointed her and her mother both. "So that meant good ol' Pam couldn't show off the work of her talented daughter in her gallery shows. And then I disappointed her by having too much energy to sit still and be a quiet little shadow she could trot out for her fancy artist friends."

"Of course not. You? Quiet?"

"Exactly!" They shared a smile, but hers immediately slipped off her face. "Anyway, today she spelled out for me again how much I embarrass her. My disappointing job, my lack of a college degree, my 'middling' talent. Just... all of it."

He tilted his head to look at her. "You know she's wrong about you."

"Is she though?" Josie rubbed a hand over her tired eyes, which were probably still pink and puffy from all the tears she'd cried. She pushed the worst part out. "Thing is, I'm still desperate for her to tell me she's proud of me. My whole life, she's made it clear how inadequate I am, but every time she snaps her fingers, I come running, begging for scraps of affection. I fight about everything in my life, but when it comes to my mom, I roll over and show her my belly. It's pathetic."

"It's natural."

Although he didn't say more, Josie knew he was thinking about the story he'd shared in the van. "I suppose it is." She sat up and wrapped her arms around her knees, huddling into herself. If only she'd reached the healthy place with her disappointing mother that he seemed to have found with his.

He drained his beer and set it aside. "As a smart woman once told me, fuck your mom. She doesn't know what she's missing with you."

His voice was as vehement as she'd ever heard it, and she let a little truth spill out.

"What's she missing, exactly? Jokes and temper and too many expensive shoes? Basically nobody in my life has the patience to put up with me. Did you know I almost broke up Finn and Tom right after they got together? I'm a life-ruiner." She tried to laugh at the weak attempt at self-deprecation, but the sound died in her throat. Sharing this much with Erik was terrifying, yet the weight on her chest felt lighter with every confession. "Honestly, I don't know how you've been able to spend so much time with... all this."

She gestured down at herself, hoping he understood everything she was referring to: her obsession with the outward appearance of success, her undying quest for validation, her unmet need for love. She couldn't joke her way through this, and what's more, she didn't *want* to. After a lifetime of rejection, her defense system was finally shutting down, leaving her weak and unprotected.

Then again, perhaps for the first time ever, she had a champion. Erik plucked the wineglass from her hand and set it on the coffee table, then swept his thumbs over her cheekbones, blotting up a stray tear that had escaped during her brutal self-assessment.

"Hey, look at me." He didn't speak again until she'd met his kind, steady eyes. "You are spectacular. Shoes and temper and all. I love every minute I spend with you."

The sincerity rolling off him was too much for her.

Too earnest, too honest, and too misguided. She cut her glance away, but he wrapped a hand around the nape of her neck and drew her close enough that he could gently bite her left earlobe to recapture her attention. Her eyes flew back to his, but even his proprietary touch couldn't chase away all the negativity inside of her.

"I'm angry, and I'm bossy."

He batted her breathless words away. "You're assertive and brave. And you're smart as hell. You helped me see that all this was possible."

He inclined his head toward the stairs that led to his bakery, and yes, true, she did feel a certain sense of pride at being part of the huge strides he'd taken over the past few months.

"You are spectacular," he said again. "Tell me you believe that."

He tightened his grip on her neck, and she just... she dropped her walls. She let his faith in her wash in like a tide, and it filled her up where she was parched.

"Okay," she whispered. "I believe you."

His thumb stroked down the column of her neck. "Say it."

When she hesitated, he delivered another ear nip that she felt all the way down to her core.

"Okay, I-I'm spectacular."

"Once more."

"I'm spectacular!" she shouted.

"Damn right. And you're going to tell your mom that the next time you see her." He kissed her hard and fast, then he shocked the hell out of her by asking casually, "Do you want to go out tonight?"

She brushed away the last of her excess-emotion tears

and looked at him in confusion. "What do you mean, out?"

Now he was the one turning pink. "Out. Like... dancing? Or dinner? What do you usually do on Saturday night?" He shifted on the couch, looking nervous, and oh. *Ooooh*. He was asking her *out* out, and he was so damn cute she might actually die.

And of course she had to mess with him a little. How would he know it was her if she didn't throw in a little snark? "Dancing would be *amazing*. You own a pair of leather pants, right? Or something really shiny and mesh? That's the dress code of the club I'm thinking of."

She let him blink in utter speechlessness for a good fifteen seconds before she dissolved into laughter. "You should see your face! God, no, I'm kidding. On Saturday nights when I don't have to work, I put on my stretchiest clothes, order in, and watch Netflix. It's the secret Josie Ryan that nobody gets to see."

He slumped against the couch in relief. "Can we do that one?"

"You want the secret Josie?" She was really asking, and she wanted a real answer.

He didn't disappoint. "I do."

The simple words, simply spoken, had her stomach performing a loop. Her emotions surged and threatened to consume her, so she groped for her sass. "Okay, but I still say you'd look great in leather pants."

"You're killing me," he said fondly. "Where are we ordering from?"

Four hours later, they were in danger of forming actual, physical bonds with the couch, they'd moved so little. Empty take-out cartons littered the table in front of them, and Josie was tucked into Erik's side, wearing one of his old T-shirts since her fancy lunch dress wasn't great for lounging.

She was content. No, she was ecstatic. He'd have to serve her an eviction notice when their time together was done because this was her new happy place.

The Netflix movie they'd agreed on chattered away in the background, and her eyes drifted lower and lower until Erik's voice called her back from the brink of sleep.

"I've been thinking."

"Mmm?" she said drowsily.

"This building is two blocks from a grade school and four from a high school."

"So many kids," she said, not clear where he was headed with this.

"So much foot traffic," he said. "And I have that big customer area in front."

"You do." She burrowed in closer, loving the rumble of his voice when she pressed her ear to his chest.

"So maybe I make some cupcakes. For the foot traffic."

The idea hit her like a thunderclap, and she straightened, sleepy brain revving. "Foot traffic. Cupcakes! Yes." She reached forward and paused the movie. "Get the moms after they drop their kiddies off. Serve coffee, let them hang out and chat. Maybe buy a premade birthday cake while they're there. This could be huge for you. *Huge.*"

Her brain was off at a gallop, racing toward a future where she'd helped build this place into the most in-demand bakery in Chicago.

"Already got a few quotes on a fancy coffee maker."

His interjection pulled her back, and she laughed in

delight. "My marketing genius! You don't need me anymore."

"Yes I do." The lightness fell from his tone, and she smiled gratefully at him.

"Okay, then I won't go anywhere." Rather than tie herself in knots looking for deeper meaning in his words, she focused on what a foot-traffic business model would do for her advertising strategy. "Did you lock in any more vendors this week?"

"Yep. I've got the suppliers all lined up to start ingredient delivery on Monday. And I took two more orders for wedding cakes."

"That's fantastic!" She rubbed her hands together and cackled. She'd never get tired of seeing her plans come to fruition. "So what do you say to a grand-opening event? Do a little advertising, invite our friends, lure the neighbors in to sample your wares?"

"Yes. Smart. And I may need to hire some help soon."

"Oh! Already?"

He nodded. "I've had a couple of inquiries, one from a current Dora employee."

"Let's definitely poach that bitch's staff." She could juggle a little revenge along with her business launch. "So how close are we to doing this?"

"Very close. Like two weeks from now close."

"I'll start making the arrangements," she said, squeezing his hand. "Erik, it's really happening."

His lips winged upward, and she lost her breath at how gorgeous he was and how frequently he smiled these days. Hadn't that expression been rare once upon a time?

"Are you ready for bed?" he asked.

"Only if you're coming too."

He hugged her close. "I wouldn't want to be anywhere else."

They raced through the meal cleanup, and once they made it to bed, he showed her that it wasn't just that indoor sex was more dignified than clawing at each other like animals against the wall of a van. He showed her how he could soothe her busy mind with sweet, drugging kisses and quiet her needy skin with the slow pass of his fingers across her arms, her breasts, her back, her *everywhere*. He showed her what it felt like to entrust your heart to someone worthy, and when he twined his fingers around hers and pushed into her so slowly that she could feel the fullness and the weight of him, he showed her what forever could feel like.

TWENTY-SEVEN

Erik woke the next morning to Josie's fingers walking across his chest.

"Tell me your secrets."

He grunted. "I told you my secrets yesterday."

"Not just the sad ones. I want the fun ones too. I want to know you."

As his brain slowly came online, it raised an alert: this wasn't a jokey request.

He pulled his eyes open to find her looking down at him with an unusually serious expression on her clean-scrubbed face.

"Sure," he yawned. "Uh, what do you want to know?" He delighted in these moments when she let her guard down, but he'd never dealt with one of them pre-coffee.

"How about these shoulder freckles?" Her fingers brushed his bare skin there, only to be replaced briefly by her teeth and then the soft press of her lips. *That* woke him up. He shifted to face her, and she took the opportunity to prop her chin on her laced fingers, using his bicep as a pillow. "My mom was always paranoid I'd be one of those freckled redheads, so she slathered me in sunblock every time I got near the front door. To this day, I loathe the smell of her expensive SPF stuff."

It was on the tip of his tongue to compliment her skin, which glowed in the bright July sunlight streaming through the windows. But that wasn't what she was after this morning. She wanted truth, and he could give her that.

"Hours on the riding mower without a shirt as a kid. Pops didn't worry much about sunblock."

Another kiss to his shoulder, then she snaked her arm across his chest. "Okay, how about the scar?" She ran her palm over the crooked pink line cutting across his torso, and he shifted to let her small hand trace the length of it.

"Cattle hoof."

She winced and looked at him expectantly, so he offered her the least gruesome version of the story. "Loading a heifer into the chute for insemination. She objected."

Her brows arched upward on a smirk, alerting him that a dirty thought had floated through her mind, but she surprised him again by keeping the comment to herself. Instead, she held up her left hand and pointed to a scar that cut along the outside toward her wrist, so thin and pale that he'd never noticed it before.

"When I turned seventeen, Mom didn't bother celebrating my birthday. Didn't even mention it. So I got drunk that night. Not with friends or anything, just alone at home on vodka and Diet Coke. I passed out in the bathroom and woke up covered in blood from where I'd dropped the glass on the tile."

"Jesus." He ran his thumb along the long, silvery line, his heart aching for that long-ago lonely girl.

She laced the fingers of her once-injured hand through his.

"I cleaned it all up the next morning between bouts of puking and then took myself to urgent care for stitches. She didn't even notice." Her smile was sad as she looked at their joined hands. "I told anybody who asked that it was a kitchen accident, and I've been careful about how much I drink ever since. Not even Richard knows the real story."

He was wrong. That lonely girl wasn't gone; she'd just grown into an adult who hid her insecurities behind a wall. And he was the person she'd let inside.

"Thank you for telling me." The words were insufficient for the gratitude he felt at her trust, but she smiled anyway, a little more brightly this time.

"Thanks for listening." Then she dropped a kiss on his chest and asked, "Okay, how about the tattoo?"

She rubbed a thumb over the lion's head on his left pec, and he swallowed a groan. No way was he getting out of this with his dignity intact.

"From high school. It's part of a matched set." His flare of hope that it was enough information to satisfy her was short-lived when she bared her teeth.

"Look, I think I've been a pretty good sport about things, but if Gina has a matching lion on her boob, I will have to kill her."

Ah, there were those walls again. But he spotted the insecurity lurking under her words and quickly punctured it. "Not Gina. It's a guy. Actually, it's ten other guys."

A beat, and then her pointy little finger jabbed at his armpit. "Explain."

He rolled over and pressed his face into the mattress

to avoid looking at her as he answered. It was almost enough to make him wish he'd kept his shirt on when she was around—almost. In actuality, he relished the hunger in her eyes when she looked at his bare chest, enough that he was willing to confess the truth.

"It was, ah, a senior varsity football team decision. We were the Liberty Valley Lions."

"*We?*"

At her delighted tone, he pressed his face deeper into the mattress. So much for the intimate moment they'd just shared.

"Erik," she said. "Maker of cakes. Guy who banged me senseless last night. Have you been holding out on me? *Were you a high school football player?*" She punctuated her last question by draping herself over his back and rolling around on top of him in a fit of laughter. As she was still naked, the squealing and writhing at his expense was an extra special form of torture.

"Yes," he grumped.

She rolled off him to flop weakly on the mattress. "What position did you play?" she asked through her giggles.

Goddammit. "Tight end."

His reluctant answer sent her into the throes of a silent laughing fit before she finally hooted, "That's no secret! I already knew *that!*" She reached down to slap his ass, bare under the sheet.

He huffed and waited for her convulsions to die down enough to explain, "It's not a big deal. High school basketball was much bigger in my town."

"Oh, it's a big deal." She wiped tears from her eyes. "So do you still have your jersey? Oh my God, can I wear it? Will you take me to brunch today and let me tell everybody we meet that my boyfriend's a jock?"

Her laughter choked to a halt as the word *boyfriend* hung in the air above the bed, vibrating like a struck bell.

This time she was the one to flip over and try to burrow through the mattress. "Oh my God, forget I said that. I got carried away. In my defense, I was picturing you in those tight, shiny pants."

The words emerged muffled from where she'd pressed her face into the sheets, and he rolled over to run a hand down the length of her spine.

"Hey, it's no big deal. I don't mind," he said soothingly.

She peeked at him warily. "Seriously?"

"Seriously. It's flattering. I love getting invited to brunch." He pressed his lips together to keep from smiling as embarrassed outrage flooded her face.

"Oh my God! I like it so much better when I'm the one teasing you," she wailed into his mattress.

"Boyfriend." He said the word out loud, and she froze but didn't roll over to face him.

Enough of that. He wanted this out in the open.

"You're better with words," he said, addressing her back, "so you tell me. Is that what you want?" Because fuck, he needed to know. He'd used his body to show her how he felt in every way that he could, and he'd even used his words to try to ease the hurt caused by her mother. But he still had no idea if she was just a tourist here or if she was experiencing the heady, confusing, overwhelming things he was.

Real things. Long-term things.

She rolled over but didn't meet his eyes, busying herself collecting her wild morning hair and twisting it into a tail that hung over one shoulder. "Can't you... can't you give me some perfect sign? Steal my house keys? Hand me your class ring? Give me a clue so it's not just me out here alone?"

He was helpless when she hit him with those big brown eyes, so he attempted to fumble his thoughts into words. "The day I met you, I risked a fight on the train, and I've been doing things that scare the shit out of me ever since." He leaned against the headboard with a soft laugh. "Let's see. I started my own bakery. I put my face on a business card. I sold my family farm. I bought a suit. I told you about Leo the Liberty Valley lion. I've spoken more words to you than I have to any other human being. I trusted you with my whole future. How many more clues do you need?"

That list, which stacked up like a mountain of evidence to him, did nothing to smooth the worried crease between her eyes. His funny, confident girl was braced for the worst, and he had the chance to be the guy who did right by her.

"Okay. Hang on." He slipped out of bed to locate his jeans where he'd flung them the night before. He pulled the wallet out of his pocket and tossed it on her lap. "Here."

She picked it up and smoothed her fingers over the worn brown leather. "And this means what?"

"Look inside."

She frowned but did as he asked, rifling through the cash, the old receipts, the coffee shop loyalty cards that he'd never get around to filling up. And then she found it.

"Is this...?" She extracted the thin, crumpled material carefully, as if it were something ancient and precious. "You kept it?" She pressed the napkin flat against her bare legs and examined her crude sketch that had turned into the face of his business.

"I did. I tried so hard to hate it, but I couldn't. In the end, I fell a little in love with it."

To his dismay, the hope in her eyes dwindled. *Shit.* He was doing this wrong.

He sat next to her on the bed and reached for her hand. "It wasn't just the drawing. It was the person who drew it. Her energy. Her talent. Her get-shit-done spirit."

This time when she looked up, he saw the glint of tears in her eyes, and it killed him that all it took to undo her was to hear someone sing her praises.

"You believed in me," he said. "But I don't think you understand how much I believe in you, sweetheart. How much I believe in you and how much I love you."

Her breathing hitched as a tear spilled from her lashes, and he leaned forward to kiss away the damp path it left behind. "I'm in love with you, Josie." He cradled her face in his palms and smoothed his thumbs over her soft skin. "I'd love you even if you'd ended up with freckles. Now, is that enough proof, or do you still want my class ring?"

That drew a laughing sob from her, and she reached up to wrap her fingers around his. "I love you too," she whispered. "I love you too."

Lightness filled him, followed by a bone-deep sense of belonging. Too overcome to keep using his words, he wrapped her in his arms and crushed her to his chest. She tucked her head under his chin and squeezed back, and they simply held one another until his leg tingled where it was bent funny underneath her. Not that pins and needles were enough to get him to let her go.

She shifted first, twisting her neck to look up at him.

"You know, boyfriends are allowed to say no to brunch provided they're willing to bring their girlfriends pancakes in bed."

Boyfriend. Girlfriend. Such simple words to fill him with such joy.

He brushed her hair back to kiss her temple. "Didn't you yell at your friends yesterday for taking advantage of my generosity in the kitchen?"

"But your pancakes smelled so good! And unlike those freeloaders, I'll totally repay you." She batted her lashes at him and he laughed. As precious as her moments of vulnerability were, he really did live for her sass.

"Okay then. One stack of 'Josie deserves good things' pancakes coming up."

She sat up and caught his hand as he walked past the bed. "You're my best thing." Sincerity vibrated through her as she brushed her lips over his knuckles, and his heart swelled.

"Ditto," he said hoarsely, then set out to show her just how much he loved her, using a griddle, batter, and some syrup.

TWENTY-EIGHT

Josie walked into work on Monday like a whole new woman.

"I am spectacular," she whispered to herself, remembering the ferocity in Erik's voice as he cradled her face and spoke those words to her. Not only did Erik say so—Erik, her *boyfriend,* who *loved* her—but more importantly, he showed her. He listened to her suggestions. He trusted her to make decisions. He absorbed her temper and dried her tears and kissed her senseless. That kind, funny, unexpected man looked at her and didn't see the underachieving, unpredictable mess that everyone else in her life did. He looked at her with affection and respect. That kind of treatment would change any woman's outlook on life.

The thought sent a shot of Fizzy Lifting Drink through her veins that propelled her through the lobby and up the elevator to her floor. But no Monday-morning good mood ever lasts, and within minutes of her arrival, terrible Val buzzed by her desk with a stack of papers that Josie recognized immediately.

"No way, Val." She crossed her arms over her chest.

The woman's lips thinned. "Somebody needs to itemize these vendor expense reports. Gil needs them by the end of the day."

"And the person to do that would be Jennifer. Remember her? You and Gil hired her after I got promoted to managing my own projects. I believe she sits at the desk next to yours and shares a printer with you." Josie kept all traces of sarcasm out of her aggressively pleasant voice, even giving Jennifer a little wave from across the room. The sturdy blonde cheerfully waved right back before returning to her computer.

Valerie flicked an annoyed finger on top of the stack of paperwork. "Jennifer's busy drawing up a launch plan for the new restaurant from Chef Andre. She doesn't have time for this kind of work."

Chef Andre opening a new restaurant was news to Josie, and it really, really shouldn't be.

"When I was promoted, we agreed that I'd be consulted on the assignment of all launch plans, and the new department assistant would be responsible for presenting itemized invoices to clients. Jennifer's the new department assistant." Josie's voice was flat because she knew with a certainty what Val's next argument would be.

Sure enough, Val tilted her head and spoke in a maddeningly patronizing tone. "But Jennifer's so well suited to that kind of work. After all, she has a hospitality management degree from—"

Josie's pleasant face fell away. No more. Thanks to an Erik-related self-esteem boost, she was done taking shit from people who disrespected her, starting with her mother. And if she was prepared to slay the ice queen the next time they met, then she could certainly handle Val, a mere snow cone pretender.

"I swear to God, if the next words out of your mouth are about Jennifer's academic credentials..." For a moment her worst Josie instincts buzzed to life and whispered to her to grab those invoices and shove them into the shredder. But in the next moment, she drew a deep breath and remembered Erik's steady blue eyes on her, the press of his fingers against her skin, his low voice in her ear reciting all the ways he found her valuable. Found her worthy.

Just like that, the buzzing stopped, and her impulse to create a fireable scene faded.

"Valerie," she began, and look at her being all adult and not calling her "terrible Val" like she wanted to, "I have been with this company for six years now, and I'd like you to stop referring to my lack of a college degree as a liability."

Valerie's nostrils pinched. "You don't need to be so sensitive. Nobody here cares about that." She sniffed.

Josie offered a smile that didn't quite reach her eyes but showed plenty of teeth. "*I* don't care, and Gil doesn't care. Our many satisfied clients don't care. The only person who seems to care around here is you. But you know what, Valerie?"

She lowered her voice, and Valerie, looking a little wide-eyed at Josie's unexpected forcefulness, leaned in to catch her next words. "I don't care what you think," she said. "I only care that you respect my position in this company and that you give this paperwork to Jennifer while I take over planning Andre's launch."

Val's mouth dropped open. Snapped shut. Dropped open again. "Well. Well, I'll..." She gripped the papers to her chest and looked around the open-plan workspace, as if to see if anyone had witnessed their interaction. "I'll just see if I can find Jennifer then."

Valerie started to back away, and Josie offered another smile, a real one this time.

"I think you'll find her four feet away from your office chair." Josie gestured grandly at Jennifer. "Oh, and Valerie? If you ever cut me out of a meeting with my own clients in the future, I'll tell Gil who *really* forgot to set the brake on his golf cart just before it ended up in the water hazard at last year's company outing." Josie laughed lightly when Val's face drained of color. "But I'm sure that won't be necessary. We're all on the same team here, right?"

Three hours later, Josie was elbow deep in possibilities for the Andre restaurant launch, which Jennifer had gratefully handed over, when the chirp of her desk phone pulled her away from her media-outreach calendar. A glance at the caller ID had her leaning back in her chair with a chuckle, stretching her legs underneath her desk and getting ready for a lengthy schmooze.

"Well, well, well, if it isn't my favorite newsman. How ya been?"

"Peachy. And how's my favorite redhead?" Yousef Bahar had the booming voice of a 1960s anchorman, but he'd made a career for himself behind the camera as a news producer. What a waste of a set of pipes.

"Oh, I'm feisty as ever. How can I help residents of Chicago be better informed today?"

She and Yousef had worked together on and off over the years after they met as baby employees, her in her first months at Dynamic and him completing a newsroom internship at the local NBC affiliate. Since then, he'd landed a sweet producing gig at the city's most-watched morning show, and he occasionally called her for help booking guests on specific topics.

"You can remind me of the name of that venue you used for that gala a few years ago."

"As always, your attention to detail is impressive," she deadpanned, casting her eyes toward the ceiling as she racked her brain for which event she'd planned that would've stuck with Yousef. "Are you thinking about the converted firehouse from the Susan G. Komen event last winter?"

"Yes! Do you have a contact there? I want to include it as a featured spot in our Chicago wedding special next week."

She was already scrolling through her database. "Sure thing." She found the name he wanted and rattled it off, but before they ended the call, she was struck with a thought. "Hey, this wedding special. Are you highlighting different vendors?"

"Yep. We're doing a best-of-the-season roundup."

"Including bakeries?"

"I mean, the cake's only the best part of the wedding," Yousef said.

She tapped a nail on her desk, briefly debating the ethics of using personal connections for her boyfriend. Then again, if she didn't use her contacts to make Erik a success, what was she even doing here? "You got room for one more?"

JOSIE BIT her tongue as she walked past the decal-less van parked behind the restaurant. One disagreement at a time. Before she pushed through the back door, she fluffed her hair at the roots, trying to restore a little bounce at the end of the workday, and reviewed the arguments she'd organized in her head on the way over. She could do this.

Inside, she found her man holding a huge metal bowl, his massive forearms flexing and bunching as he worked a whisk. Her cheerful greeting died on her lips with a "Guh."

He looked up, and his frown of concentration dissolved into a smile. The rest of the world might get a glower, but she got the teeth and the eye crinkles and the breathtaking beauty of his face when it lit up to greet her.

The thought sent a bolt of shyness racing through her. For some reason she was the one he allowed into his innermost world, and now that she was there, she was terrified of screwing up. Screwing up like she was potentially about to do.

He set the bowl down and beckoned her toward him.

"Isn't this a health code violation?" she asked as he wrapped his huge hand around her neck.

"I don't see the health inspector here." He pulled her in for a kiss, his tongue sweeping across her lips until she opened her mouth to give him access, twining herself around him like a vine and only worrying for a split second that he might have flour on his apron that would get all over her silk blouse. He was worth a dry-cleaning bill.

When she pulled away, her eyes fell on the mixing bowl he'd set down. "Oooh, don't move." She grabbed the DSLR camera she kept stashed in the bakery kitchen and snapped a few shots of the batter-covered whisk resting against the side of the shiny bowl. "Perfect."

"What's with all the pictures? I thought the website was finished." He picked up the bowl and resumed his task but kept his gaze on her as she worked. A few strands of hair had slipped from his elastic, and he looked every inch the rock-star baker she could market him as. She held up the camera and snapped a handful of shots, then tucked it away before he could object.

"It is. This is for a special project. You'll see. And speaking of." No time like the present. "I've got a lead on an amazing opportunity to get the word out about your new business."

He grunted and maintained the pace of his whisking, which she took as a signal to continue.

"So I've got a friend who books segments for *Wake Up, Windy City!,* and they're planning a week's worth of wedding content with a different topic every morning. One of those days is what's on trend with wedding cakes this year. How do you feel about showcasing one of yours?"

He frowned and stopped to add a little sugar to the bowl before resuming his motions. Damn, no wonder he never got tired when he planted his forearms on either side of her head and stroked into her until they were both panting and out of their minds. Her cheeks colored at the memory of their particularly energetic session that morning, which had carried over into the shower until the hot water gave out. But *that's* not why she was there. She shook off her sex trance, and when she did, she saw the smile had dropped off his face.

Of course. She was talking about television to *Erik*, for God's sake. She held up her hands soothingly. "You won't be on-air or anything. The plan is for the host to talk to Darlene from Chez Bakes since that's the most in-demand shop in town. They'll just put up graphics with the bakery names for the rest of the cakes as they pan across. They actually had a full roster already, but I talked him into squeezing your cake onto the stage too."

His whisking had slowed. She wasn't sure if that was good or bad, so she rushed onward. "It's win-win! You get to show off your cake and your bakery name, but you won't have to come bail me out of jail for murdering every woman who sees you on TV and tries to steal you away." More stoniness. "Because you won't *be* on TV." Not even a flicker of facial-muscle movement. "Just your cake. On TV."

So much for projecting breezy confidence to get him to agree. She'd trailed off like the dying whistle of a teapot taken off the heat.

He set the big metal bowl down with a clunk. "TV exposure is good."

It wasn't a question, so she didn't bother answering as he worked through the proposition on his own.

"And I don't have to talk on camera," he said slowly, still frowning.

"Correct. This will be great for you." Then she said in a singsong voice, "People will visit the website and learn about next week's grand opening..."

He looked around the shop, at the shelves waiting to be filled with product, at the room beyond waiting to be filled with customers. She didn't doubt that he knew what the correct answer was, just like he knew he needed to put the damn magnet on the van, but she couldn't predict where his stubborn self would fall on this.

"Erik." She set her hand on his flour-covered wrist. "Do you trust me?"

She held her breath until he grunted and snatched the bowl up again and resumed his motion.

"You know I do." And then, so quietly she could barely hear it over the scrape of this whisk against the bowl: "Thanks for setting it up."

TWENTY-NINE

Erik felt like he was heading to an execution. *His* execution. And he was doing it willingly, although he wasn't sure what percent was for his business and what percent was for his girlfriend. Agreeing was smart on both counts, even if the very act of stepping inside a TV studio made his palms sweat.

There were cameras and cords and lights and people everywhere, all pointed at flimsy sets that looked substantial when you watched from home but would probably topple if a guy like him brushed past too aggressively. He felt like a cat in a roomful of rocking chairs, as Pops used to say.

He followed in Josie's wake as she grinned and waved and Josie-ed her way through the building, apparently on a first-name basis with every last person working under the roof at 7:00 a.m. on a Tuesday. How in the world had he landed himself the grown-up equivalent of the prom queen? He trudged behind her with the temperature-controlled cake transportation box he'd made out of corrugated cardboard and sheets of insulation with ice packs stashed inside. A little cash at Lowe's would allow you to build a container that would keep a cake from sweating even at the most humid of outdoor weddings. Or in this case, under fearsome studio lights.

If only he'd made a box for himself. By the time they arrived at the kitchen set where the segment would be shot, moisture had collected between his shoulder blades under the white chef's jacket. The sweat wasn't from the lights though; his own nerves were launching his body temperature into overdrive. Christ, would this marketing shit ever get easier? Could they just fast-forward to the part where word of mouth was enough to keep customers coming through the door?

"I regret everything," he muttered, eyeballing the counter where he'd be setting up his cake next to three more that were already in place.

"This is going to take you to the next level." She squeezed his bicep, then squealed when she caught sight of someone over his shoulder. "Be right back!" She ran to hug a guy in, yep, an expensive suit. Her appreciation for men in ties was going to give him an ulcer.

"Well, this is a surprise."

The snide tone hit Erik like a ball-peen hammer to the eardrums, and he turned away from Josie's animated conversation to face his old boss.

"Dora," he said flatly.

"I heard a rumor you were setting up your own bakery." She folded her arms across her chest with a scowl. "How charitable of the studio to include one that isn't even open for business yet. How'd you pull that off?"

Her gaze moved across the room and landed on the wildly gesticulating Josie.

"My, my," she said. "I'm seeing things more clearly

now." With a mean little laugh, she brushed past him to fuss with her cake, which was already in place on the counter. Being in her orbit again spiked his anxiety even higher, and out of habit, he reached into his pocket but came up empty. Damn. He hadn't needed his earbuds to block out his surroundings since he'd left Dora's, and he really could've used them right now to crank the music and pretend he was anywhere but here.

From a few feet away, Josie grinned and waved, then pointed to the open spot on the counter next to Dora's creation. He exhaled a thin stream of air and forced himself to step on the set and worked quickly to unpack his cake and position it precisely as he wanted it to appear on camera.

He took grim satisfaction that the sleek sophistication of his cream, mint, and gold leaf geometric creation would overshadow Dora's fussy display of baby's breath and icing flowers. And he knew Dora knew it too; her lips flattened so much that they disappeared when she glanced his way.

"Still looking for a replacement decorator, I see."

"How did you...?" Her voice trailed off as she narrowed her eyes and studied his face, searching for the insult. Oh, it was definitely there, and the audience would spot the difference in her cake and his. Without deigning to respond, she squeaked away in her sensible shoes while he savored getting in the last word without having to say anything at all.

He looked at his four-tier creation one more time. No flaws. All perfection. To his right, the slot for the fifth cake remained unoccupied. The big clock on the wall told him there was six minutes to go before the segment was set to be filmed, so that bakery was cutting it awfully close.

He'd just stepped away from his masterpiece when Josie bustled up, breathless and beaming in her flowy brown pants and white shirt.

"Oh em gee, amazing news! Denise and her cake got stuck in traffic across town, and they need somebody else to feature, so I talked them into using you!"

The rest of her words were lost in the rush of blood to his head. Something about showcasing a new bakery and amazing opportunities for growth. She twinkled up at him, more thrilled than he'd ever seen her, as his skin tightened in terror.

"So you'll be on with Donnie Parker," she was saying. "He'll ask you about your favorite flavors and decorating techniques. Talk about the business location and the open house. It'll be just like when you helped me write your bio."

"That was me talking to you though." His voice creaked like a rusty hinge, but she waved away his concerns.

"Nah, you can give these answers in your sleep. I mean, it's either you or Dora, and I'll be damned if I let that bigot get a moment of extra airtime." She called to the guy she'd been hugging. "Donnie will be gentle. Right, Yousef?"

The man stuck out his hand with a big, phony smile. "Yousef Bahar. Thanks for stepping up. You're a lifesaver."

With a clap on Erik's back, the suit spun around and disappeared behind the corner of the set, leaving him alone with Josie again. She tugged on the hem of his chef's coat and smoothed a wisp of hair back into his bun, beaming at him the whole time. "You look great. The coat, the hair, the scruff. You're going to be amazing. I've always said that you're as big a selling point as your cakes."

That's when he realized she had no idea what this was doing to him. No fucking idea. He could actually feel the blood freezing in his veins, and all she could do was talk about marketing opportunities. He opened his mouth, but his throat was too tight for him to speak.

"Just think how many people will hear about your new bakery. This is gonna be *huge.*" She wrapped her arms around his waist and stretched up to kiss him, and even in his state of abject horror, he melted briefly at the press of her lips, soft and pliant against his. He couldn't help it; his body was hers to command. But when she pulled away, the terror crashed in again.

She had to know how impossible this was. How awful he'd be on camera. Why was she doing this? His growing panic finally freed up his vocal cords.

"Jos, no way can I—"

"Here you are! Erik, right?" A plastic-looking man with rock-hard silver hair and enormous chompers approached with his hand extended. "Donnie Parker. We'll be live for three minutes, and I'll keep things open-ended so you can guide the conversation."

"Actually," Josie interjected, "he might do better with some direction. It's his first time on camera. Here." She whipped a notepad out of her purse and scrawled a few words. "New business location, where he trained, decorating inspiration, favorite flavors. Anything else, babe?"

She flicked her eyes Erik's way, practically bouncing on her heels in excitement, but his joints were locked up and he couldn't move his head to nod or shout at her that this was an awful fucking idea. With a wink in his direction, she tore out the sheet and handed it to Donnie as a crew member clipped a microphone to his jacket and herded him toward the set.

"This is it!" Josie called after him. "Your business is gonna explode!"

"Ten seconds!" the man behind the camera called.

Erik squinted into the bright lights, searching for Josie amid the jumble of people meandering around in front of the set. Instead, his eyes locked on Dora, watching from the sidelines with an evil, anticipatory smile on her lips. *She* knew how bad this was going to be. He desperately pulled his gaze away until he found the red of Josie's hair, directly in his line of sight next to the main camera. She offered him her widest smile, a thumbs-up, and a mouthed, *I love you.* And in that moment, a tiny part of him hated her.

Then the red light on the camera turned on, and Erik did his best not to puke all over Chicago's most beloved morning-show host in front of tens of thousands of viewers at home.

THIRTY

Josie couldn't stop grinning. Her man was out there crushing it. He frowned a little as he listened to Donnie's questions and nodded earnestly as he spoke about his favorite flavor profiles and what decorating trends were poised to take off next season. His initial stiffness softened into a bashful charm, and when he crossed his arms over his chest and his forearms flexed, she heard the woman who'd mic'd him up heave a gusting sigh.

"So does that mean people wanting a cake tomorrow are out of luck?" Donnie beamed.

"Not at all. We're taking orders now, and our grand opening is this Saturday from two to five." Erik looked right to the camera, expression serious.

"Take me now, Lord," the microphone woman breathed. Such was the power of those bright blue eyes in that ruggedly pretty face.

"Give me a break," muttered a voice behind her as Donnie tossed the broadcast back to his cohost in the main studio.

Josie turned to see a pissed-off Dora and offered a

sickeningly sweet smile in return. "Oh, I'm so sorry, did you not bring your personal marketing expert with you to make sure you got good placement on the morning show?"

"I taught him everything he knows," the woman hissed, and Josie just laughed.

"Oh honey, we both know that's not true." She didn't break out the "oh honey" very often, but Dora had richly earned it. Without waiting to see how her barb landed, Josie moved forward to greet Erik when he stepped off set.

"You were amazing!" she squealed, flinging her arms around his neck, then moving away to let the crew member reclaim the lav mic. Erik was sweaty and frowning, and she dropped her hands to his shoulders, squeezing those lovely muscles to chase away the tension there. Her mind spun as she starting thinking up new marketing strategies. "This is just the beginning. We could have you do web videos. Short little things demonstrating your different techniques. How-tos. Tours of the kitchen. Oh my God, the audience reach would be incredible."

"Josie," he said, reaching up to grab her hands, but she was too excited by the ideas crystallizing in her brain to stop. She pulled free and gestured in the air as she kept spinning plans.

"Think how great a series of videos would be to drive content for web and social, and we could—"

"Goddammit, Josie, shut up for one minute!" he roared.

The woman with the mic froze in the act of winding the cord back into its case while around them, all action in the studio paused for what felt like an eternity. Mic woman scuttled away wide-eyed, and soon enough the rest of the station employees shrugged and turned back to packing up and moving out of the kitchen studio. Josie, however, was rooted to the spot in shock.

Erik had yelled. *Yelled.* He'd yelled *at her*.

She stepped forward, but he flinched away from her, turned on his heel, and stormed out of the studio. Her heart hammered in time to the tapping of her high heels as she hurried after him. What had just gone wrong here?

She caught up with him in the hallway, where he was leaning against the wall, body rigid.

"Erik, what's—?"

"Next time, *ask*." His jaw barely moved, and each word pierced her like a knife.

"What do you mean? You were great!"

"I was terrified."

She fell silent, processing his words, his clenched fists, his stiff shoulders. "And now you're mad."

"I'm fucking *furious*." He yanked open his chef's coat with a sharp tug to reveal the sweat-stained T-shirt underneath. "Do you think any part of me wanted to do that?"

"Well, n-no. Not at first," she stammered, "but I thought you'd—"

He turned his glittering eyes on her. "Thought I'd do whatever you wanted?"

"Yes." She answered honestly, without thinking, and hastened to add, "When it comes to marketing, *yes*. You said you trusted me!"

"Yes. I trusted that you knew me."

"I *do* know you."

He shook his head once, sharply. "Then you should know that I would never *ever* want *that*."

Of course she had. *Of course*. But the opportunity had been right there, and dammit, she'd been absolutely certain that he could do it. Absolutely certain that he'd be amazing if she could just get him to stand in front of the camera and *do it*. Like with opening his own business and posing for website pictures and the millions of things she'd lovingly bullied him into for the good of the business.

She took a tentative step closer. If she could just touch him, he'd remember what a good partnership they had. But he twisted away, leaving her hand grasping at empty air. "I'm sorry, Erik. I just wanted—"

"What, exactly?" His voice cracked through the empty hallway.

"Success," she managed to say. "For you to be a success."

"Why?"

Why did he think? "Because I love you."

"Bullshit." The retort shot from his lips. "You want to be the person responsible for my success. You wanted that way before you knew me at all. Remember? *'Because I can'*?"

"No, I..." She started to correct him, but then she *did* remember. This had all begun as a way to prove that she was capable of launching a business from scratch. She'd shoved her way into Erik's life to prove that she could do it. To prove it to herself and Valerie and her mother.

Erik must've seen the memory click into place, because he stepped closer and lowered his voice as a pair of station employees strolled down the hall, clutching coffee cups. "Exactly. You had something to prove. But I'm not your show pony, and I won't let you use my business to inflate your self-worth."

"What? *That's* not why I did this." When he leveled a disbelieving look at her, she forced herself to be honest. "Okay, maybe I like how it feels when a business takes off because of me. But lots of people get satisfaction from their jobs. *You* do."

"Yeah, but I don't need to prove anything. You though?" He looked pointedly at her leopard-print heels and Gucci bag. "You put on a costume every day. You're obsessed with broadcasting success to the outside world, and today you pushed that shit on me."

"At least I'm not too scared to go after what I want."

His face reddened at the cheap shot, and she regretted it immediately. But he'd made her believe that he loved her, fashion sense and all. Instead, he thought she was *obsessed*.

"I never said I don't have my own shit to work through," he said tiredly. "For fuck's sake, I know how hard it is to let go of the past, but at least I'm trying. You? You're spending your life chasing the wrong kind of approval, and it's never going to make you happy."

Did he not think she was happy? "You're wrong. I'm happy with *you*." Her panicked heart slammed against her rib cage.

For the first time since they'd left the studio, he looked at her with the soft expression he saved only for her. But it disappeared a moment later, replaced by the unreadable aloofness she remembered from their first interactions.

"I wish you *were* happy," he said finally. "Just like I wish you could build your sense of self from inside and not outside. But I'm not sure you can."

He might as well have slapped her. She wrapped her arms around her waist and pitched herself forward as she processed his words. Erik was her champion, the person who believed in her. He knew the secret hurts in her heart, and now he was telling her that she was broken.

She struggled to pull enough air into her lungs to

speak. "Maybe at first I wanted to help you to prove a point. But even if that's how it started out with you and me, with your bakery, it's different now."

She was begging him to believe in her, but he just shoved his hands in his pockets.

"Is it?" He pressed his lips together before speaking again. "What if I told you I want to take a step back, cancel the grand opening. Just focus on wedding cakes. Stay small. Rent a portion of my kitchen to another baker to share expenses."

"You wouldn't," she breathed, drifting close enough that his good vanilla-and-Erik smell went straight to her head.

"If I did, would I lose you?"

"As a client? Yes," she said immediately. "I can't let you waste all that potential."

His face hardened. "I'm not your client."

She opened her mouth to assure him that of course not, he was her boyfriend and she wasn't going away. But something about what she'd just said scratched at her memories.

Potential. Wasted.

Her mother had said that to her at their horrible lunch, had accused Josie of wasting her potential. She pressed a trembling hand to her mouth as she revisited everything that had happened over the past twenty minutes. She'd pushed Erik to be something he wasn't so she could claim the glory. She'd done to him what Pamela had spent a lifetime doing to her. Commodifying him. Using him to boost her own image.

Cold horror trickled down her spine, and she glanced over to find that he'd pulled the elastic from his hair and let it fall forward to hide his features. She was pushing him away. She was losing him.

"You need all this"—he waved a hand in the direction of the studio but didn't turn toward her—"to feel good about yourself, but I don't want it." His whole body sagged against the wall, like this fight was leeching his essence, the thing that made him so big and vital and precious to her.

"So I guess that means you don't want *me*." Her voice was tiny and scared. *She* was tiny and scared.

He looked at her with no trace of warmth on his face, and ribbons of pain unfurled in her heart. Every cell in her body cried out for him to deny it, to tell her that of course he wanted her, needed her, *chose* her. But his gaze dropped to the floor, and his shoulders lifted on a massive inhale.

"I never asked for any of this." He lifted his head, but he fixed his eyes on a point beyond her shoulder. "I never wanted to want you."

She gasped. She actually gasped as those baldly stated words stung her skin and sank into her blood and her marrow. This man had convinced her it was safe to pack away her defensive armor, and now she had nothing to protect herself from the fatal blow he'd just landed.

"Then I guess we're done here," she managed to say. "I-I hope you get whatever it is that you do want."

But he'd already retreated into his own world, the one he'd been in the night they met, and his expressionless face hurt her almost as much as his cutting words had. She choked back a sob and spun on her heel to leave the building before she dissolved entirely.

Unfortunately, the moisture started to leak from her eyes once she reached the end of the hallway, and there was goddamn Dora, lurking around the corner, clearly having caught enough of their argument just now to account for that smirk on her face.

"Well. I guess we'll see how well he does without someone there to pull his puppet strings."

Josie blotted the tears with her wrist, gratified that she had the strength to fight at least this unworthy opponent.

"Please. He doesn't need me to crush you in the baking department, you hateful cow."

And with that, she sniffed back her tears, straightened her spine, and got the hell out of there to mourn the implosion of her relationship in private.

THIRTY-ONE

"Hey. Hey!"

Erik's head snapped down at the sharp words to find Gina draped in paper banners and peering at him in concern.

"Sorry," he muttered, pressing pause on yet another replay of his fight with Josie three days earlier. He grabbed one of the strings of brightly colored pennants and stretched it along the top of the plate glass window in the dining area, wrapping it around a nail to hold it in place.

"Are you sure you're okay?" Gina handed him another strand.

He wasn't, and they both knew it. Instead of answering her question, he said, "I'm glad you're here."

"Of course." She plopped into a café chair to pick apart the tangle of the remaining banners, draping them over the shoulder of her denim overalls as she separated each one. "When you called me last night, you sounded so..."

Lost. She didn't say the word out loud, but it's how

Erik would finish that sentence. He was lost in a churning, seething ocean, and he didn't know how to stay afloat.

He grabbed the strings from her shoulders and finished looping them around the walls of the shop, stepping back to survey the effect. "Looks good."

"Mmm." Gina's noncommittal answer bordered on irritated, and Erik jammed his hands into his pocket.

"What?"

"Testy," she said. "I can't help but notice that since I got here, all we've done is talk about grand-opening stuff."

"I asked you how the new job is going."

"Oh, sorry. Five minutes on my exciting career debugging laptops, and the rest on grand-opening stuff."

"Right, because you came over to help me get ready, and it's happening tomorrow," he grumbled.

"No, I came over because you've been hurting for days, and when you finally reached out, I came running over to let you pour out all your troubles. But all you've done is deflect and avoid."

Erik growled and stalked to the kitchen, where he continued to deflect and avoid by grabbing a tray of unfrosted key lime cupcakes from the fridge and banging them onto the countertop. Gina followed and calmly handed him the icing bag. He snatched it from her and started aggressively piping green-tinted icing onto half a dozen naked cakes before she spoke.

"I actually did have better things to do with my Friday night, you know," she said. "New gal in town. Lots of social options. I turned down a date with a lawyer to hang out with you."

He slammed the bag down, unconcerned about the icing that shot out to cover the countertop in a sticky layer of sweetness.

"Ah, so you're pissed," she said calmly.

"Yes, I'm pissed. She didn't stop to think about me. Only herself."

Gina moved around the counter to grab a towel. "Oh yeah? Because she's the one who benefits financially when this place earns a profit?" She moistened the cloth and began wiping away the green smears.

Erik's jaw tightened, but he refused to acknowledge her point. Instead, he recalled yet again the sick dread of looking into the lens of the camera and knowing he was being broadcast across the city in all his tongue-tied awkwardness. And then the even sicker dread when he realized that Josie needed a partner who would happily step in front of a million cameras for her.

"She doesn't want to be with someone like me." He bunched his shoulders and pushed the words out even though they hurt to say out loud. "I can't make her happy."

"She said all that? 'Erik, you're a big, silent man-ape, and I hate it. What I need is a silly, shiny, shallow man to make me happy.'"

"Of course not." He nudged her aside and grabbed the cloth to finish wiping up the icing explosion. Gina's sarcasm burrowed under his skin. It was minor league compared to Josie's MLB-level skills, but it still rankled. Then again, he hadn't seen Josie lose control of her temper at all recently, and in that last, awful conversation, she'd looked downright defeated. The Josie he'd met four months ago probably would've lunged for his eyes.

"She's always going to be chasing some new kind of validation." He addressed his words to the green streaks of icing on the towel. "I can't be with her knowing I'll never be enough."

And fuck, he'd known that from the beginning. Known that women like her craved something more exciting than men like him. He'd just let himself forget for a little while.

Gina wrapped her arm around his waist and gave him a squeeze, her head barely clearing his shoulder. "Listen, the girl isn't stupid. She knows a good man when she sees one, and you're a good man. She'll come around."

"Maybe."

"And if she doesn't, that just means more grand-opening leftovers for me." She released him and selected a cupcake, peeling away the wrapper with a grin.

"Remember when I said I was glad you were here to help? I changed my mind."

"Yeah, well, I didn't actually have any better plans tonight. That lawyer seemed totally boring. Although..." Her face reddened.

He tossed the towel into the sink. "Although?"

"Christine left me a voicemail." She too casually adjusted the strap of her overalls and didn't meet his eyes. "She wants to talk about things. Relationship things."

"That's good," he said, glad that one of them had positive news to share. Then he noticed Gina's frown. "That's good, right?"

"Yeah. I love her. I miss her. It's... complicated." She looked up, a wan expression on her normally friendly features. "I'm hoping we can move past all our shit, including my post-breakup rendezvous with Closing-Time Timmy."

Chagrined at the reminder that he wasn't the only person in pain in this kitchen, he pulled her into a hug, sticky green icing be damned. "I'm sorry."

"That's what I've been wanting to say to her." Her

soft laugh ended on an even softer sigh. "So we'll see how it goes when we talk."

"Say the word and I'll bake all her favorite desserts for you to give her. If she's anything like you, the way to her heart is through her stomach."

"Damn straight," Gina said. Then the bell above the door jangled, and she pulled away. "Expecting anyone?"

"No. You?"

She shook her head, and he tried to quash the flutter of hope in his chest. What if it was Josie, here to apologize? Or to let him apologize. He wasn't sure which was more necessary, but at this point he'd be willing to try either one if only to ease the pain in his heart at the thought of never seeing her again.

Yet when he walked into the front of the shop, he found a dark-haired woman where he was hoping to find a flame-haired one.

"Hey!" Lily crossed to the center display case with a vase of purple tulips in one hand and a large cardboard box tucked under her arm. "I wanted to drop by with good wishes for tomorrow. Sorry I can't make it; the Cubs are in town, and going to the games keeps the spark alive in my marriage."

Erik wasn't too keen on pondering someone else's happy relationship at the moment, but he was touched by her thoughtfulness. "Thanks." He accepted the flowers and set them next to the cash register.

"No pollen, no scent," she said, pushing her dark, shaggy hair behind her ear. "And this was on your front step." He stepped out from behind the counter to accept the long, flat box while Lily turned in a circle to take in what he'd accomplished with help from his friends. Well, his ex-girlfriend and her friends. The pain intensified.

"Great floor." She ran a battered sneaker along the mellow gleam of the refinished wood. "Did Josie help pick out the wall color? And is she here? I was hoping to say hi."

The pain turned into a wave of bleak despair that threatened to pull him under, and all he could manage was a short "No."

Lily's smile vanished. "Oh, I'm sorry. That sucks. You two were cute together."

He forced himself to hold still while she patted his arm in sympathy.

"But hey," she continued, "at least she helped free you from Dora. Oooh, do you think the old bat'll swing by to wish her favorite former employee good luck?"

"If Dora walks through my door, I'm torching the place and starting over."

Lily snorted, then cocked her head. "Josie made you funnier, you know."

"I'm sure it'll pass." That prompted another burst of laughter, followed by a flower-scented hug.

"I've got a few more deliveries yet, so I need to run. Good luck tomorrow!"

With a last squeeze, she slid out the door, and Erik turned over the package she'd handed him as he walked behind the counter to grab a knife. He didn't recognize the return address, and when he slit open the tape, he discovered a dozen oversized black-and-white photos packed inside. He picked them up, being careful not to smudge the glossy surfaces, and flipped through the high-contrast shots of the tools of his trade. A pastry bag on its side. A spray of flour across a countertop. A cake mid-icing. The images emerged from the soft-focused background to glow as if they were lit from within. These weren't photos; these were art.

"Oh cool." Gina emerged from the back and peered over his shoulder. "Where'd those come from?"

Josie. It had to be. Who else would've captured his livelihood with such care? "Her special project. She must've ordered these before..." Regret locked up his vocal cords, and Gina rubbed a soothing circle on his back in a gesture similar to Lily's. Since when did a breakup give the women of the world the right to maul him with their sympathetic touches? It just reminded him of the woman whose touch he missed every day.

"Shame not to display them," she said. "They'd look great framed and hung up."

She pointed to the yellow walls flanking the dine-in area, and damn, but she was right. The stark images would stand out against the bright backdrop. Was that what Josie had intended? His fingers twitched to text her—hell, to *call* her—and ask. But he stopped himself. What they'd said to each other had felt pretty fucking final, and making it through tomorrow's event would be hard enough even without official confirmation that his stolen time with her had truly ended.

He again pictured her laughing with the guy in the suit at the TV station on Tuesday. Yet more proof that he wasn't the man for her in the long run. But he'd accept this gift from her, this precious glimpse of her talent. And he'd hang them in the business she helped create. His heart might crack every time he looked at them, but they'd also remind him of the woman he loved but hadn't been able to keep.

THIRTY-TWO

Josie heard her apartment doorknob rattle but couldn't muster the strength to pull herself up from her sprawl on the couch to see if it was a friend or a serial killer. Honestly, either would be fine.

"'Sup?" She flopped her arm over the back of the sofa in a half-hearted wave. "If you're a stranger here to kill me, make it quick."

"'Sup?" came Richard's amused voice. "That's how you greet possible murderers?"

"Yes." Gravity pulled her arm down, and she tucked it back under her cheek and resumed staring into the middle distance. "I welcome death."

"Oh geez." He moved around the couch and surveyed the scene in front of him with a wrinkled nose. "What's happening here?"

"I'm wallowing." She flopped to her back and propped her head against the sofa arm.

Richard brushed a few stray chip crumbs off the couch cushion next to her leg. "Clearly."

"You're a happy newlywed. You don't get to judge

me," she said dully. Finn and Tom were off doing an out-of-town couply thing, so she'd called in sick and devoted the day to her private grief. She would've thought so much crying would leave her hollow and empty, but instead she was heavy. Leaden. A dense monument of sorrow who just wanted to be left alone.

"Why are you here?" she grumbled.

"Byron's having dinner with his brother tonight." Richard moved an empty ice-cream container from the couch to the coffee table, flipped the bottom of his suit jacket up, and perched gingerly on the cushion next to her. "And you didn't answer my last five texts."

"I've been busy."

"Right." He nudged an empty wine bottle on the floor by his foot. "I was worried, so I used my key to check on you."

"That's supposed to be for emergencies."

"I think that's what this is, sugar bum." He leaned close to study her face, and she didn't have the strength to slap a hand over her puffy eyes and oily T-zone. "The last time you had a breakup, you were closing down bars and dragging us all to sushi joints over the Indiana state line just because you could."

"Yeah, well, last time my heart wasn't destroyed."

Richard rocked back in surprise. "That's... incredibly honest. Where's the sarcasm? Where's the Josie sass?"

The concern in his tone made her swallow hard. "I don't think I have any left. I'm broken."

He made a sympathetic noise low in his throat. "Want to tell me what happened?"

"No." With a soul-deep sigh, she pulled herself into a sitting position and reached for a magazine just to have something to do with her hands. She thumbed through the pages, aware that she was miles away from conveying "just enjoying my casual Friday night at home, thanks."

"So are you going tomorrow?"

Her heart lurched. "No." The word narrowly escaped her tight throat.

"Are you really not going to go see all that hard work pay off?"

The mild disapproval in his voice rankled. "Of course I'm not." She sniffled miserably. "We b-broke up."

"Help me understand what happened here." He reached over and pulled the magazine out of her hands. "Because I've spent some time with him, and I'm here to tell you that Erik the Viking is wild about you."

She exhaled a shuddery breath and dropped her chin to her chest. "He told me we weren't happy."

"He *did*? That shocks me."

"Well, he told me *I* wasn't happy." She impatiently brushed away a tear. How did she still have moisture in her body left to cry out? "He said I measure my self-worth by how much I help others succeed."

She looked to her friend for commiseration, but Richard merely tipped his head fractionally to the side before he said gently, "Oh sweetie. Did you not know?"

"I..." She looked at him helplessly. The nightclub launches, the galas, the open houses. Even his and Byron's wedding. Had she really used the accolades from all the events she'd spearheaded to paper over the neediness inside her?

"Poor Erik." Richard stood and walked to the kitchen. "Want some water?"

"Excuse me?" The words hit her like a slap to the face. "Poor *Erik?*"

"Yeah, I think you want water," he said calmly, grabbing two glasses and filling both. "And yes, poor Erik."

"So much for loyalty," she huffed.

"Oh stop." Richard returned to the couch and handed over one of the tumblers.

"Why are you taking his side?" She swiped at her eyes with her shirtsleeve. "He dumped *me*."

Richard didn't answer right away, taking a sip first. "Let's take a second to think like Erik."

"No."

"No?" His perfect brows arched.

"It hurts too much." Her voice broke, and she tilted her head down so Richard wouldn't see the misery in her eyes. He nudged her chin up and tucked a lank strand of hair behind her ear.

"Your light is gone. It's hard to see." Richard patted her cheek, then leaned back. "So let's imagine you're an introvert who just wants to bake cakes. One night you run into a fire demon on the subway who entrances you with her heart-stopping beauty and her indomitable spirit."

"That's a generous interpretation." She bent to scrounge around the floor near the couch in search of a hair tie. She'd given up caring about her normal grooming standards a few days ago and probably looked like she was wearing a fright wig.

"And then you quit your job and agree to work with the bossy fire demon to open your own bakery. She takes your picture and makes you a website and wants to put your face on a van. Is any of that something you thought you wanted?"

She paused with a fistful of straggly curls in one hand and an elastic in the other. "I suppose not." She turned that idea around in her brain. "But he was *so angry*, Richard."

The memory of their fight was a punch to the gut, even days later. It was like he knew exactly what to say to cut right to the heart of every insecurity she harbored. Unwanted. Unwelcome. Unchosen. She'd told him about her mom, about her past. She'd laid herself bare in all her fashion-loving, impulse-following frivolity, and he'd held her and soothed her and accepted her as she was—until he hadn't. Yet again, she hadn't been worth the trouble, and that knowledge made it hard to breathe.

"It sounds like he was unkind, yes." Richard nodded. "But he'd just been on television. *Television.* Imagine you're Erik talking into a camera."

She reclaimed her glass but couldn't bring herself to do more than stare into it. "He hated every second." Her cheeks flushed in shame yet again that she hadn't thought it through.

"I'm sure he did." Richard charged ahead with his logically laid-out argument. "I'm sure he felt like you were pushing your version of success on him. Has it occurred to you that he might have just wanted *you* and not your help with his business?"

Someone wanting *her*. What a novel thought. Her clients wanted her for her marketing savvy. Her mom wanted her as a daughter accessory. Was it possible she'd let herself believe that Erik only wanted her if she was helping him?

Maybe Erik and Richard both had a point. Maybe she got her self-worth from helping others succeed. Maybe accepting that Erik loved her meant accepting that she was good enough on her own. And maybe she'd reacted so badly when the man she loved brought all this to her attention that she'd tossed a bomb into the middle of their relationship.

"I ruined everything," she whispered.

Richard pursed his lips. "Do you think he was going to break up with you on Tuesday, regardless of what happened?"

"Well ... No." In truth, he'd given her zero indication that he'd planned in advance to end things. Which meant...

"Maybe it was just a fight," Richard said. "And you both jumped to the worst possible conclusions."

Josie's brain turned this new idea around and pulled it apart to study its guts. They'd been happy. More than happy. This had just been a fight.

But that burgeoning spark of hope fizzled out when she remembered his words. *I never wanted to want you.* She loved him with her *everything*, and he resented his feelings for her. She wanted to lie on the floor and howl at the unfairness of it until she dissolved into dust.

If he didn't want to want her, she wouldn't force her way back into his life. But there was one thing she *could* do: she could show him that she'd heard what he'd said and that she was walking away from their relationship as a slightly better person. She could show him that she wanted him to have his business on his terms, not the ones she'd insisted on.

An idea formed in her mind, and she drained her glass and peeled herself off the couch, her mind clearer than it had been in days. "I've got a plan."

"Is it a shower?" Richard eyed her stained shirt. "Because that might be a good place to start. You smell like the bottom of my gym bag."

"Too mean," she muttered as she shuffled toward the

hallway. "You're legally obligated to be nice to me until I sort myself out."

"Be sure to wash your hair too!" was her best friend's compassionate response.

In the bathroom, she stood under the spray and let the hot water wash over her. She'd learned to accept Erik's love. That meant she could also learn to love herself, right? She could find her worth outside of work successes or her mother's approval or any of the countless ways she'd spent her life seeking validation. Finn loved her regardless. So did Richard and Byron. Even Jake was fond of her in his own way. That was something. That was the start of thinking of herself as a person of value on her own merits.

Fifteen minutes later, she was clean, sweet-smelling, and seated in front of her laptop. While Richard clicked through the Netflix offerings and settled on *Barbarian Time Brigands: The Quest for Dragons*, she opened her design program, took a deep breath, and got to work on an apology the best way she knew how.

THIRTY-THREE

Everything was perfect, and Erik had never been more miserable.

"You ready?"

Gina stood next to the door with a red Have Your Cake apron wrapped around her waist, her hand on the CLOSED sign, and anticipation on her face. Erik took one more look around his shop with a mixture of pride and sorrow. The glass display cases were crammed with plump cupcakes wearing hats of pastel icing, and an array of glossy single- and double-tier cakes covered the countertops. The colorful chalkboard hanging behind the cases boasted the day's specials, and the colorful pennant banners gave the shop a festive feeling. He was standing in the middle of what should've been a triumphant moment, but he was as hollow inside as a baked meringue.

Gina heaved an impatient sigh and announced, "You're moping. Let's go." She flipped the sign on the glass door over to OPEN and moved to stand next to him in front of the display cases. The grand opening was officially underway. They stood shoulder to shoulder, expectation thick in the air as... nothing happened. The bell above the door remained stubbornly silent, and the only movement on the sidewalk in front of the building was a kid skateboarding past in ripped jeans. Erik reached for his phone to check the time, but his pocket was empty, which meant he'd left it upstairs when he'd changed into his service clothes. If he went up to retrieve it, he might be tempted to hide there all afternoon, so he forced himself to stay put.

"This is going great so far."

"Yeah, good thing I'm here to help with crowd control." Gina bumped his arm, and he looked down at her and tried to muster a smile.

A few more moments passed in silence as they both stared at the door.

"How'd your talk with Christine go?" Their prep for the open house had been intense, so this was his first opportunity to ask.

She turned from the view of the empty street in front of the store and flashed him a brilliant smile. "Good. Better than good. She apologized, and then I apologized. She misses me. Next step is her coming to Chicago for a visit."

"Guess I better get baking then. What's her favorite—"

The jingle of a bell interrupted his question, and he straightened to greet the first customers. The pair of sixtysomething women offered him wide smiles, which he returned as best as he could. "Welcome to Have Your Cake bakery. Let me know if you'd like to sample anything."

The taller woman dug her elbow into her petite friend's side. "See anything you'd like to sample, Joyce?"

"Shush!" the second woman admonished before turning to Erik and patting her short curls. "We saw you on the news and thought you were too adorable to believe, so we had to come see for ourselves."

Gina snickered, and a flush spread from the roots of his hair on down. Every last misgiving he'd ever had about making himself the face of the bakery zoomed front and center.

"Take your time," he muttered, turning on his heel to hide in the kitchen. Gina could deal with the two silver-haired thirst buckets. But within five minutes, he heard the bell jingle again, and then again and again. He closed his eyes, groped for his inner calm, and stepped back out to the public area.

He stopped short and blinked in surprise at the dozen people milling in the waiting area while a maniacally enthusiastic Gina tried to organize them into a line.

"A little help, big guy?" she called over her shoulder.

He jumped into motion and stepped behind the counter to start fielding questions about gluten from a woman in yoga pants as he boxed up a dozen chocolate ganache cupcakes for a sandy-haired man in a plumbing company T-shirt. Out of the corner of his eye, he saw Gina package two Boston cream cakes for the first two women through the door.

The taller one winked at him as they paid. "Don't worry, cutie. I'll be back next week to pick out a birthday cake for my niece!"

The crowd kept up a steady flow over the next three hours, a mix of curious neighborhood residents and *Wake Up, Windy City!* fans who'd made the drive to check out his shop—and, occasionally, him. Which he hated. But weirdly, he didn't once burst into flames or sink through the floor in agony at being forced to interact with strangers who were there to gawk at him rather than his creations. In fact, no matter what brought them in, most ended up leaving with a cake here or half a dozen cupcakes there, and he didn't hate that. At times he'd almost say he enjoyed it—or he would have if he weren't heartbroken over the person who was conspicuously absent. Still, he managed to bury his discomfort and stepped around the counter to pose for selfies when customers requested it, at one point telling a trio of teenage girls, "Be sure to tag us. It's @HaveYourCakeBakery."

He barely recognized himself, but it's what Josie would want him to do.

His feet ached by the time things finally slowed to a crawl with five minutes to go before the end of the event. "Thanks again for your help," he said, but Gina just waved him off from where she was collecting dirty plates and wiping crumbs from the café tables.

"Don't mention it. Besides, I know it's not what you pictured." She brushed past him with a tub of dishes to take to the sink in the back, leaving him to his thoughts.

She wasn't wrong. He'd pictured working side by side with the woman he loved. The woman he'd pushed away in anger. And he *was* still angry with her, but then again... at least two-thirds of the people through the doors had mentioned the morning show, and he'd booked eight appointments for wedding consults. It felt good. Looking around and knowing his place was full of satisfied people felt good. Success felt good.

He'd done that, yes. But so had Josie. And she deserved to be proud of that.

He was in the middle of inventorying the remaining

supply of raspberry-lemonade and chocolate ganache cupcakes when the bell above the door tinkled and a dour, rail-thin woman in a severe black jumpsuit entered the shop. She looked around with pinched lips before turning her cool gaze on him.

"Is my daughter here?" she asked without preamble.

It took Erik a long moment to connect the dots. "Mrs. Ryan?" he asked in surprise. She inclined her head and continued her unimpressed inspection of the bakery while his brain struggled to explain how this brittle woman had brought the vibrant ball of energy that was Josie into the world. "She's not here."

Pamela breathed hard through her nose. "Isn't that just like her. Changing plans on a whim without bothering to tell anyone." Then a wisp of interest moved across her face for the first time since she'd entered the bakery, and she crossed to the far wall where Erik had hung Josie's photos in plain black frames.

"These are lovely. What a smart use of exaggerated lighting to elevate everyday objects." She leaned closer to examine a shot of a row of eggs, one of them cracked and bleeding its yolk onto the counter. Next to it was an image of a glass bottle of heavy cream dotted with condensation, luminescent as it emerged from the darkness surrounding it. "Who's the artist?"

"Are you kidding me?" He stormed around the counter to jab his finger at the photos. "It's your daughter. Your *middling-talented* daughter did that."

"Really? I'd never have guessed." Pamela brushed her straight, dark hair back to peer closer but didn't take the bait.

Erik's teeth snapped together. Was it possible she didn't recall the specific insult that had sent Josie careening into his arms that hot afternoon in the delivery van? He'd thought nothing could hurt worse than a mother who abandoned you, but it seemed he'd underestimated the other kinds of hurts a thoughtless parent could inflict.

She turned away with a final sniff. "I guess every hobbyist gets lucky once in a while." She stalked away from Josie's art on her sky-high heels. "Do you expect to see her later tonight?"

"I don't."

At his brusque words, something almost gleeful moved across her brown eyes, so like and yet unlike her daughter's. "Well, that didn't take long," she said with a dismissive wave. "I suppose that means I'll just have to track her down some other way before I leave town."

"No. You won't."

She froze at the unexpected whipcrack of his voice.

"Pardon me?" she asked incredulously.

Erik drew himself up to his full height, which gave him a good foot on the tiny woman. "You will not call Josie until you're prepared to treat her and her work with respect." Pamela's thin lips dropped open as he continued. "She's smart and talented, and she sure as hell deserves more love than you've ever given her."

Her eyes narrowed. "Just where do you get off—"

"I'm the one who *does* love her," he said. "She's got the quickest, funniest mind and kindness that she clearly didn't inherit from you. You're lucky to have Josie in your life. You don't deserve her. *I* don't deserve her. But she sure as hell deserves us both trying harder than we do."

He was breathing hard by the end of his unexpected speech, and Josie's mother stared at him in shock for what felt like an eternity before she coolly lifted her chin.

"Typical. She attracted a man just as hotheaded as she is. Good luck with your little business, Mr. Andersson." Without another word, she spun on her pointy heel and minced from the store, brushing by two men as she did. When one of them started a slow clap, Erik's awareness returned to his body, and he recognized the people standing at the entrance with amazed grins on their faces.

Byron continued his dramatic clapping while Richard crowed, "Bravo! I've been wanting to give that harpy a piece of my mind for years."

Gina appeared from the back with wide eyes. "Is it safe to come out?"

"I don't know. Are you done shouting at everybody?" Richard asked Erik, who groaned and slumped into a chair at the nearest table.

"Richard, Byron, this is my friend Gina. Gina, these are the newlyweds who started it all." Erik gestured around the shop, then pointed the newcomers toward the display case. "Flip the sign to Closed and help yourselves."

They were all seated around the table and slicing into the strawberry-champagne cake Richard had selected when Gina asked, "Was that Josie's mom who called you hotheaded? *Hotheaded?*"

The other three dissolved into laughter as Erik grumbled, "I fucked up."

"No, Pam needed to hear that," Richard said decisively.

"He doesn't mean with Pam," Byron said, and Erik looked up to find himself the object of the man's kind gaze. "Do you really love her that much?"

Erik took a deep breath. "Yes." For the first time ever, talking about his emotions with a group felt *right*. "I was pissed at her, sure, but I also get why she did what she did. And I said some things..." His voice trailed off as he replayed the crushed look on Josie's face in the station hallway, and once again, he lost hope of ever making things right. "I hurt her."

His hands clenched into fists at his own stupidity. There wasn't a moment of the fight that he didn't regret, except the part where he'd tried to get her to see that she didn't need other people's approval to love herself.

"She's ridiculously forgiving, you know." Richard paused in the act of slicing himself a second piece of cake to brandish the server at him in a threatening fashion. "But you have to mean it. Do you mean it?"

Erik pushed the pointy end of the server away from his chest with the tip of his finger. "Yes. Of course. I just don't know if she'd be willing to listen."

"Oh, that won't be a problem," Gina announced. "I grabbed your phone when I ran upstairs for a fresh apron. She texted."

He snatched it from her to read the message Josie had sent earlier that day, and a trickle of optimism moved through his veins. "She wishes me luck on the grand opening, and she sent me a..." He swallowed convulsively before he could continue speaking. "A new logo."

He turned the screen to the others so they could see the text-only logo featuring his bakery name in a spare, masculine style that once upon a time he might have chosen for himself.

"That really does look more your speed," Gina said. "I like it."

"I hate it," he shot back. And to his surprise, he truly did. Not only was he attached to the current logo for sentimental reasons, but he *was* the face of the bakery he'd built with help from the people he loved. Making peace with the upheaval of his childhood had helped him embrace that. He wasn't his mother. He wasn't Pops. And now he was ready to build his future on his own terms. He just hoped it would include his favorite redhead.

"I'm keeping the first logo my girlfriend made for me," he announced to the table. "Now I just need to get her back."

Richard looked up from his own phone with a grin. "I might be able to help with that."

THIRTY-FOUR

Of all the weekends for Josie to have zero evening work events, why'd it have to be this one? Instead of brandishing a clipboard and overseeing a chichi cocktail party or handing out oversized scissors for a cheesy ribbon-cutting ceremony, she was pushing her way through the crowd gathered near the entrance of the Wicker Park bar where she'd promised to meet her friends for a night out. Lucky her.

Bass-heavy music assaulted her ears once she was inside, and she was jostled by no fewer than four aggressively cologned men before she joined Finn and Tom at their booth. Her roommate took one look at Josie's wan complexion and turned to ask Tom sweetly, "Could you grab us another round?"

He pressed a kiss to her palm and vanished into the crowd, and Finn shifted closer to Josie on the bench so she wouldn't have to shout over the ambient noise. "What's wrong? He still hasn't texted back?"

Josie swallowed the crushing pain over her phone's daylong, heartbreaking silence.

"So why not just show up at the bakery this afternoon?" Finn asked.

"I'm sure it was hard enough for him to get through. No need to introduce our emotional baggage too." It had killed her to stay away though. She pulled her phone out and checked it one more time. The bakery open house had ended hours ago, which meant there'd been plenty of time for Erik to text back. But there was nothing, not even from Richard, even though she'd texted him a summons to join this barhop of despair.

Looked like she was well and truly dumped.

"I hope he had a few familiar faces there at least," Finn said. "Tom and I were going to go, but his boss's birthday party ran superlong and we missed it."

"You two are a couple of Disney characters," Josie muttered.

"Lady and the Tramp, right?" a new voice asked.

The women looked up to see that Jake had joined Tom while he was at the bar, so they shifted again to accommodate a fourth at the table. Once they were seated, the men started sharing highlights of that afternoon's Cubs game while Josie stared moodily at the group occupying the adjacent table, who were laughing and clinking glasses and passing around a box of cupcakes. Everybody at *that* table looked like they were having a great time, while Josie was suffocating under the weight of Erik's absence. He might not talk as often as anyone else in her social circle, but she adored his quiet contributions: the upward tilt of his lips, the crinkle at the corner of his eyes, the well-placed, if infrequent, quip.

Had he not gotten what she was telling him with that new logo? She now understood that his wants were different from hers, but apparently it was too little, too late. She cut her eyes upward to control the burn of tears, then lifted her drink to her lips, tasting neither the gin nor the tonic inside but in need of some activity to keep herself from screaming.

"Okay, this is weird."

Jake's voice in her ear startled her, and she turned to find him with a beer bottle halfway to his lips, eyebrows raised.

"What?"

"You. Completely ignoring me tonight. So weird."

It *was* weird. The demise of her relationship—the best relationship she'd ever been in—should leave her itchy and ready to explode. She should be pestering Jake and scoping out the best-looking guys in the club. She should be standing on the bar with a bottle of tequila in each hand, pouring drinks for everyone in the room. She should be picking a fight with a bouncer. Anything she could do to stop the buzzing in her head, no matter how bad the idea might seem the next morning.

Except her head was quiet. Erik had shown her what calmness meant, and he'd shown her she was capable of not giving in to each wild impulse. But right now all it really left her with was sadness.

Still, tradition was tradition. "You wanna get out of here, go someplace a little more quiet?" she asked indifferently.

"Sure. Let's do it." He leaned back in his seat and stretched his arm along the back.

Even though it was the first time he'd ever agreed to her jokey come-ons, she just sighed and rested her chin on her hand. "Nah. Thanks though."

"That's what I thought." Jake shook his head. "Man, that baker really did a number on you."

She considered denying it, but what was the point? "Yeah. He did."

His thick brows pulled together in a scowl. "Do Tom and I need to beat the shit out of him?"

"As if you could," she said hotly, coming to life for the first time all night and slamming her glass on the table.

"Tom!" Jake called over her head, forcing the other man to quit nibbling on Finn's ear. "We could take Josie's baker in a fight, right?"

"Absolutely not," Tom shouted cheerfully over the EDM nightmare blaring through the speakers. "That guy's a tank, and I want no part of whatever you're planning."

"Nobody's beating up anybody!" Josie yelled, but Tom had already returned to exploring Finn's neck with his tongue. "And he's not *my* baker," she shouted at Jake.

But he was though. He was hers, as much as she was his, no matter how improbable a couple they might be. Unfortunately, she might be the only one of them who felt that way. Just as another wave of grief threatened to carry her away, she noticed two club kids strutting past their table with a cupcake in each hand. Weird. This place was known for high-end martinis, not baked goods. In fact, she didn't think it even had a food-service license.

She leaned around Jake for a better view of the other tables and noticed several patrons noshing on cupcakes. And not just any cupcakes, but exceptionally beautiful ones.

"Hey," she called to a goateed man who was about to take his first bite of what looked quite a bit like a key lime creation. "Where'd you get that?"

He paused with the treat halfway to his mouth. "Some guy's giving 'em away from a van parked outside."

Buzzing. In her head. But the excited kind, not the destructive one. She shoved Jake's muscly shoulder and ordered, "Move it."

As soon as he complied, she slid across the bench and darted for the exit. She had no idea if her friends were following her, nor did she care. She needed to find out for herself whether she'd let her imagination run away with her. On her way through the crowd, she saw a raspberry cupcake and another that looked like a chocolate ganache, and her heart started to beat harder. Those were the flavors Erik had planned to serve at the grand opening.

She finally made her way to the door and burst onto the sidewalk. And there it was, double-parked on the street directly across from the bar: a white van with a huge caricature of the man she loved affixed to the side. And there was the man himself, standing at the back next to... Richard? Handing out cupcakes to an enthusiastic crowd alongside Byron and Gina?

As if he sensed her presence, Erik's head snapped up, and his eyes sought hers out. He immediately handed off his tray to Byron so that by the time she made it across the street, her best, favorite person in the world was standing in front of the magnetic logo, waiting for her.

"Hi," she said breathlessly. "Is this legal?"

"Not even a little." His beautiful mouth twisted in amusement. "But I had to do something to get the attention of a woman inside that bar."

"Oh yeah?" She shifted closer to him. "Did it work?"

He leaned a shoulder against the van and crossed one ankle over the other. "So far, so good."

She was so overwhelmingly happy to see him that the tears she'd struggled to hold back all night started to leak out of the corner of her eyes. "Erik, I'm so sorry about everything. The logo, the TV thing, all of it. I swear I'm not a fame-obsessed monster. I'll never push you again."

She drank up the heat in his eyes when he said, "Keep pushing. It's good for me. And I'll be better about saying no when I need to."

He wanted her to keep pushing? Did that mean he wanted *her*?

As if he'd seen the question float through her mind, he said, "*Since you asked,* you need to know that when I said I didn't want to want you, what I meant was that I wasn't prepared for you. I never thought someone like you would be interested in someone like me."

She stiffened and wrapped her arms around her midsection, braced for the insult, the dismissal, the gentle letdown. But instead, he gripped her arms and rubbed his thumbs above her elbows. "All this energy, this life." He reached up and ran a hand along her hair. "How would I even know what to do with you?"

She took a leap of faith and whispered, "You could love me." Hope pulsed through her body with every beat of her heart as she waited for his answer.

His smile bloomed, that perfect smile he kept only for her. "I do. It turns out what I thought I wanted doesn't matter. You're what I need."

He'd pulled her into his arms and leaned down, a hairbreadth from kissing her, when a voice intruded on their moment.

"You da ones widda cupcakes?"

Josie whipped around to confront the source of the thick Chicago accent. "Does it look like we have cupcakes?" she snapped. "God! Read the room!"

"Step around the back," Erik calmly told the ruddy-faced man in the Bears shirt. "My folks'll take care of you."

Once the interloper was gone, he chucked her under the chin. "Looks like I'll be spending the rest of my life finishing the fights my girl starts." Then he pulled back, his brow creased. "Assuming that's what you want too?"

The vulnerability in his voice melted the last of her doubts, and she twined her arms around his waist. "I want that. So much." Her words chased the last of the doubts from his face, and he pulled her close and pinned her to the side of the van, kissing her until the whistles and cheers of the people in the cupcake line penetrated their little bubble.

Once their breathing had slowed a tick, Josie realized he'd pressed her against the logo magnet. And yeah, it was a little weird to be kissing the real man when she was plastered against the cartoon one. "Please don't keep using this for my sake! I know how much it bothers you."

"Honestly, it's grown on me." And then he shocked the hell out of her by moving directly in front of the huge caricature and striking an identical pose.

The easy way he joked about it was the last proof she needed that this was real. "You love it." She lifted her chin and shot him a triumphant grin.

"Damn right I do." His lips sought out hers again, and this time no amount of cheering from the cupcake line could get them to stop.

EPILOGUE

SIX MONTHS LATER

"Want company?"

Josie's red curls peeked around the shower curtain before the rest of her followed.

"Always." He shifted away from the spray to let her step under the hot water and to give himself a better view of her soon-to-be wet body.

"Everything set for today?" She brushed against him as she reached for her body wash, and his hands automatically dropped to her waist and tugged so her back was pressed against his front in all kinds of interesting ways. It thoroughly chased the subject he needed to discuss with her from his head, but he was happy to let it go for now.

"Yep."

"I see we're having a talkative morning." She tilted her head back and looked up at him with a grin, and he seized the opportunity to pluck the bottle from her hand with a grunt.

A sharp citrus scent filled the shower as he slicked the gel over her skin, and as always, he experienced a mild state of awe that he was the man allowed to put his hands on her in the shower every morning. Just one of the perks of cohabitation with the woman he loved.

She purred in appreciation as he stroked his fingers under her breasts, then sighed. "I still can't believe Finn and Tom planned their engagement party for my birthday weekend."

"It's not all about you." He spun her so she could rinse under the spray.

"It's a *little* about me," she said matter-of-factly. "Turn, please."

He did as instructed and stood still as her fingers invaded his hair, the pads massaging shampoo along his scalp in languid strokes that he felt in each nerve ending.

"Is your mother going to make it?" he asked as she worked.

"No." Her answer was short but more rueful than bitter. "It's okay. We had coffee last week, and I only got shouty once. You've mellowed me."

"Or social justice has mellowed her."

Although Pamela hadn't gotten the Art Institute residency she'd been angling for, she'd secured a grant to work with an organization collecting stories and photos of Chicago's homeless population. By some miracle, the project was making her marginally better at basic human decency when it came to her daughter.

"Nah, I'm pretty sure it's me." She stroked conditioner through his hair now, taking her time to work it in the ends before sliding her arms around his waist and pressing her cheek to his back. "How did I end up with an Iowa farm boy who has more haircare products than I do?"

He turned in her embrace. "That's what happens when you pick fights on public transportation."

She laughed and then she kissed him, and then they communicated in nothing but sighs and caresses for a time.

Afterward, they managed to get dried, dressed, and downstairs with an hour to spare before the first guests arrived at the shop for the low-key friends-and-family celebration of love. As Josie filled a tray with mocha espresso cupcakes, Erik fetched the centerpiece cake from the fridge and debated how to bring up a potentially touchy subject.

"So uh," he began, and she groaned.

"I know that tone. What is it? Gina's not coming after all, is she?" She gestured impatiently at the cupcake in her hand. "She and Christine got stuck in Iowa, so you made these gluten-free for nothing."

"No, they're still coming. And Jake's bringing his girlfriend, last I heard." Hey, just look at that personal growth: nothing but happiness that the guy in the suit had found his own happiness. Of course, it helped that it was with someone other than Josie.

Josie, who was looking at him with curiosity all over her face. Time to jump in.

"So I got a call from your TV friend Yousef this week."

Her hands stilled over the outer circle of cupcakes, and he rushed to banish the apprehension creeping across her features. "He asked about doing a monthly segment on baking techniques"—deep breath, push it out—"and I told him yes."

The only sign that Josie had heard him was the slight flicker of her eyelids, so he continued as if she was absorbing the news like normal. "I guess the station manager liked that god-awful first appearance I did. It was popular with viewers."

More silence. Even her eye twitch had fallen still.

"Oh no. I've broken you." He bent down to her eye level, a flicker of concern growing. "If you hate it, I'll tell him no. But I thought—"

"You don't have to do this for me," she blurted. Now that she was talking again, she burst into motion, wringing her hands, biting her lip, and all but crumpling with pink-cheeked anxiety.

"No, I... I want to try it. People still mention that segment sometimes when they come in. Let's grow the business. We've got that second location to pay for after all."

A slow-growing smile replaced the apprehension on her face. "That we do." Then, like the sun coming out from under a cloud, she threw back her head and hooted. "You hear that, Deplorable Dora? You 'retire early,' we swoop in and buy your building, and my man's about to be a TV star!"

"Okay, let's not get carried away," he cautioned her. He might be bolder with risks, but he was still, well, *himself*.

"A star!" she shouted, flinging her arms out. Then she dropped them and cocked her head. "Hey, you're gonna marry me someday, right?"

His heart stopped, then started up in double time. "What if I crash and burn on-air?"

"Then you'll *have* to marry me so I can support us both."

She tossed her hair, all Josie Ryan sass, but he saw the there-and-gone flash of nervousness in the quiver of her lower lip.

Well, that wouldn't do. He took her by the shoulders and walked her to the far wall of the kitchen, the one where he'd hung the framed napkin sketch that had started this all. Below it was the small wall safe where he kept cash and other important paperwork. Without a word, he spun the dial, reached inside, and extracted a velvet box.

He opened and held it out to her. "I'll marry you tomorrow if that's what you want." He'd been waiting for the perfect moment. Why hadn't he realized that every moment with her was perfect?

"Yes, please," she whispered. With a tremulous smile up at him, she dashed a stray tear from her velvety brown eyes and ran a finger over the single diamond embedded in the gold band. Then a flash of teeth showed against her lower lip. "But... let's put it away until then. No sense having dueling engagements tonight. It's Finn and Tom's day."

He raised his brows in surprise, and she sighed. "I guess it actually *isn't* always about me." Then she sobered and said almost to herself, "I can't believe I'm going to have your big blond babies."

He laughed and wrapped her in his arms, holding her close. "Yep." He pulled her against his chest once more. "And?"

"And I love you," she said, melting against him.

His smile turned wicked, and he bent to nip her earlobe. "Say it."

His growled command had her shivering. "I love you, Man Bun."

Maybe, in the end, he was a little bit of a nickname guy after all.

*Will any woman be able to shake up Jake Carey's all-work, no-play life? Find out in **Tempting Talk**, available now!*

> *If you're hungry for more Erik and Josie, head here for a sweet bonus epilogue:*
> ***www.sarawhitney.com/taste***

Dear reader,

As I was finishing up book 1 in the Cinnamon Roll Alphas *series—after months of edits, revisions, stress-chocolate, and wine—I was ready to move onto Jake's book. Then an author friend casually said, "Finn's roommate is fun. I bet you could write her a great love story." And wide-eyed people-pleaser that I am, I said, "You love Josie? I WILL GIVE YOU JOSIE."*

Thus Tempting Taste *was born, and you know what? I would stand down a pack of hungry badgers to protect Erik from harm, and I would follow Josie into any shopping expedition, marketing pitch, or public transportation throwdown.*

Of course I feel that way about all of the characters who live in my head, my laptop, and now your Kindle, but these two are special, and I hope you think so too. I also hope you'll pick up Tempting Talk, *the third book in the series. (For the record, I would fight badgers for Jake and Mabel too. You'll see.) For information about all of my upcoming releases, be sure to sign up for my mailing list:* ***sarawhitney.com/newsletter***

Stay sassy, and stay in touch!

Sara Whitney

ALSO BY SARA WHITNEY

The Cinnamon Roll Alphas Series

Tempting Heat

Tempting Taste

Tempting Talk

Tempting Lies

Standalone novellas

Game On

Ghosted

Praise for Sara Whitney

Tempting Lies

"Sweet and funny and sexy all at once. I couldn't put this down." *Marianela Aybar, Mari Loves Books Blog*

"The right blend of sass and steam. Sara Whitney's smooth, upbeat prose is a delight to read. I devoured it fast. Too fast." *Elle Greco, author of the LA Rock Star Romance series*

"The roller-coaster ride the author takes us on getting to their happily ever after left me feeling slightly broken but so happy and hopeful." *Kristen Lewendon, Renaissance Dragon Book Blog*

"Thea and Aiden (loooooved these two together!) were unputdownable in so many moments, unforgettable in a lot of the others. If you love a fake relationship trope in romance, then you will adore this duo." *Briana, Renee Entress's Blog*

Tempting Talk

"A sweet, witty, and engaging story featuring likable, complex characters." *Laurie, Laurie Reads Romance*

"The interactions are hilarious, while the sparks are flying everywhere. I was all in cover to cover." *Jennifer Pierson, The Power of Three Readers*

"A fun, sweet and passionate romance. I loved these two, individually and together." *Valeen Robertson, Live Thru Books Blog*

Tempting Taste

"Sara Whitney has pulled together the most fun you'll have in a bakery with this one! I loved the cupcake-baking, cinnamon roll hero who looks like the God of Thunder. Hello to my new book boyfriend." *Christina Hovland, author of the Mile High Matched series*

"Sexy, sassy, and downright delicious! Whitney's pint-sized heroine and strong-but-silent hero make for the perfect pairing. Tempting Taste brims with her trademark wit, humor and warmth." *Kate Bateman, author of This Earl Of Mine*

"I love a broody hero, and Erik was amazing! Sweet, humorous and full of so much sexual tension." *Messy Bun Book Blog*

"A fun, sexy read full of humor and heart." *Sarah Hegger, author of Positively Pippa and Roughing*

Tempting Heat

"It made my heart squeeze and my cheeks flush. Finn and Tom are 100% guaranteed to make. you. swoon." *Blair Leigh, author of What Comes After*

"A brilliant read. I adored it from beginning to end." *Sandra, Jeanz Book Read & Review*

"The perfect amount of tension, smoldering heat, unexpected twists, and satisfying conclusion." *Sarah, Paranormal Peach Reviews*

"Seriously juicy, swoon-worthy, and light-hearted romance." *Jasmine, Reading with Jax*

ABOUT THE AUTHOR

 Sara Whitney writes sassy contemporary romance that's always sunny with a chance of sizzle. A multiple award-winning author, Sara worked as a print journalist and film critic before she earned her Ph.D. and landed in academia. She's a good pinball player, a great baker, and an expert at shouting her TV opinions to anyone who'll listen.

Sara lives in Illinois surrounded by books, cats, and half-empty coffee cups. Keep up with the latest news by subscribing to her mailing list here.

- bookbub.com/profile/sara-whitney
- facebook.com/sarawhitneyauthor
- goodreads.com/SaraWhitney_
- amazon.com/author/sarawhitney
- instagram.com/sarawhitney_
- twitter.com/sarawhitney_

Made in the USA
Las Vegas, NV
27 October 2021